D0427048

Winter Passage

by
Paul Raymond Côté
and
Constantina Mitchell

Behler
PUBLICATIONS

California

Behler Publications
California

Winter Passage
A Behler Publications Book

This is a work of fiction. Names, characters, places, and incidents either are the product of the author's imagination or are used fictitiously. Any resemblance to actual persons, living or dead, events, or locales is entirely coincidental.

Library of Congress Cataloging-in-Publication Data is available
Control Number: 2005921333

FIRST EDITION

ISBN 1-933016-19-1
Published by Behler Publications, LLC
Lake Forest, California
www.behlerpublications.com

Manufactured in the United States of America

Much of what follows is true, and much is fiction.

Bordeaux, 1794.

They tell me today is the 30th of Prairial in the year II, yet I know not what that means. I know only that it is mid June, and this is the last day of my life.

Reason has succumbed to hysteria. The Tribunal has become a killing machine—Saturn devouring his own children. No one is spared. Most are sentenced without even the semblance of a trial. Rivers of blood flow in the streets. The new social order has failed. Only witch-hunts and madness prevail.

Clanking metal broke the silence. A key was jiggling in the lock again. Pierre shoved the unfinished letter under a pile of damp straw and looked up. The dank enclosure reeked of urine. The steady influx of prisoners left little room to move. The creak of rusty hinges sent rats scurrying to their nests. A shadowy form pushed open the heavy wooden door. His indistinct features were those of every jailer. How could one prison guard be different from another? Weren't they simply the collective instruments of a greater force?

"Move back! Make room!"

Three men stumbled into the chamber, flinching with each jab of the guard's musket. The firearm glittered, ablaze in the light of the setting sun that filtered through the grated vent near the ceiling.

The door slammed shut and the double click of the lock echoed once more as the bolt snapped back into place. It was the sound of destiny. Dying red-gold rays illuminated the profiles of the new detainees. Pierre stared at the stout figure nearest the door, still crumpled on the floor. The once familiar face was now almost unrecognizable. What remained was a haggard expression that betrayed a broken spirit, a soul in agony. Pierre stood and walked toward him through the maze of bodies.

"Monsieur le Marquis?"

The mere mention of a title of nobility was an act of treason, yet Pierre, Baron de Montigny, could not bring himself to address as *citoyen* the man he had known ever since he could remember, could not relinquish centuries of tradition, much less his own identity.

"My God, Pierre. You here too? I thought you'd be in England by now with your son."

Pierre helped the Marquis de Bouillet to his feet.

"Charles never made it. The bullet pierced his heart. I don't know what has happened to Armande, Françoise, and Eugenie—or any of the others."

Bouillet placed his hands gently on Pierre's shoulders. The answer was in the marquis's eyes. Words did not come easily for him. So much had transpired in such a short time. The world was upside down. Perhaps he was already dead, in one of the inferno's lower circles. He managed to find the courage to utter what no one wanted to hear. "They took them down to the Garonne early this morning...weighted their clothing with stones...threw them into the water. My wife was among them, too."

Pierre stared blankly as he listened and imagined the horror.

"There's no one left for either of us now, Pierre. Our lands are gone. Lunacy roams the country. It leaves nothing in its wake but suffering and destruction."

It was the voice of a man who had died to this world and renounced life in the face of the inalterable. The hack of the guillotine's blade would be little more to him than a near superfluous blow to an existence that had already ceased to be. Yet his eyes were still lit by the flame of dignity—the only remnant of his being the Insurrectional Commune had been unable to take away.

Pierre could not react. He wedged his way back to the pile of straw that hid the letter. Well before Bouillet spoke, he had known there was no chance of escape for himself. His only son had been killed, but he had held the meager hope that his wife and daughters might somehow be spared. It had sustained him throughout the endless night of his despair. Now that, too, was gone. His limbs pulled his torso down onto the cold slabs. He remained there, motionless for minutes—or hours. What did it matter? Time was devoid of significance.

When he came out of his daze, darkness had enveloped the crowded cell. Sleep was momentarily delivering Bouillet and most of the others from their torment. Brushing the straw aside,

Pierre retrieved the letter, placed it in his pouch of belongings, and quietly moved to the opposite side of the stone chamber. A dim light from the torches in the corridor shone through the door's small barred opening. It would be enough to allow him to continue to write without being seen by the guards, now lost in a game of *tarok*. He would make no sound, not draw their attention.

Reaching for the letter, his hand fell instead upon a packet of loosely tied pages. They were among the few things Pierre had been allowed to keep with him. He had only recently discovered their existence while sifting through family documents in anticipation of the interrogation that never took place, the defense he was never allowed to present.

Untying the packet's crimson ribbon, Pierre pondered the hurried script that so resembled his own. Sporadically dated notes and unfinished paragraphs alternated with eloquently formulated reflections that evoked distilled moments of a life. These were not lines from a novel or a play, but instants recorded in defiance of time's effacement—a dialogue between the mundane and the sublime. Jean Luc, Baron de Montigny, had never been one to expose his deepest emotions. Had he buried glimpses at a hidden part of himself within the predictable entries of his diary only to remove them later? Could that explain the journal's incomplete state? Or had someone unlocked the secret door before Pierre and stolen, for some unknown purpose, the events and emotions they held?

Pierre was moved by what the fragmented text revealed, intrigued by what it might conceal. His letter was still not finished, yet death's approach compelled him to set out for those remote shores where the distant spirit of his father dwelled. To reach them, Pierre would need to free the ship of his memory from its moorings and wake the oarsmen. Only then could he fill the journal's gaps and relive the adventure in his mind in preparation for his own passage into the void.

~~~

Aboard the Goéland, off the coast of New France on this Monday the 30th day of September 1734.

White gulls circle high above. The gentle wind brings with it vague sweet sounds. Voices beckon, entreating me to abandon all and follow, surrender to the wine-dark sea. These are not ordinary sea birds, but sirens calling, casting their spell to lure me. Were it not for Pierre, I would cut the bonds that hold me to this life, respond to the summons, and be spared the ceaseless battle against the beasts that plague me from within. "This is no mortal being, but an immortal woe." Of all the great thinkers, it is you, ancient poet, whom I chose to accompany me on this journey. It is your epic that I pulled from my shelves. Odysseus in his wandering and desolation speaks to me. He is a kindred spirit, yet he cannot appease my soul or mitigate my anguish. It is inside the confines of my being that I must brave the obstacles Poseidon has placed on my path. But I possess neither the courage and cunning of Odysseus nor the protection of clear-eyed Athena. May this ocean crossing beguile my imagination and hold the monsters in abeyance.

Quebec City, on this Tuesday the 1st day of October 1734.

We followed the coast for some time after making our way into the gulf. On our approach to the port, the outline of the fortified city came into view, nestled high on a rocky summit covered with radiantly colored trees against a background of low rising mountains—an almost theatrical setting, unlike anything I have ever seen, at once real and unreal, inviting and foreboding.

I know not what awaits me. In any event, it is of little consequence, now that they are gone. I am but a shell, a moving reflection with no substance.

The port seemed impervious to time, as though it had always been and would forever be. Crews unloaded trunks, barrels and wooden cases, and lined them up along the dock. The frenzy and commotion was like a swarm of ants protecting their colony from attack.

Montigny carried Pierre down the plank in his arms. The child's governess followed close behind. They were among the first to disembark. The baron was in his early thirties. An alabaster complexion enhanced his strong profile and charcoal eyes. His dark hair, longer than usual and unkempt from the rigors of the voyage, was blowing across his face as he paid a black man and an Indian to hoist the trunks onto the carriage he had hailed. He fumbled through the pockets of his waistcoat for the address of the inn the notary had recommended, and then handed the scrap of paper to the coachman, who acknowledged his recognition of the establishment with a nod.

Pierre's governess, a plump matron whose patience with children had earned her excellent references, was not an adventurous woman by nature. Her surprising willingness to participate in this expedition into uncharted territories stemmed, in large part, from her very real affection for her young charge. She looked down in embarrassment as she passed the Indians mulling about the port, some wearing little more than feathered headdresses and green face paint. Yet she could not resist taking furtive glances at the almost nude bodies glistening in the late morning sunlight.

Montigny helped the governess into the carriage and lifted Pierre up to her before climbing in himself. A tug at the reins made the coachman's two steeds whinny as they trotted away from the harbor and through the narrow winding streets. From within the moving vehicle, the three voyagers beheld the autumnal brilliance. Maple trees were unknown to them. The reds, yellows, and deep oranges entranced them as much as the city's clamor and bustle. The horses had barely pulled to a stop in front of the *Auberge du Roy* when Montigny motioned to two men. They smiled broadly at the sight of the shiny silver coins he proffered, lifted the trunks onto their shoulders, and carried them inside. As they did, the sounds of a crowd caught Montigny's attention. He hastened to get the boy and his governess settled in and then set out in the direction of the noise.

The cobbled square he entered was lined with houses and a church, all built of stone. Stalls had been set up around the outer edge. It was market day. Farmers and merchants were hawking their produce and meats. Yet the confusion was not due to the ordinary din of tradesmen and peddlers vaunting their wares.

Officers of the law were circulating in the crowd to make sure the vendors kept to the square's perimeter and did not rig their scales. The presence of extra recruits meant the square was to serve an additional function that day. In the middle, loomed a large

wooden structure in the form of an X. Montigny recognized it
immediately. It was a Saint Andrew's cross. Next to it stood a
crudely constructed gallows and a large pile of kindling. Serpentine
swirls of smoke the color of mercury billowed from a small fire
burning off to one side. Two burley men dressed in red were
leading a young Indian woman toward the tiny flames battling the
wind. Montigny was struck by her features, so different from those
of the faces he knew. Long straight blue-black hair hung like two
folded raven's wings on her russet shoulders. She resisted. A third
man, shorter and stockier than the others, laid a branding iron in the
flames, waited for the tip to turn white, then pulled it from the heat,
shook off a flurry of ashes, and stepped toward the terrified woman.

There was a drum roll. Eyes turned to the squat figure
unfurling a document that bore a large wax seal.

"By order of the High Council and His Royal Majesty's
Intendant in these territories of New France, you, Charlotte...17
shillings and six pence from one Catherine Tissot..."

The voice was barely audible as it sank beneath the yelling.
"...law-abiding subject...King of France...sentenced...grievous
offense visible to all."

Shouts echoed the accusation.

"*Voleuse*! *Voleuse*!"

One of the men in red jerked the woman's right arm
forward and forced open her fist. The tip of the branding iron
pressed firmly into her flesh. A piercing scream drowned out the
jeers as the trembling hand was raised high to display the burn,
the letter *V*, seared across the palm's lifeline. The histrionic
inflection of the town crier's voice competed with the Indian's
shrills as he read on. "In addition...prison...five and one half
months."

The branded Indian was led away. A horse-drawn wagon
filled with garbage pulled into the square. Montigny noticed
something move high atop the putrid mound. The form was
human. It was a black woman. The guards yanked her from the
wagon and prodded her to the gallows. A filthy ankle-length
chemise was all she had on. Montigny could see she had trouble
walking. Her feet were bare and bruised. Pain contorted her face
with each step she took. A sign dangling from a chain around her
neck covered her breasts. Another hung down her back. Both

bore the word *INCENDIAIRE* clumsily printed in large red letters.

The scarlet-clad executioners piled the kindling around the base of the gallows. Again, the drummer played. Again, the town crier read. And again, Montigny could hear only fragments.

"By order of the High Council ..you, Marie Claire Angelique, property of Therese Decouagne, widow of Francheville, did willfully and maliciously...night of the 10th of April...destruction of all her earthly possessions...great damage...city of Montreal."

The town crier was no match for the mob. He stopped to adjust his white wig, a pretext of protocol that allowed him to catch his breath and muster his stamina.

"You furthermore did attempt to flee and seek refuge in the southern colonies...King of England...walk the streets in atonement...burned to ashes."

In seconds, she was hanged and fire set to the gallows. A dark stench-filled vapor swirled around the lifeless body swaying in the wind. Leave. Get away. Anywhere. But how? There was no escape from the nauseating odor. The crowd and the spectacle held everyone captive.

The executioners were now carrying a large pasteboard up to the wooden cross at the square's central point. Montigny studied the scene depicted on it as the men secured the board in place. It was a primitive drawing of an Indian tied to a cross that resembled the one in the square. Two other figures in the drawing were holding objects that looked like clubs, as if readying to strike him. The drums thundered a third time.

"...cruelly and hatefully murdered on the banks...Duchesne River...seigneury of Deschaillons...night of the 12th of May...sentenced...death...victim's widow, Madame Marie Claire Lambert, née Perreault...ignoble and reprehensible crime..."

Heads turned toward a young woman in black standing in the crowd, holding the hand of a little girl at her side tightly in her own. A gossamer veil shadowed her face. Montigny's eyes met hers for a moment but she quickly shifted her gaze back to the pasteboard attached to the cross. Fists shook in anger. Rotting fruit and vegetables soared over the heads of the onlookers and splattered the drawing. Someone took aim at the woman. Red juice soaked her sleeve, darkening the black fabric like blood seeping from an open wound. Looking ever more intently at the caricature, she clutched her arm in silence.

The barrage subsided. Emotions settled down and the crowd slowly dispersed. Montigny's freedom of movement was restored, but dense smoke and the smell of burning flesh lingered in the air. Cinders and soot flecked the white linen handkerchief he held over his mouth and nose as he left the *Place Royale*.

He closed the door behind him, shut out one dimension and stepped into another. He had to remind himself he was not in France, but had simply crossed the threshold of the tavern at the *Auberge du Roy*. At a long table, men and women, their metal goblets lifted high, filled the space with cacophonic attempts at harmony. *"Goûtons voir si le vin est bon!"* The last time Montigny had heard the drinking song was in another life, where pain and suffering did not exist, or at least seemed eclipsed by light and joy.

Noise and the haze of tobacco permeated the tavern's every crevice. Despite the room's expanse, the low-beamed ceiling created an atmosphere of warmth. Empty seats were a rarity at the *Auberge*. Montigny spied a vacant spot across the sea of faces and made his way there, weaving in and out of the tables and benches arranged in no apparent order. He sat down near two men playing piquet at the next table. They joked and laughed as they slammed the cards onto the worn pine planks. In a corner, lovers whispered and embraced. Close by, men were casting dice to see who would buy the next round. On the opposite side of the room, the finesse and precision of a pair of serious billiard players had drawn a small gathering of idlers who watched transfixed as the long wooden sticks scattered the ivory balls to their desired targets with a single blow. More drinking songs periodically interrupted the banter as food and wine were downed heartily.

"Sylvie! Another round."

The barmaid nodded with a smile, though it was difficult for her to hide her fatigue. The day had been unusually long and the demand for her services was increasing as the night progressed. It was hard work but the innkeeper and his wife ran a clean business and treated her decently. She was grateful for the steady income. The tavern was among the city's most popular—a fairly large watering hole that drew its clientele from all the colony's social strata. Sylvie showed Montigny the same concern she bestowed on the regulars, describing the evening fare, enumerating the kinds of wine and beer on hand, making certain to let him know the *Auberge du Roy* was renowned for its fresh warm bread. Such good-natured attentiveness. Perhaps she was one of the Graces, a daughter of Zeus. But her penchant for exchanging witty remarks with those whose thirst it was her function to quench likened her as well to Thalia, the comic muse. And while she enjoyed the parade of customers and the news they brought from near and far, that evening, more than most, she looked forward to hearing the bell in the adjacent square that signaled closing time for all the city's drinking establishments.

Montigny finished his supper but was reluctant to leave the company of strangers. He did not want to return to his room and the solitude that sat waiting for him there. He would sip one more cup of wine and add an entry to his diary before going upstairs for the night, before extinguishing the candle of consciousness and staring into the eyes of his inner demons. He took a quill and small flask of ink from his pouch and began to write.

I hear your voice in the wind. See your soul in the evening star, eternally present, forever absent. How can I capture the ocean's crests in my hands or caress the summer breeze with my arms? You...

"Pardon me, Monsieur. Might I take the seat across from you?"

The intruding voice came out of nowhere. It had no place in Montigny's universe of selected memory. He nodded distractedly without looking up.

"Allow me to introduce myself. Desjardins. Auguste Desjardins. I saw you in the town square today."

Montigny set his quill on the table. The tall husky gentleman smiling down at him raised his wine cup as if to toast him. A black three-cornered hat was tucked beneath his left arm, as was the silver-tipped walking stick he carried more for adornment than support. "If I may say so, you appeared a bit confused."

"Jean Luc de Montigny." He stood to extend his hand to the

stranger. Montigny speculated the man was nearing sixty, yet his grasp was firm and steady. "Please join me. Yes, I suppose I did look confused. I just arrived this morning and..."

"Ah! Well of course! I should have guessed. You're Louis's nephew, aren't you? A good friend of mine, a wonderful man. My sincerest condolences."

Montigny was dumbfounded. The first person he had occasion to speak with in Quebec City knew his uncle. An odd coincidence. And why had he offered his condolences? Was he somehow aware? But how could he be? Desjardins saw the consternation on Montigny's face.

"You didn't know?"

"Know what?"

"Oh, I'm so sorry, there was no way you could have. You were in the middle of the Atlantic at the time. But I assumed from your dark attire... Your uncle died two weeks ago. I regret having to give you such news on the day of your arrival. It goes without saying, if I can be of assistance in any way..."

"That's very kind of you. I had no idea his illness was so serious."

Desjardins had apparently not been informed about what had happened on the other side of the ocean. He did not know that a world had ended. And Montigny wanted to keep it that way.

"His last two years were not easy. I visited him in Beau Val as often as I could."

"Is it far?"

"A few hours down river."

"But from what I understand, his notary is here in Quebec City."

The statement was left unacknowledged and rejoined instead by an unrelated question. "So, did you make the voyage alone?"

"No, but perhaps I should have. I came with my son. He was worn out from the journey and all the excitement. I had his governess give him supper and put him to bed early."

Montigny panned the disparate assembly in the tavern. It was as if an early painting by Franz Hals, one he admired for its palette and the mood of spontaneity it captured, had come to life.

He turned back to Desjardins. "I was surprised when the notary sent for me. In any case, I was glad to get away." He paused, realizing where the conversation would lead, and tried to change the subject. "That scene in the town square today was unbelievable." He was well aware that it was not as unbelievable as all that. Authoritarian displays of brutality designed to instill fear and obedience in the monarch's subjects were customary throughout Europe. France was no exception and apparently neither was Quebec.

"And why did you want to get away, if the question is not too impertinent?" asked Desjardins, gliding over Montigny's reference to the *Place Royale*.

"There's been so much unrest, ever since I can remember. My father still talks about the Spanish succession. The war... Then there was that damn Scotsman and his paper money schemes."

As Desjardins listened politely to what he deemed an implausible response, he deduced that Louis's nephew was attempting to skirt his question by diverting his attention, but indulged him nonetheless. "Oh yes, that John Law fellow. We haven't stopped licking our wounds from the jabs of his follies either, even though it's been over ten years now."

Montigny made every effort to push the conversation further away from the subject he knew he could not face. Not that evening. Never go back to that wasteland. Never confide in anyone. "He had Indians brought over to Paris from the southern territories, draped them in gold, and paraded them around the city. Told everyone Louisiana was overflowing with silver and emeralds. And now that the king of Poland has died..."

Desjardins continued to play Montigny's game. "Well I hope you don't think things are any easier here. You'll be disappointed if you do. We've simply imported the problems to this continent, and added a few of our own of course. The only difference is that the rules aren't the same. Sometimes there aren't any rules at all. And if there are, they're more visceral than judicial, so to speak. Behavior dictated by primal instincts. Survival at any cost. The veneer of civility tends to chip away rather quickly."

Desjardins took out a plaster pipe and pouch of tobacco and

started to fill the pipe's bowl with a few pinches of the pouch's fragrant contents.

"Do you mean the events..."

Loud voices cut Montigny off. A brawl had broken out between two chess players. Desjardins put down his pipe to watch the outburst. One of the men grabbed the other by the front of his shirt and knocked over a chair. Threats were exchanged. When bystanders started taking sides, the innkeeper intervened. Like Desjardins, he was a portly man of considerable size, although much younger—just the other side of forty. Patrons knew better than to challenge him, especially in the late hours when his patience was worn.

"Now there's a perfect illustration of what I was saying. At least nothing worse came of the incident. Ah, when the nectar of Dionysus flows... A while back, one of the lieutenants had a few too many and killed a man in a duel. He was apprehended. They cut off the poor fellow's right arm and speared it to a barricade as a lesson to others not to do likewise. Such violence everywhere... If only there were doctors who could cure the afflictions plaguing society."

"I studied medicine in Bordeaux, but I assure you I'd be at a loss to treat the ills of human nature."

"Oh, how rude of me! Do you smoke, Monsieur de Montigny? May I offer you some tobacco?"

"No, I don't, but thanks just the same." Montigny took another sip of wine. His thoughts were taking him elsewhere and everywhere all at once. To a church in Bordeaux—Saint Andrew's Cathedral. To the market square and the cross of Saint Andrew he had seen earlier that day. He thought of the pasteboard drawing, the widow with the small child, and his own secret that would give him no reprieve. But just when Montigny was certain Desjardins had forgotten the remark he knew he should not have let escape his lips, the old gentleman looked him squarely in the eye and said, "If I'm reading you correctly, coming here at your uncle's request was more or less a pretext." He lifted the candle from the table and moved it toward the pipe in his mouth. A pungent odor wafted through the air. The blue-gold flame that illuminated his lips as he spoke gave his words an oracular aura. "The real reason you've come here is to forget."

Montigny's hands and face turned to ice as he pondered the possibility that Desjardins had gained access to the book that was his soul. He was eager to hide the message its pages contained, but the man persisted. "My experience has been that the past never leaves us completely. The harder we try to run away, the more we end up running right back into it. It becomes a form of bondage in its own way."

Montigny was silent for a moment. Then, forcing a smile, he spoke. "You're a keen observer, Monsieur Desjardins. What do you do for a living, might I ask?"

"Fur trading. Learned the craft from my father—and the Indians. Father did quite well, thanks in part to all those puppets whose strings the old king pulled at Versailles. They had little choice but to embrace his extravagance. Everyone who was anyone, or at least wanted to give the impression of being someone, had to be seen wearing furs—mostly beaver, with fox, raccoon, and sable not far behind. But alas, fashion is a fickle business partner. What's stylish one day is commonplace the next. Oh, I do all right, but the demand is not nearly what it used to be."

Montigny needed to play his part, recite his lines convincingly, not retreat inward, but he could find nothing to say. Finally, he bridged the gap. "When I saw the red and gold coastline this morning, I thought the forests were on fire."

"Indian summer."

From Montigny's look, Desjardins realized he hadn't the slightest notion what the term meant.

"The last balmy days of autumn. Cold nights and warm sunny days make the leaves change color. Winter's unusually late this year, but the frost and snows will soon be upon us. This is a land of extremes. Indian summer is one of nature's ways of reminding us of that. I like to think of it as a superficial manifestation of profounder mysteries."

Montigny was now completely enveloped in the smoke wafting from the fur trader's pipe. He had the sensation that the colony was closing in on him as he listened to Desjardins continue. "Life here may not be what you expect. Distance makes royal authority less absolute. As you can see, few pay attention to the ban on playing cards in taverns or the regulation restricting natives to designated drinking establishments. The Church's condemnation of dancing has done little to quell the vogue of the quadrille and minuet. But we do have laws. When broken, the consequences can be heavy."

"Are you talking about the woman they burned today?"

"Well actually, that slave could have had it much worse."

"Slave? I know slavery exists in the southern territories, but..."

"That's right," Desjardins cut in. "Settlers down in the Antilles petitioned the king some fifty years ago to legalize it. They'd been watching the Spanish and English colonies thrive for the simple fact that their economies were built on slavery. Still are. The king bowed to their request and enacted the Black Code. From that point on, the sugar cane industry flourished."

Montigny caught sight of Pierre's governess zigzagging her way to their table. She had not planned to leave her room and come down to the tavern so late in the evening. Her hair had been hurriedly clasped, not with the care that was one of her distinctive traits. And she was not wearing her garnet earrings. She had obviously settled in for the night when the visions surged from the shadows.

"Monsieur, Pierre's had another nightmare."

"Monsieur Desjardins, let me introduce you to Madame Seguin, who graciously agreed to make the journey with us."

Desjardins half stood and gave a friendly nod. "Madame."

"Pleased to meet you," she replied, somewhat embarrassed by her appearance and the brusque intrusion on their conversation.

Montigny turned to Desjardins. "Would you excuse me a moment? I do hope you'll still be here when I return."

"Most likely," he answered, lifting his now almost empty cup to his lips. "I've got the whole evening ahead of me and this is as fine a place as any to spend it."

The sobbing grew louder as Montigny opened the door of his son's room.

"Mama. I want mama. Where's mama?"

Montigny took the boy in his arms, and rocked him back

and forth while he searched for an answer.

"She's not here, my lamb. She's somewhere else. But she's watching us and smiling. Come on now, smile back at her. I know she wants to see you smile."

As Montigny spoke, he stroked his son's golden curls, but then stopped abruptly. The softness of her silken blond tresses between his fingers...

You were a bird in the sky. But your wings have been clipped. Our love cannot be reborn. The wind has stolen our hopes and dreams. A boat has taken me far, so far from you. I would leave a candle burning in the window if I thought you might come to me.

"Papa's here. Papa won't leave you." His voice wavered. Pierre's tears slowly subsided. Montigny quivered. The night air had turned cold. It was probably working its magic on the leaves of the maple tree near the window. "Indian summer," he thought, as he brushed his hand over his son's cheek. Or had ghostly spirits followed him from the other side of the globe to breathe their icy sighs in his ears? He gently laid Pierre back in bed and pulled the downy blankets up to his chin.

"Go to sleep now. And tomorrow, I want you to notice as many new things as you can. Then I'll ask you to tell me everything you saw. Promise?"

The boy nodded as his father kissed him on the forehead. Madame Seguin was waiting anxiously in the hallway by the door. For all her eccentricities she was an exceedingly kind woman and loved Pierre as if he were her own grandson. She had watched over him through long sleepless nights on the *Goéland* and during the months before the voyage. Now she feared that it was beginning again, that the child might never find peace.

~~~

Pierre lifted his eyes from his father's journal. It had been years since he had recalled the loving face of Madame Seguin. His paternal grandmother had died in 1735 when he was just a child in New France with his father. And since his maternal grandmother rarely left her estate in Brittany, he had barely known her. It was therefore Madame Seguin who, through chance and circumstance, had provided a feminine presence in the patriarchy comprised of his father and his father's father during the early years of his existence. Upon their return to Bordeaux, she was the one who told him stories of the distant land of snow and Indians, a place that slowly became a fantasy in his memory—more a forgotten dream than a reality.

A faint light illuminated the dark corners of Pierre's mind. He remembered the room at the inn where he had slept and the maple tree outside the window, brightly colored when they arrived but stark and bare soon after. He could see Madame Seguin reading to him to help pass the time, inventing tales that opened his imagination to horizons he would never have discovered on his own. Such a kind, patient woman, his dear Nounou. He could still feel her warm hand on his face drying his tears, her loving arms holding him tightly at night to shield him from the threatening shadows, from the monsters lurking in the creaking armoire, the phantoms that hid in the forest and cried out with the wolves and owls. If only she could be here now, he thought, to protect him from harm as she had so often done. The little boy she had watched over, his hair now sparse and gray... In the last few years, he had come to terms with his mortality. He knew death would strike, but had never imagined it would come this way or that he would see his children murdered and his grandchildren dispersed.

Pierre returned to his father's script before it would be forever inaccessible to his consciousness, before there would be no consciousness.

~~~

Sorrow and rage... Were it not for those two emotions, I would feel nothing.

Montigny walked back down the corridor to the straight narrow staircase. He hesitated before re-entering the tavern. His body was rigid, a machine accomplishing the motions of daily existence. Did he have the energy to pretend he was part of the race of the living? He pushed on the tavern door. His seat was still waiting for him.

"Is everything under control?" he heard Desjardins ask. The question seemed to come from another galaxy. Could he find a thread to cling to, a fiber with which to weave words, any words to form a net over the void and hold him in the here and now?

His answer betrayed no feeling. "Tell me about that...that...Black Code."

Sylvie arrived with two cups of wine.

"I hope you don't mind, but while you were upstairs, I took the liberty of ordering another." The touch of gaiety in Desjardins's voice hinted that the liquid was intended more to regale his spirit than quench his thirst. "Unlike some of his cohorts, the innkeeper here doesn't water it down. He leaves that to customers with tight purse strings and those who can't afford drinking straight wine all evening. Now, where was I? Oh yes, not long after the king's proclamation, our islands in the Antilles were teeming with slaves, thousands of them. They get them from Africa. It's called..."

"Importing ebony wood."

"Ah, so you do know about it."

"It would be difficult not to."

Bordeaux was only one of the cities whose middle class had built its wealth on the triangular trade routes. Sculpted heads of slaves were beginning to appear on the *mascarons* adorning the window cornices of the newer buildings down by the port and on *rue Fernand-Philippart*, alongside phantasmagoric stone renderings of Bacchus, river gods, and courtesans. Montigny remembered the unusual coat of arms of one of the city's most prosperous families, whose fortune had been built on the commerce of humans. The blazon depicted the profile of a black man, and had been designed a number of years back for the family's patriarch—a famed slave trader—when Louis XIV granted him nobility.

"But no one speaks of the Black Code," continued Montigny, almost mechanically.

"That's no surprise. It spells out the particulars of the relationship that binds slaves to their masters and vice versa. The intention was to limit slavery to the territories. But then, some of the colonists began taking their slaves on board ship with them during their voyages back home. And so, Monsieur, what happens when a slave sets foot on the shores of *la douce France*, where slavery does not exist, at least technically speaking? Does he instantly become a free man? Or she a free woman?"

Montigny had no answer.

"I see you understand the complexity of the issue. Precisely because of that ticklish conundrum, yet another royal edict was enacted. It guarantees that owners retain legal rights over slaves they bring to France so long as they register them properly with the authorities. Some cities enforce the edict, others don't bother."

"You seem well informed on the subject."

"I studied law for a while in Paris. Did I forget to mention that?"

Montigny liked to think of Bordeaux as a seat of intellectual enlightenment. The city had always fostered humanist ideals. He recalled the story his father had told him about a sea captain from Normandy who docked in the port some sixty years earlier with a shipload of slaves. It was a floating prison. The city parliament blocked the sailor's attempts to sell his human plunder, and the captives were set free. But now, legal loopholes were making a mockery of those values. Growing numbers of ships setting out from Bordeaux headed to the Gulf of Guinea or the Angolan coast where cloth and weapons could be exchanged for slaves. Once the live cargo was sold in the colonies, the boats returned to Bordeaux laden with sugar and coffee, only to begin their journey again. Montigny was aware of all that. But he had somehow imagined that the snow and ice of France's northern colonies had spared them the degradation of the human commerce that flourished in the steamy tropics.

Plaisir d'amour ne dure qu'un moment... Someone had begun to sing. No guitars, no flutes, just a sweet, silken voice. Montigny could not see her. He did not know if she was real or somehow a part of the confused vision beginning to unfold in his mind. The sound of clinking cups snapped his attention back to the tavern. A hush slowly fell over the room until nothing but the crystalline voice could be heard. Montigny saw Desjardins turn in the direction of a small table by the windows and followed suit.

There she was, surrounded by an assortment of wet-eyed cronies who'd fallen into a sentimental stupor induced more by their drinking than the song's lyrics. Their faces faded from view

as Montigny steadied his gaze on the singer, and then turned
away in disbelief or pain. He was not sure which. But he could
not keep himself from looking at her once more. Her features
and her voice had been transformed.

The meadow is flooded with sunlight. She is picking
wildflowers. She likes the larkspur and columbine best.

Plaisir d'amour ne dure qu'un moment... Each note struck a
separate chord in his soul, calling up dormant emotions. Could
he wake them? Did he want to wake them? Before he could
decide, he was back in the smoked-filled tavern. *Chagrin
d'amour dure toute la vie.*

The song's end brought with it empty silence, until a fiddler
convinced the spoon player at his table to join him in a jig. The
rhythmic tapping chased away the melancholy mood and the
vision in Montigny's mind. He'd been spared this time.

No one had caught sight of the boy with flaxen hair and
brown eyes at the tavern's entrance. The young messenger
spotted the intended recipient of the note he was carrying and
approached. Desjardins unfolded the paper the boy handed him
and read silently, his lips taking the shape of partial words now
and then, but not distinctly enough for Montigny to deduce the
note's contents.

"Well, my friend, I'm afraid I have to leave." He tucked the
note into the pocket of his waistcoat. "Unexpected business. And
at this late hour."

Desjardins's claim of some unforeseen nocturnal
engagement could not disguise the mirthful expression the
message had brought to his face. Perhaps a lady friend had
summoned him. "I hope nothing's wrong," said Montigny with
feigned concern, masking his distress, for he knew that with
Desjardins's departure he would be forced to wage a battle in the
black pit of his dreams.

"No, no. Not at all." Desjardins stood and reached for his
hat and cane. "Thanks for the wine. Next time, you'll be my
guest. I insist."

Montigny rose to bid him goodbye. "Don't mention it."

"Will you be lodging here during your entire stay?"

"I suppose. I was planning on spending time at the estate
with my uncle, but now..."

"It's not bad, really. It's central, relatively safe, and far more respectable than some of the other establishments. And despite the climb to the upper city, it's within reasonable walking distance of Bourville's office."

Desjardins saw Montigny's eyes widen. "You're surprised I know the name of your uncle's notary. Louis asked me to take care of paperwork for him occasionally, especially towards the end when he couldn't travel. He lived so far out in the country, and I was right here in Quebec City. There's a clause in the will—your uncle and I discussed it—that you'll find somewhat peculiar, I'm sure."

"Really. What?"

"I don't think Monsieur Bourville would appreciate it if I revealed the contents of the will to you. After all, that's his job. Good night, Monsieur de Montigny. And my condolences, once more."

The tavern's merriment sent a shiver of loneliness through Montigny. He looked deeply into the wine in his cup.

It is by your light alone that my world exists. You appear in my glass and pain wakes in my soul, cutting me like a knife. So many roads in the night, so many paths in my heart... Where can I go? Tears flow into my wine and drown your image. Now that you are gone, I will drink an early death.

He pulled out his money purse and hardly had time to throw some coins down by the two empty cups before the innkeeper's stubby hand scooped them up. "Thank you, Monsieur. Your change." The hand slapped the table with the speed and deftness of a magic trick. Before Montigny knew what had happened, the innkeeper had disappeared into the back room. Two worn playing cards lay on the table. Each bore a handwritten number and had been stamped with some sort of seal. Montigny surmised they were part of a credit system the innkeeper had devised for transactions with his lodgers, but he was too tired to ask. Besides, the amount was so small it was of little consequence to him. He slipped the cards into his coat pocket.

The wavering flame of his candlestick barely illuminated the corridor, a tunnel of uncertainty. The ruckus from the tavern below was still audible as he struck the door's gray painted surface with the knuckle of his forefinger.

"Come in, Monsieur, if you wish."

Pierre was sleeping in the low trundle bed. The governess was sitting up in the large canopied four-poster, reading the letters of the Marquise de Sevigné. Montigny had taken the finely bound volume from his library at Loublanc before leaving France and placed it in one of the coffers that accompanied them to Quebec City. He remembered his eagerness to purchase the edition some years back. It was the first, not counting the private copy printed much earlier for the exclusive enjoyment of Louis XIV. More than the renown of the letter writer and her illustrious lineage—her father, the Baron de Chantal, had met his death in 1627 fighting against the English not far from La Rochelle—what had piqued Montigny's curiosity was the idea of peering into the correspondence of a woman who had intended each of her letters to be read solely by its recipient. She could never have imagined they would one day be printed and bound for the world to see—the uncensored expression of human nature in all its dignity and baseness, all its wit and melancholy, laid before the eyes of strangers. The personal gazette of this sometimes superficial woman who delighted in the gossip and diversions of Paris, who counted among her intimates Madame de Lafayette, was not without sadness. As he watched his son's aging governess deeply absorbed in her reading, Montigny recalled one of the Marquise de Sevigné's letters to her daughter. "You ask me, my dear child, if I still love life. I admit to you that I find much sorrow in it, but I am even more disheartened by death."

"How is he now, Madame Seguin?"

"Poor thing. He's had such a long day."

Montigny tiptoed to the trundle bed to observe the serenity of his son in slumber.

He closed the door to his own room. The dim glimmer from the lone candle intensified. He placed the candlestick on the pinewood table. Pulling one of his leather traveling bags from the armoire, he reached inside for the letter he had brought with him, and looked once more at the distinctive handwriting on its outer fold:

Monsieur Albert Bourville, Notaire
34, rue Saint Louis
Québec

Exhausted, he sat on the bed and removed his long jacket, vest, and black leather boots. Beyond his window, the steeply pitched rooftops formed a jagged line against the radiant luster of the moon shining through a curtain of quickly moving clouds in the night sky.

I miss your perfume. My lips are chafed from the salt of my tears. How can I pretend that I have forgotten you, that yesterday never was? Once again, you have come into my mind and I cannot sleep. We were the blue and green of the sea, the sun and the earth. If only I could depart in a dream, but my thoughts hold me captive. The night is a prison.

Montigny blew out the candle. In the moonlight, the room took on an unreal bluish hue. He finished undressing and sank under the covers.

Obscurity, then sunlight. I am moving slowly as if under water. Lying on meadow grass, I watch her pick the irises that grow by the pond. *Plaisir d'amour...* She makes her way towards me. She is within reach. I grab her ankle as she laughs and pull her down onto me, unlace her dress and caress her. Flowers fall from her hand, crushed by our embrace. She is in my arms. But what is happening? Cries of agony. Light, joy, tranquility are gone. Only tears and anger remain. So much anger. *Plaisir d'amour ne dure qu'un moment...*

Cold sweat covered Montigny's face as he sat up in bed. Rain was pounding on the windowpanes.

Quebec City, on this Wednesday the 2nd day of October 1734.

I spent a night of torment. I did not find the rest and solace I long for. The rain has stopped but the overcast sky lingers. The barking of a stray dog in the street echoes the emptiness that remains within me.

Though my uncle's death is a sorrowful occasion, I must confess my emotional detachment. Had I arrived in time to make his acquaintance, perhaps it would be different. I need to inform Father. He will be much grieved. His only brother...

Madame Seguin was hesitant to go off on her own with Pierre for the day, but I rented a carriage for her. The barmaid told me of an area where there are a few shops of interest and a well-frequented tearoom.

When I stepped out into the morning air, a flood of sights and sounds enveloped me: sailors, prostitutes, beggars, soldiers, merchants, nuns. The tiny spiraling streets were a confusion of carriages and wagons, some pulled by harnessed dogs. I've been told they are called "the poor man's horse" here. Cows, chickens, and pigs everywhere made it difficult to move about. A group of three or four Indians with their hands tied behind their backs walked past me. Another, armed, was directing them somewhere.

And there were all manner of street performers...

The red and blue balls kept rising and falling. One color dominated the space above the juggler's painted face for a few seconds only to be replaced by the other. Red and blue, blue and red alternated until finally all the blue disappeared leaving only red, moving up and down. Montigny asked one of the onlookers the way to the upper city. Without diverting his gaze, the man pointed left. Montigny started out, but turned on impulse to catch a last glimpse of the juggler.

"Oh, I'm very sorry. How clumsy of me."

"That's quite alright."

The woman he'd bumped into looked familiar but he couldn't place her. Perhaps she reminded him of someone back home. Or was it the barmaid from the tavern? No, it was the widow he'd seen the day before in the *Place Royale*. But now, a veil did not shroud her face. Her expression told him she recognized him, too.

"I didn't harm you, did I?"

"Not at all," she said with a faint smile, looking down at her little girl.

She put her arms on the child's shoulders and led her around him so they could continue on their way. She was more simply dressed than the previous day. Her loosely tied auburn hair fell against her somber poplin bodice. There was a paleness to her complexion that was not unpleasing, offset as it was by the intense green of her eyes.

She wears the color of solitude. She must turn her heart into a stone until the pain subsides. But what mermaid has taught her to be so lovely in her sorrow?

As she disappeared into the crowd, he noticed her stride—a slow syncopated gait, too graceful to be considered a limp. He could call out to her, share her mourning. No, she would think him impertinent...and Bourville was waiting.

Montigny headed toward the *Côte de la Montagne*, the road leading to the upper city, whose wider streets were lined with professional offices. It was there, high above the port's hubbub, that the wealthy resided, including the colony's two foremost figures of authority: the Intendant, Gilles Hocquart, and the Governor, Charles de la Boische de Beauharnois. It was there, as well, that the pomp and circumstance of government business and official socializing transpired. Indian chieftains could on occasion be seen attending receptions at the Governor's residence, the Chateau Saint Louis, in full native dress.

In the last few years, Beauharnois had set up secondary offices further south along the Saint Lawrence River in the city of Montreal, which until recently had been known as Ville Marie. Its population was increasing more rapidly than that of Quebec City. The Governor now spent four or five months each year there, but his absence from the capital hardly detracted from its social life. Seeing and being seen were obligatory rituals that lent an air of frivolous pageantry to the comings and goings of the more status conscious locals. Many of those indulging in these parades of vanity, it was said, preferred to spend their last coins on a new pair of gloves they could flaunt in public rather than use the money to quell their hunger pangs. Exposed feminine shoulders and plunging necklines were regularly the subject of reprimand during Sunday sermons. Visitors to the city marveled that the young ladies who wore the fashionable high-heeled wooden shoes covered with tooled leather or fine fabric managed to keep from teetering over.

Regardless of how one was shod, accessing the upper city from the lower was not easy. The road's angle was so sharp that Montigny was surprised horses could make the ascent with the heavy loads they pulled. He was even more in awe of the ability of the coachmen to control their descent on the reverse trek.

Once at the top of the steep incline, Montigny stopped to catch his breath. He observed the port below, the expanse of the Saint Lawrence, and the Ile d'Orleans on the northeastern horizon. Scores of gulls coasted over the water's surging crests like wispy white cotton strips swirling in the wind. The clouds were darkening overhead and the air was getting cooler. He hoped Pierre and Madame Seguin were safe inside, she having her tea and he eating a warm bun. A fine drizzle began to fall. In no time, he was on *rue Saint Louis*. The notary's wrought iron sign was swinging in the wind at number 34. Montigny approached and found himself face to face with the head of a lion. He lifted the brass knocker and tapped several times.

A clerk showed him into the main office. The room was dank despite its two tall windows, one partially open. Fresh, cool air and the sounds of boys playing tag cascaded through it. The walls were lined with leather-bound books and worn ledgers stacked in disarray. Amid the sparse but massive furnishings sat a white-haired gentleman, slight of build, behind a long table that functioned as his desk. It was covered with green damask tapestry that draped to the floor. On one side was a candelabrum in the style that had been favored by Louis XIV. Its candles were nearly burned down to their *bobeches*. Some of the melted wax had trailed along the straight gilt arms and onto a large pewter charger placed under the candelabrum for that purpose. The table was piled high with papers.

At the sight of the office door opening, the notary stopped sharpening the brightly colored quill he was holding and rested it in the groove of the ormolu inkwell directly in front of him. The bronze object was a source of great pride. It sat on four low acanthus leaf feet. Ornately worked floral patterns were embossed within the square surface's concentric ridges. Curved handles in the form of swans' necks set off the left and right sides. A hinged lid, on which stood a small griffin, capped the globe rising up from the center that housed the porcelain ink cup. A stick of red sealing wax rested diagonally on the outer right corner. The notary's silver engraved stamp lay on the table next to the inkwell. From their richness and fine craftsmanship, it was evident that writing instruments held special importance in this otherwise dreary decor.

Looking up from his work, the notary rose and darted around the table. His profession had given his shoulders a noticeable hunch, yet he maintained an almost mercurial stride.

"Good morning, Monsieur de Montigny."

As soon as Bourville saw the black crepe hatband, the dark coat devoid of pocket or sleeve buttons, and the discreet white linen weepers on the coat's cuffs, he knew Montigny had been told. He was in mourning for his uncle. At least that was the notary's assumption.

The two men shook hands. "Pleased to meet you at last. Let me begin by expressing my condolences. I'd known your uncle ever since he came to Canada. He was a dear friend. Here, let me have Edouard hang your things in the antechamber to dry. He's built a fire to take the chill off. I must say, the cool air is quite a change from yesterday. I trust your journey was not too difficult."

"The seas were rough at times but on the whole it was bearable."

"How long does it take to make the crossing these days?"

"Two months more or less from port to port, depending on the winds."

As Montigny spoke, Bourville's hand gestured toward an old Louis XIII style armchair upholstered in worn maroon and green striped velvet. The bull's blood the woodworker had applied to stain the chair's frame gave it a luxuriant red-brown luster that time had not dulled. "Please be seated. May I offer you anything? A brandy to warm you up perhaps."

"That's very kind, but no."

Bourville began shuffling through the piles of paper on his desk until he found what he was looking for. Clearing a spot, he placed the documents in the center of the table and reached for his reading glasses. The metal rims holding the thick lenses were connected by a bridge that the notary constantly adjusted to keep the device from falling off his nose. He was unaware of the new English invention gaining popularity on the continent—lenses equipped with rigid arms that rested on the ears.

"Well then, let's get down to business, shall we? From what I gather, you had no contact with your uncle."

"None at all. He left France before I was born. I do remember the letters he sent, though. When I was a child, my father used to read parts of them aloud to me. They filled my imagination for days on end."

"To a boy so far away, I can see how Canada would seem like a place of enchantment. But it was very real to Louis. He saw the potential and used it to his advantage. The personal fortune he brought over allowed him to purchase extensive parcels of land. Agriculture was his passion of course, but the mill turned out to be more lucrative. There are fifty-two sawmills in the colony now. But Louis's mill has prospered in spite of the competition. He was one of the suppliers of lumber to the royal ship builders."

"I'm sorry I didn't arrive in time to meet him."

"His wife Emma—your aunt—died two years ago. I presume you heard about that. It was quite a blow to him. There were no children to help him overcome his grief."

The playful yelling outside had become louder, forcing Bourville to raise his voice.

"A few years after the marriage, Emma had a baby. It was a difficult birth. It took her months to recuperate. The infant died the following spring and she was never able to have another after that."

Bourville stood and closed the window. Absolute silence descended on the office.

"After his son's death, Louis became more attached to the land, as did Emma. I believe it took the place of a child for them."

"I see. But why did he send for me after all these years?"

"Because, Monsieur de Montigny, you are the primary beneficiary in his will. It was his intention to give you the news himself. Aside from a few personal items bequeathed to friends named in this codicil," the notary pointed to a separate page, "everything that comprised your uncle's estate at Beau Val has been left to you."

"Everything? Is there no one else?"

"Neither Louis nor Emma ever mentioned anything to that effect. And, in any event, no one else is named in the will. However, it is my duty to tell you Louis imposed conditions that must be honored before the deed can be transferred to your name."

Montigny heard the rapping of the lion's head at the front
door followed by movement outside Bourville's office. Muffled
voices exchanged hushed utterances against the notary's clearly
articulated words. "You must live in the house, continue farming
and running the sawmill, and essentially carry on in your uncle's
place, as he would have wanted his own son to do."

Montigny remembered what the gentleman in the tavern had
told him the night before about an "unusual clause." Should he
be thankful that a new life was being offered to him or was it a
machination contrived by some gorgon to tempt him to abandon
his Ithaca forever? He felt like Odysseus in the land of the lotus-
eaters. But Odysseus resisted the honeyed fruit.

"And if I don't care to do that? Can't I simply sell the
property?"

The knock at the door was timid. Edouard entered carrying
a stack of documents. "Monsieur Bourville, the papers for the
Talbot estate have arrived."

"I'm with a client at the moment, as you can see." The notary
was visibly perturbed by the intrusion. "Take them to Bellemare's
office," he snapped, waving his hand at the young clerk as if to say,
"You should know better."

The scolded employee exited obsequiously, closing the door
softly behind him. It was at that point that Montigny noticed
Bourville's facial twitch, an almost imperceptible quiver of his
left eye—the result of years of close reading well into the night,
deciphering long documents written in dissimilar styles of
penmanship.

"There's another contingency. If at any time you sell the
property, all monies received as a result will be placed in escrow.
You'll only be allowed to keep any sums exceeding the present
worth of the estate. The rest must be donated to the Basilica."

"I never expected anything like this."

"I was bewildered by that clause as well since I knew your
uncle and can attest to the fact that his religious beliefs were
rather ill-defined to say the very least. But he did appreciate art.
The proceeds would be earmarked for the acquisition of
paintings and sculpture for the Basilica and a few other churches
in the region."

During our conversation this morning, the notary misunderstood my astonishment. Whether or not I receive the inheritance is not the issue, but rather the heavy responsibility that has suddenly been placed upon me—being saddled with the eccentricities of someone I have never even met—especially at this juncture.

"I believe, Monsieur de Montigny, that you have a sizeable inheritance coming to you from your father. Consequently, am I right in assuming, if I may be candid, that you are not in urgent need, if indeed you are in need at all, of your uncle's property? At least from a financial perspective."

A nod cued the notary to continue.

"If you should decide to accept the terms outlined in the will and take up residence here, it would represent a radical change for you. I suggest you inspect the estate but, more importantly, take the time to weigh the implications."

Montigny had brought liquid assets and small objects of value that could be sold for cash, but the total sum might not be sufficient for an extended stay. It was indispensable that he ensure himself access to supplemental funds should he need them. He broached the subject with the notary.

"Oh yes. Shortly after Louis's passing, I entered into contact on your behalf with Monsieur Robert Langlois, a merchant of considerable wealth accustomed to offering credit, for want of a better word, to people of standing who find themselves in situations like yours. I've dealt with him over the years and know him to be an honest gentleman. Might I suggest you call on him in a week or two, after you've had a chance to visit the estate? You'll be in a better position to assess your needs and make the appropriate arrangements with him. I've taken the initiative of drafting this note. Once he sees it's from me, you'll have no difficulty whatsoever. Let me give you his address."

Bourville lifted the golden griffin, dipped the finely sharpened quill tip into the porcelain cup, and scribbled the information on a piece of paper which he blotted and folded neatly before handing it to Montigny along with the note. The moment Montigny felt the paper's heft and texture between his fingers, he knew Bourville used only the finest French vellum.

Beau Val, on this Wednesday the 9th day of October 1734.

After Madame Seguin put Pierre to bed this evening, the majordomo informed me that there was an occurrence here not long after Louis's passing. I am surprised he did not tell me of it the day we arrived at the estate. It seems there was a failed burglary attempt on the 21st of September. His wife thought she heard noises in the middle of the night. He inspected the premises but found no one. Nothing was out of place. The following morning, he noticed the kitchen door had been forced. The intruder may have been frightened off before he could take anything. Later that day, the majordomo's daughter came upon a silver button while sweeping the kitchen floor. It belonged to no one at the manor. The majordomo insisted on giving it to me. I was touched by his honesty, but told him I had no use for it. He decided to retain it for safekeeping, in the event its owner might one day be found. I am more concerned with the safety of the premises than with finding the owner of a tiny button. I suggested he bring one of the dogs into the manor each night for his own security and that of his family.

This week at the estate has revealed many things. Much more than I'd counted on.

Quebec City, on this Friday the 11th day of October 1734.

We left Beau Val yesterday in the chill of the early morning. Frost clung to the blades of grass and reeds along the way. Indian summer is no more than a memory.

A brilliant shaft of afternoon sun cut the tavern into two distinct spaces of light and shadow. Montigny took off his cloak, scarf, and hat, and hung them on a wall peg.

"Monsieur de Montigny, over here!" It was a familiar voice. The fur trader was sitting by the windows. He nodded toward the empty seat across from him.

"They told me you'd gone away for a few days."

Montigny waved to Sylvie and pointed to Desjardins's cup.

"I went to visit my uncle's property."

"And? Have you decided what you're going to do?"

"Not yet."

"You're right not to be hasty."

"It's going to be complicated. It's not just a question of

property and possessions. There are people involved. Slaves. There was no mention of them in the will. Bourville said nothing about it. But you knew my uncle had slaves, didn't you?"

"Yes, of course. I also know he treated them decently."

"There are more than two dozen of them, counting the children. They're hoping I'll take over so nothing will change. They're afraid of being sold."

A cup of liquid garnet appeared on the table. Montigny looked at it distractedly. "Settling the estate will take time."

"Believe me, you'll have lots of that," smiled Desjardins. "With this cold snap, we'll be getting snow before you know it. Once the Saint Lawrence freezes over, there'll be no more boat traffic till spring. I'm afraid you're marooned."

"I'll never forget my uncle's descriptions of the winters here. Their severity—and their beauty."

"You'll get a chance to see for yourself. You know what they say here: there's just one season in Canada—winter. The rest of the year is spent talking about it and waiting for it to come. But enough about the cold, that will be the main topic of conversation soon enough. What was your impression of old Bourville?"

"The consummate notary, right down to his spectacles..."

Screams from outside interrupted his response. Sounds of panic, the neighing of a horse, and the clatter of falling objects made the two men bolt outside.

A woman was lying unconscious in the street. Casks and barrels were strewn everywhere. The contents of a large wicker laundry basket had spilled in all directions.

I pushed through the crowd. The cooper driving the wagon claimed he hadn't seen her until it was too late. She came out of nowhere.

When I drew near, I saw it was the widow.

"Quick, someone get some brandy," Montigny shouted. He sat on the ground and gently raised her torso, bracing it against his arm. Sylvie rushed out of the tavern with a tall brown bottle. He poured a few drops of its contents on the injured woman's pale lips. Her eyelids fluttered. Color returned to her face.

"There's no way to be sure how badly hurt she is until I can examine her thoroughly."

"I'll get a carriage," yelled Desjardins, disappearing down a side street.

Montigny looked up at the crowd. "Does anyone know where she lives?"

"Not far from here, with her sister, on *rue de Meulles*." It was Nicolet, the blacksmith's son, who had responded—a young man with reddish hair and cheeks scarred by a bout of smallpox that nearly took his life two years earlier.

"Can you show us the way?"

Moving closer, Nicolet tipped his head forward in an affirmative nod. Desjardins returned, seated at the reins of a black four-wheeled carriage. By now, the woman was standing but still groggy, supported by Montigny on one side and Nicolet on the other. They helped her into the carriage. Sylvie raced over once more with Montigny's things. He draped his cloak over the widow and hoisted himself inside. Nicolet climbed up beside Desjardins. They were about to pull off when a voice stopped them.

"Wait!"

Bent figures were gathering the spilled linens. Nicolet took the filled basket and placed it on his lap while Montigny held the widow's hand gently in his. Desjardins gave the reins a tug. The journey had begun.

Neither of the passengers inside could tell if the great wheels were rolling on the ground or if the carriage had taken flight. Houses, trees, people flashed by like ghosts. That was the effect of the vehicle's speed, so swiftly did everything appear and vanish on either side. The movement was dizzying. The widow closed her eyes to keep from losing consciousness but she wanted the odd sensation to go on forever. She was in a space where time did not exist, where obligations were effaced by whirling delirium.

The carriage made a turn and the pace slowed. *Rue de Meulles*. Within proximity of one another were the butcher, baker, wigmaker, hatter, tailor, cobbler, chimney sweep, and locksmith. The craftsmen were further down: carpenters, cabinetmakers, stonemasons, tanners, and metalworkers. Nicolet pointed to a small house that had appeared on the left. Desjardins brought the carriage to an abrupt halt, climbed down, and gestured to Nicolet to hand him the laundry basket. Balancing it on his hip, he tapped on the front door with the silver knob of his walking stick.

Steam and vapors filled the back room. A fire had to be kept burning to heat the iron. The faded brown cotton pinafore of the tall, slender woman working there was moist with perspiration. Her drawn features placed her in that nebulous phase of life called middle age. She had spent the morning tending to the bulk of the washing. A large vat was filled with soap and lye, another with rinse water. Years before, when her mother started taking in laundry, her father dug a well behind the house to spare his wife the arduous task of fetching water at the pump down the street. It was a small luxury, but a luxury just the same since most city dwellers, especially in that part of town, depended on public wells. The laundry was hung to dry on the room's far side where a series of ropes suspended from opposite walls wove their way back and forth.

The fire helped speed the drying time, but a few damp garments still hung on the lines from the previous day. Piles of clothes and linens surrounded her, some in haphazard wads, others stacked and ready for delivery. There were sets of white tablecloths and napkins of varying quality and wear, sheets and bolster pillowcases, Nîmes cotton drawnwork fichus, gauze aprons, cotton and wool stockings, chemises and camisoles in all shapes and sizes, gentlemen's and ladies' handkerchiefs—most with handsome floral motifs. It was a behind-the-scenes look at the lower city's private life. The laundress associated each piece she ironed with its owner and imagined the articles as costumes for a play, accessories in an intimate daily drama. The performances were endlessly rehearsed in her mind. But she needed to pay constant attention to her work. It was easy to scorch the more delicate fabrics. One unfortunate mishap a month or two before had cost her dearly. She was accustomed to putting in long hours and always returned the clean, neatly pressed linens and clothing promptly. Her reliability had built her a longstanding clientele.

A girl of almost four was playing with a rag doll near a large hamper. A cat dozed unperturbed on a heap of washing, ready to pounce or flee according to the dictates of any unexpected situation. The loud tapping at the front door caught them all by surprise. The cat opened its eyes sleepily. The sound was not near enough to pose a threat. The laundress put down her iron, took the child by the hand, and went to answer.

She knew something was wrong as soon as she saw the basket. "Oh my God! Marie Claire! What happened to her?"

"Your sister had a slight accident, but there seems to be no cause for alarm."

The woman looked past Desjardins, released her grip on the child's hand, and ran toward Marie Claire.

"Are you alright? Let's take her to her room."

Montigny and Nicolet helped Marie Claire through the main room into a smaller one and onto the bed there. Her sister heard Desjardins clear his throat. She turned. "Oh, you can put that down anywhere. Anne Perreault," she said, wiping her hand on the front of her pinafore before extending it to him. A worried smile crossed her lips. He set the basket on the floor and shook her hand warmly. "Auguste Desjardins. Pleased to meet you, Madame." Assuming from her age that she was married, he had addressed her as such.

His eyes quickly scanned the premises. He was accustomed to judging unfamiliar surroundings in a matter of seconds. His trade required it. The dwelling was far from lavish—comfortable at best. There was a spinning wheel in one corner near the open hearth. The cupboards, cabinets, and linen chests were made of pine, less costly than hard oak or walnut.

Anne, Desjardins, and Nicolet waited in the front room for the diagnosis. The moment had come for Montigny to join them, take leave of his patient and the pain of her secrets. As he reached the threshold, he brushed against a small chair in his path and stopped to reposition it. The gesture gave him time to shake the images from his mind.

Her wounds were deep, like theirs. She managed to slip from the grasp of Thanatos. Why had they not?

"She's still suffering from the injuries she sustained last spring. They haven't completely healed. She shouldn't have been out delivering laundry."

"I know, Doctor, but she's stubborn. I can't keep her down. She's frightened of being alone yet when she's in the company of others, she becomes withdrawn. It's as though she longed to be nowhere. I worry about her. Perhaps she'll listen to you."

"She had a bad scare today," he said. "Her ankle is very tender. She must have twisted it trying to jump out of the cart's way. It's a miracle she wasn't crushed. She'll need to stay off her feet for a few days."

Hearing the doctor, Desjardins concluded that their role at the Perreault household had ended. "Well, I guess we'll be going, Madame, and leave you to tend to your sister."

"Thank you all so much for everything. If you hadn't been there..."

"I'd like to stay a little longer," Montigny interrupted. "If you don't mind. To be sure there are no complications."

"I'll serve you both supper in her room," Anne said, once Desjardins and Nicolet had gone. "Nothing fancy, I'm afraid. I made some pea soup this morning." She was unaware that she was addressing a baron whose *Saint Cloud* porcelain dinnerware bore the family crest and was regularly laden with pheasant and truffles.

"I'm sure it will be delicious."

Anne seemed convinced by his response. "Let me feed Suzanne and get her ready for bed first. It won't take long."

In the late afternoon silence, Montigny sat on the small wooden chair by the bed, pondering the soft features of the woman resting calmly by his side. What momentary peace had she found? And what horrors remained locked in the chambers of her mind? When Anne brought in the supper, he thought only seconds had passed, but the sun had almost completely set. The last glimmers of twilight, that uncertain moment that is neither night nor day, shone through the small window.

Anne set steaming bowls of thick yellow soup and a pile of dark bread on the pine table. When she lit the tin oil lamp next to the bowls, its golden flame transformed the space. The Italian painters whose works Montigny contemplated whenever he had the occasion were masters at creating similar illusions. They could transfigure a flat surface into a multidimensional world complete unto itself, where everything is in its place and nothing can be altered without destroying the beauty and magic of the whole.

Artemisia Gentileschi's self-portrait as an Allegory of

*Painting. Rosabla Carriera's Allegory of Spring. The two works,
the two women, have captured feminine beauty as no other
artists or paintings can. Anne adjusted the pillows, helped her
sister sit up in bed, and placed the tray of warm food on her lap.
Art in movement. The sensation has stayed with me.*

~~~

A noise broke the heavy silence and pulled Pierre from the
temporary refuge he had found in his father's past. Another
prisoner was maneuvering through the sea of breathing corpses,
making his way to the corner furthest from Pierre, where there
were buckets lined along the wall. Most were overflowing with
urine. Rarely did the guards empty them. The sound of a tiny
stream hitting the bucket's tin surface echoed in the obscurity.

The prison cell and degradation were in sharp contrast to
the environment in which Pierre had been raised. Over the years,
he had come to understand, at least in part, his father's views on
the function of art. Possessing objects of beauty was not a goal in
itself, but rather secondary to the contemplation of the harmonious
world such objects suggested, a world of perfection and order.
They were representations of an ideal whose very existence
meant that the ideal could be achieved and should be accessible
to everyone. Pierre had been unable to fully reconcile that
esthetic vision with the fact that his father never completed the
work he had begun on the chateau of Loublanc. At the age of
twenty-four, Pierre had married Armande and left Loublanc for
Cinqfontaines, the estate bequeathed to him by his grandfather.
That is where Charles, Françoise, and Eugenie were born.
Loublanc remained in an unfinished state up to the time of his
father's death. Montigny spent the rest of his years alone there,
in a castle frozen in time. He would not, could not allow
Loublanc to change.

The cell was again silent. Pierre picked up the loose pages
once more.

~~~

Her sister left us alone. She had pushed back the bed drapes.

Prussian blue. So soothing. I moved the oil lamp slightly away from my bowl. The change of position cast a glow on her face, revealing the same tranquility I've seen in paintings by Georges de La Tour.

Montigny admired how La Tour had succeeded in infusing *Saint Sebastian Tended by Irene* with an atmosphere at once simple and mysterious by placing the light source in the center to lend a smooth, wax-like quality to the figures, how he had illuminated the reds and blues of the clothing by the accordant flame of a torch in *The Discovery of Saint Alexis*. But at that moment, it was the auburn gleam of Marie Claire's hair and the hints of jade in her eyes that magnetized Montigny.

"Your name... The slave woman's was the same. The one they burned."

"You remember?"

"I haven't been able to forget what I saw that day in the square. It's engraved in my mind."

"I found it ironic that we shared the same name. I identified with her. With all of them."

"What do you mean?"

He noticed a glint in her eyes. Had they welled up with emotion or was it simply a reflection of the lamp's flame?

"You know...my husband and son... They were murdered. Butchered. Their bodies were never found. The wolves devoured them, no doubt. Without a decent burial, their spirits will never be at rest. Nor will I."

Montigny reached for her hand in an awkward gesture of consolation. She continued, "The killer is still on the loose. He needs to die a terrible death. That's the curse I wish on him. He wasn't even at his own execution. But I was. It was as though I were the one being put to death instead of him. And they call that justice. It brought back such awful memories, as if they were beating my body with the iron bar intended for him. Each memory hit me like a separate blow. I've been marked like the slave woman they branded that day. I don't just mean the scars. People lower their voices when they see me coming."

Montigny remained silent. The intensity of the moment needed to dissipate before he could speak. But it was she who broke the stillness. "You're wearing the color of death, too.

You've lost someone."

He turned pale. "My...uncle...died a few weeks ago."

Montigny would not admit, would not reveal more. Finally, he said, "The pain must be... Perhaps if you talked about it..."

Marie Claire did not react. She seemed distracted, her thoughts elsewhere. At first, Montigny was not sure she had even heard him. Then he saw her swallow and take a deep breath. She was entering another region of her psyche, one to which she would not return without good cause. Montigny thought again of La Tour, of his *Magdalene at the Mirror*—a visual representation of life's riddle. It was perhaps the most perfect work of its kind. Seated at a table, the repentant Magdalene gazes pensively into a looking glass, her chin resting on her right hand, her left hand on a skull partially obscuring the light of an oil lamp. Shadows envelope her. Time is transcended, erased. Tears etched the crimson of Marie Claire's cheeks as she went on, her voice altered.

"In this land, nothing is what it seems. Nothing is simple. I loved a man, but he's dead now. Gone forever. Did he deserve to die? Perhaps. I don't know anymore." She stopped, unsure where she was, unable to separate past from present. "Jacques was so handsome. And I was very young. I met him here, at the port. He had come in on a ship from Acadia. It was the most splendid summer of my life. He was loading cargo on the docks one morning when I walked by with a basket of laundry. The wind took a petticoat from the top of the pile and blew it to the ground by his feet. When he bent down to pick it up, he smiled at me. I'll never forget how large his hand appeared to me as he gave me the delicate garment. The whole thing seemed so ridiculous. I was a bit embarrassed. I saw him every day that summer. Mornings when I went by the docks to pick up linens or make deliveries. And evenings if he had free time."

Marie Claire's mind raced back to that Edenic period before her initiation to misfortune and evil, the innocent simplicity of her early existence. It was the last barrier separating her from what should not be spoken. She could see herself helping her mother with the laundering. She remembered the neighborhood children and the chunks of bread and cheese she always gave to the poorer ones. And there was Felicien, the wigmaker, pinching the tips of his whiskers between his thumb and forefinger as he prattled on about everything from the weather to the rising prices at the market, his walking stick swaying left and right. He used to chase the urchins away from the side of his house with his stick raised. One day, the children found a bell. "Get old Felicien to hang it on his front door so we'll be warned," they told her. Yet no matter how she tried, he stubbornly refused. She could still hear Jacques's advice to her. "Tell him, 'Your house is the grandest on the street, Monsieur. This will make it even more so.' " The ploy worked. Whenever Felicien opened his door the bell would ring and the children would scurry from his garden. Their laughter was already far, far away...

The wall protecting her suddenly crumbled. She had no choice but to continue on the path before her. "Summer came to an end." There was a weariness in her voice now. "Jacques was to return to Acadia. But we'd become inseparable. We married in September and moved to Port Royal. I thought that was where my life would be. Jacques did what he could to earn a living: fishing, dock work, anything and everything, depending on the season. We lived in a little house by the water—just a shack really. It was a fishing village. I can smell the sea air even now. It reminded me of the port here, where I grew up, but it had a newness to it. I loved that smell."

She fell silent, perhaps reliving a moment of pleasure and the calm it brought. Montigny said nothing as he felt the serenity along with her. She went on. "Life was hard, but there were good times. Simple times. Bright warm afternoons." She spoke of sitting in the shade, knitting a blanket for the baby she was expecting, the needles interlocking loops of yellow yarn. She tried to describe the heavy, comforting sound of the axe as Jacques chopped logs for the coming winter. "He continued his work for a while, then stopped, looked up at the blistering sun, and wiped his brow. He put down the axe, walked toward me, and gently placed his hands on mine. I felt the knitting needles leave my grasp."

As Montigny listened, Jacques and Marie Claire faded. He saw himself—with her. They were together again. He had to force himself back and concentrate on the voice telling the story, the voice that had been eclipsed by another.

"Jacques laughed and pulled me to my feet. I smiled and caressed my stomach thinking 'in four months we'll have a child.' "

She rested her other hand on Jacques's shoulder.

"Let's go inside," he said with the softness of a warm breeze.

She laughed coyly. "And why would we want to do that on such a pleasant day?"

"To see if the grass is greener in there."

"You know, once there are three of us, it will be harder to keep watch over the color of the grass."

"That's why we need to check on it now!"

They laughed as they held each other by the waist and walked slowly toward the house. Jacques pushed the door closed with a slam.

A loud thud startled Marie Claire and Montigny. The small chair near the room's entrance was lying on its side.

"Oh, I'm so sorry. I didn't mean to alarm you." Anne was carrying a large tray with a pot of soup and deep ladle. "That silly chair really is too close to the door. We should find another spot for it once and for all."

Montigny sprang to his feet and set the chair back on its legs, further away. "Let me help you, Anne. May I take anything?"

"I think I can manage now. I just wanted to know if either of you would like some more soup," she said with a nervous laugh as she put the heavy tray down next to the empty soup bowls on the table.

"How sweet of you, Anne. Not for me, but perhaps the doctor would like another bowl."

"Thanks, but I couldn't." Quickly realizing his negative response might be construed as a sign he hadn't liked Anne's cooking, Montigny added almost in the same breath, "But it was good. Very good indeed."

Marie Claire's slight smile conveyed a complicity that Anne did not share.

"Well, I'll go check on Suzanne," Anne spouted to break the almost merciless stillness that had descended on the room. Her sister and the stranger from across the Atlantic had momentarily severed ties with the present. They could not pursue their faltering course so long as she was there with them, for either knowingly or unknowingly, the two were beginning a ritual of their own making. Anne had unexpectedly become a stranger, and she had sensed it. Her footsteps echoed as she left the room and Marie Claire's voice pronounced the words sadly and ever so softly.

"It seems very far away now. I was in love and nothing else mattered. I don't know if you've ever been truly, deeply in love." Her glance in Montigny's direction forced him to respond.

"Yes...but it's over now. Or at least it's not the same as it was before."

"Things have a way of changing without our wanting them to. Jacques had the thickest blond hair. And the wind and salt air made his skin rough. I liked the way it felt. He was tall and strong, but was always unsure of himself. He was thrilled when Thomas was born. A son! Jacques was so proud. We had no money to speak of, or possessions for that matter. Just the bare essentials: a bed, a cradle, a table, a few chairs. It was enough, though..."

She remembered a cold Acadian morning in autumn soon after Thomas's birth. She could still feel Jacques's touch. It was passionate and sensual, rugged yet gentle. There was a fire burning in the hearth. The bed was warm. Jacques's body enveloped her as his large hands caressed her entire being, his body pressing ever tighter against hers. She alone was destined to be with him, to feel his touch that way as they glided freely into the unexplored. But what intermittent sound was calling them back? It was barely audible. They needed to descend, had to return to ordinary existence.

The crying went from sporadic and soft to loud and constant. Jacques stopped. They took a moment to delight in listening to the baby, and then Marie Claire put on her woolen robe, went to the cradle, and gently lifted her son in her arms. "There, there, Thomas. Don't cry. Mama's here to take care of you. Good boy. You're hungry, aren't you, my little robin?" As she moved toward the rocking chair, gently coaxing Thomas's tiny mouth toward her breast, she turned to Jacques. "We need bread and molasses. And if there's enough change, some eggs."

Jacques pushed off the covers, slipped on his pants, and went to the cupboard. Pulling down the earthenware pot from the top shelf, he removed its wooden lid, pretended to fish out some coins, and put them in his pocket. "There's not much left. I'll pick up a few things this morning. They'll have to last us to the week's end."

Had Marie Claire fallen for his bluff or did she say nothing because she didn't want to wound his pride?

"The captain's taking the *Belle Aurore* out tomorrow for another catch. Wants me to help pull the nets. He still owes me for the last time. If he gets around to paying me, we should be set till the end of the month. Then I'll see what I can do."

"We'll manage. We always have." The infant was suckling at her breast.

"Once the fishing season ends, it'll be even harder to get by. Sometimes I'm not sure we'll make it. This is no way to live. Not for you and the baby."

Their eyes met in surprise at the sound of an unexpected knock at the door. No one ever came by that early unless something was wrong. Jacques grabbed his shirt. As he was putting it on, he went to the window to look out. "It's Martin. What could he want at this time of day?" He threw Marie Claire her shawl, and then opened the door. A blast of cold air filled the room. Martin entered hurriedly, rubbing himself to warm up. "Mornin', mate. Mornin', M'am Lambert. Sure is a cold one out there. But it's nice and warm in here."

Martin was a lanky man with salt-and-pepper hair. His eyes were starting to lose the intensity that had made him so striking in his younger days.

"Hello, Martin. What brings you around at this hour?"

"Got a piece of news that might be of interest to you."

"You do, eh? Well come on over here by the fire."

Jacques pulled a chair out from the table. Tilting his head in Marie Claire's direction, Martin gave him a knowing glance, and whispered with a grin, "Hope I didn't interrupt nothin'."

Only slightly embarrassed, Jacques returned the smile. "No, Thomas just woke up."

"I was afraid I might catch you at an awkward moment, if you know what I mean."

"So what's this information you think I might be interested in?"

"Well, you know old man Bedard?"

"Yeah. Don't care for him much. Never have."

"You mean you *didn't* care for him. *Didn't*. He just died. Caught pneumonia about a week ago."

"What's that got to do with me?"

"Think about it, mate. You need money comin' in. Old Bedard just kicked. The magistrate's already lookin' for someone to take his place. It's steady pay, whether there's any executions or not. It's pretty quiet in these parts. Can't remember the last time there was a hangin'. Sure, you might have to do a floggin' every now and then or put some rabble-rouser in the pillory. But an execution? Nah, won't happen. When you think about it, old man Bedard had it pretty easy. I know the stipend ain't a lot, but it's guaranteed. It'd sure help make ends meet, specially in the off season."

Jacques looked down at his hands as he weighed the consequences of accepting against those of refusing. Finally he said, "I don't think so, Martin. But say, why don't you do it?"

"Can't. Promised my wife I wouldn't. Besides, I really don't need the money the way you do. My kids is all big now. They pull their own weight whenever they can. Next season, the boys'll be goin' out on the boats. But you're just startin' out. Think about it. Think about the future. Your family's future."

Suddenly Jacques and Martin were gone. Anne was there instead. Neither Marie Claire nor Montigny had noticed her enter the room. The evening had come to an end.

"I really should be going. Marie Claire needs to rest," Montigny said with reluctance. "With your permission," he uttered almost inaudibly, "I'd like to stop by in a week or so to make sure that ankle is healing properly."

Anne turned to her sister.

"It's so kind of you to take such an interest."

Picking up on Marie Claire's approval, Anne responded, "Of course, Doctor. You're always welcome here."

He bid his patient good night and followed Anne to the hearth in the main room. She helped him on with his cloak, then handed him his hat and scarf.

"Why don't you come for supper next Thursday at around the same time? Strange how she opened up to you. Ever since it happened, she's been awfully distant. Keeping all those terrible memories bottled up inside..."

As she lifted the wrought iron door latch, she paused. Montigny could see she wanted to say something but was having difficulty finding the words.

"I'm worried about her, Doctor. I know that wasn't an accident today. This isn't the first time."

Montigny waited impatiently for her to go on.

"About a month ago, she disappeared. The search party spent hours looking for her. They found her in the woods by the river. She was just staring at the currents. When they got close, she didn't move, didn't even realize they were there. They spoke to her, but she didn't answer. They had to shake her to bring her back from wherever it was she had traveled to in her mind. She claims she was lost, but I'm sure that's not true. She knows these parts like the palm of her hand."

The situation was serious; otherwise Anne would not have been so quick to confide her fears to him, a total stranger.

"Keep a close eye on her and let me know if there's any change. She's lucky to have such a caring sister."

Montigny had responded as consolingly as he could. What else could he say? He hardly knew the women. And he knew even less about what had occurred before his arrival in New France.

He walked back to the *Auberge du Roy* by the light of the moon, but in his imagination he was still in her room, watching the color of the bed drapes deepen with the changing incandescence of the oil lamp's flame. He hadn't been alone with a woman his age for almost half a year. He hadn't wanted to. He thought he would never want to again. Thursday seemed an eternity away. But why? Why should he care? Wouldn't she simply continue her own account of sadness and death? He was caught in a spiral of ambiguous emotions, dreading every heartbeat that separated him from what was gone, eager for what was yet to be.

The inn's front door was locked, but Montigny could make out a corpulent profile through the fogged panes of glass. He knocked.

"Why it's Monsieur de Montigny. Or should I say Monsieur le Baron? I trust you had a pleasant evening."

The innkeeper was friendly enough, but his temperament could change abruptly if he thought someone might be trying to hoodwink him. He shared all the tasks related to running the inn with his wife, who was his female double in both appearance and disposition. The two of them were caricatured incarnations of the art of inn keeping. The fact that the baron had reserved rooms for the entire season helped assure their financial stability over the coming winter months. They were particularly happy to rent Montigny not two but three large rooms, at his request. The third served as private quarters where the baron could retire from the company of others and tend to his affairs. Situated at the end of the corridor, the improvised suite afforded both space and seclusion—at least as much as could be had under the circumstances.

"We have to close at ten. That's the law. Of course, if the night's especially merry, we pretend not to hear the bell. Just once in a while, mind you. We don't want to get fined. Anyway, I'm sure you'll not wish to be left out on the street till dawn with the young ruffians. They'll knock you down and steal your money purse in an instant, so do remind me to give you a key to the front door. There are always candles in the metal box by the entry if you need light."

Montigny looked in on Pierre. The boy and his governess were sound asleep. He gently removed the volume of the Marquise de Sevigné's letters from Madame Seguin's hands and set it by the candlestick on her nightstand. The wick had gone out on its own. Stepping over to the trundle bed, he kissed Pierre on the forehead, and then walked the short distance to his own room. He would record another entry in his journal before submitting to forces beyond his control.

Each step I take brings me deeper into the labyrinth. My journey is without direction. I know not where or at what moment I will encounter the monster. Unlike Theseus, I have no golden thread to guide my passage from the maze. Who is she? A beacon in the darkness or an instrument of fate placed on my path to draw me into the web?

Quebec City, on this Saturday the 12th day of October 1734.

I ran into Desjardins again this afternoon. He is an extraordinary man...

"Murder. Last spring, a Pawnee killed him and his son. Just a boy. He tried to kill her, as well, before running off. She managed to make her way out of the woods to a clearing with her daughter. Some field workers found them and brought them to the hospital here."

"Despite her sadness, she's rather pretty."

"Indeed. A good woman, too, regardless of what some may say. These days, that's a rare combination. And I speak from experience."

Desjardins continued his account between sips of wine. If anybody could tell Montigny about Marie Claire, he was the one. "She's been through an incredible ordeal. She's lucky to be alive. It was hard for her to talk about it, but she knew she had to make her deposition if she wanted even a modicum of justice to be done. A trial was held, though the accused was long gone. He was judged guilty and sentenced to be executed by having his bones crushed. But since he was nowhere to be found, the sentence was carried out in the manner you saw in the town square on your arrival. An execution in effigy."

"I gathered that's what it was. What an absurdity." Now it was Montigny's turn to speak from experience. "Any crime of violence that goes unpunished is a blot on the social fabric. A moral failing."

"Perhaps, yet what's the alternative? An example must be set. The crime and the criminal have to be recognized."

*Chagrin d'amour dure toute la vie…*Color left Montigny's face. He needed to latch on to the first thought that came into his head. "You never finished telling me about the other incidents in the square that day. Or the Black Code."

"I suppose I didn't. Well, to begin with, slavery in these parts is different than in the other territories. The king was reticent to allow it here. It was a poor investment, he claimed. Africans wouldn't survive the winters. But the proponents used a clever strategy to change his mind. They promised to outfit slaves of color with beaver pelts to keep them warm in winter."

"What's so clever about that?"

"Wait, I haven't finished. The real reason the king was finally persuaded had little to do with humanitarian concerns. The slavery advocates told His Royal Highness that if the

Negroes wore the pelts, the value of the furs would double."

"And why would that be?"

It was so obvious to Desjardins. Then he remembered that his drinking partner was a stranger to New France.

"The pelts would absorb the slaves' body oils, of course."

Montigny stared across the table for a moment, and then smiled skeptically. "Are you making this up to see how gullible I am?"

"Not at all. Any fur trader worth his salt knows there are two types of beaver pelts: dry and oily. Wearing dry pelts for a time allows sweat and body oils to soak into them. It makes the fur soft and plush—and highly prized by furriers. It's an old Indian practice. The king finally gave in, but we never got an active trade going with Africa. There were too many wars. So the Black Code has never been made official here. If it had, the slave woman accused of stealing, the one you saw in the town square, would have been hanged after they branded her palm."

"But she wasn't an African. She was an Indian, wasn't she?"

"Indeed, a Pacotas. Negroes are scarce here, so traders have turned to the natives. There's nothing new about it. It's been going on for hundreds of years. Even the Indians themselves do it. Some native languages make no distinction between 'prisoner' and 'slave.' On occasion, they give their slaves to us or to other tribes as gifts. But generally, they sell whoever they capture or trade them for goods. Most are Pawnees. They're easy to get, but they're a bad risk. They have a reputation for running off the first chance that comes their way."

Montigny caught Sylvie's eye. She gave a hurried nod before stepping up to the wooden keg to fill her pewter pitcher.

"The Negress who was hanged and burned that day..."

Desjardins peered at Montigny over the brim of his empty wine cup. "She was the slave of a merchant's widow in Montreal. Her owner had no more need of her and was planning to sell her instead of freeing her—a common way of terminating ownership here. The slave had little hope of ever being released from bondage. That's why she decided to run away. Down to New England with her lover. A white man. Before fleeing, she wanted to get even with her mistress and destroy any evidence of her escape, so she set fire to the house."

Sylvie poured their wine. Montigny saw Desjardins give her a wink before taking a long sip.

"Did more damage than she'd intended. The night watch rang the tocsin the very second the flames broke out, but there was a strong westerly wind that evening and the fire spread. In just three hours, a good part of the city burned to the ground—a church, a hospital, a convent, and nearly fifty houses. It's amazing no one perished. Her lover managed to get away. She wasn't so lucky. The mounted guards picked her up not far from Montreal. She confessed to the crime, yet never admitted her lover had any part in it, even when questioned under torture. They crushed her knees and ankles in a vice."

Montigny stared blankly.

"Yes, my friend," continued Desjardins, "I suppose our methods are just as dubious as anywhere else. The whole of Montreal was enraged by the damage the fire caused. The magistrates feared a riot. That's why they moved her execution up here."

"It was horrible."

"Yes, but her fate would have been worse under the Black Code. Wherever the Code is law, slaves have no more rights than do minors. They're at the complete mercy of their owners. But up here, they can appeal any charges levied against them, which is precisely what she did. There was never any question of setting her free, of course, but she did succeed in having her sentence revised. The initial one was far more gruesome."

"That's difficult to imagine."

"Well listen to this. Before transporting her to the square in the rubbish wagon and burning her at the stake, the executioner was supposed to lead her to the door of the parish church where she was to hold a torch and repent her evil deed before having her hand axed off."

The violence of the image blinded Montigny.

But it is only by your light that my world exists.

Desjardins noticed the change of expression on Montigny's face. "Please excuse me. I have a tendency to rattle on."

"It's... I was just...thinking about my son." Montigny had become accustomed to inventing excuses.

"Perhaps you'd like to check on him."

"I'm sure Madame Seguin would alert me if there were a problem." He quickly pushed the conversation back across the table. "Please go on."

"As I was saying, she was spared the agony of having her hand chopped off. Oh, and they hanged her *before* they lit the kindling under her. More merciful than being burned alive, wouldn't you agree?"

The current of air that rushed through the tavern was cold. A Montagnais entered, closed the door behind him, and stood motionless. The shallow straw basket in his hands was filled with multicolored ornaments and tribal jewelry—dreams and traditions. Some of the drinkers put down their cups and stopped talking. The innkeeper looked the other way, as he usually did when natives came into his establishment. The chatter and drinking resumed as the Montagnais moved quietly among the tables, selling his wares.

"We strive for justice, in our own way," continued Desjardins.

"Justice? In a land where slavery is condoned?"

"I told you the colony was full of contradictions, did I not? The Indians learn from us and we from them. Both good and bad. The natives teach the bushmen how to make lightweight bark canoes and go straight to the source for the finest pelts, how to wrap their feet with strips of cloth for warmth. When they fall ill, it's the herbal remedies of the medicine men that they drink. We tend to focus less on idealism and more on immediate needs, the pragmatic over the philosophical if you will." He took a deep puff on his pipe. "So where do you stand, Monsieur de Montigny? Are you a philosopher or a pragmatist?"

The question emanated from a cloud of smoke.

A pause. Silent reflection.

"My first instinct is to say I'm a pragmatist, but someone said—a woman if I'm not mistaken—'to philosophize is to render to reason all its dignity...to shake the yoke of opinion and authority.' I do believe that to be true."

When the ornament seller came by, Desjardins peered into his basket with an eye of expertise, pulled a cloth pouch from his waistcoat pocket, poured some coins onto the table, and took a carved bone amulet on a long leather cord from the basket.

Placing the small warrior figure on the table next to the coins, he
looked the Montagnais in the eyes and pronounced a few words
Montigny did not understand. The Indian nodded, picked up the
money, and proceeded to the next table of drinkers, who shooed
him away with a distracted wave.

"I'm not sure what the right answer is to the question
you've asked me," continued Montigny.

"Perhaps my question may be too simplistic. We need to
look deeper into ourselves. Otherwise, we're dragged along by
the tides of change. The native peoples can teach us much about
going beneath the surface."

"You can speak their language. When you bought that
trinket…"

"This is no trinket, I assure you. Oh, I know a bit of
Algonquin. That's what the Montagnais speak. It's similar to
Cree. The best fur traders negotiate with the natives their way, in
their vernacular. There must be more than fifty languages. I can
only get along well enough in four to do business with them."
Desjardins picked up the amulet and rolled it between his
fingers. "The complexity of their rituals escapes the
comprehension of outsiders. We tend to brush them aside as
mere superstition, but I've seen some of them with my own eyes
and I can tell you otherwise. Do you know what a *shaman* is?"

The question caught Montigny off guard. The term had
been planted somewhere in his memory, but evoked only
imprecise notions. "I've come across the word in books. Isn't it
some sort of tribal medicine man?"

"It's more than that. We think of them as a cross between a
priest and a doctor because those are callings with which we're
familiar, but shamans have attained a form of enlightenment—
and therefore power—by confronting a personal crisis. They're
the first target whenever a tribe is attacked because they are the
keepers of sacred tribal traditions. I'm not talking about puberty
rituals or men with painted faces dancing around a campfire. I
mean a profound awareness, mightier than death itself."

Desjardins was now gazing intently at the amulet. A flood
of phantasmagoric images flashed before his eyes.

The young warrior has broken free from the carved bone.
His smooth body glistens in the hot sun. An ochre-colored cloth

covers his loins. A string of blue beads adorns his neck. The all-powerful eagle swoops down, carries him to the realm of shadows and flickering fires where the white bear devours him. A maiden, the Healing Spirit, lays herself on the warrior's bones. Soon they take on flesh. He is regenerated. Ecstasy transfigures him. Deeper into the cavern he descends. In its depths, a skull turns to dust in his hands. Bright sunrise. Return to life. The white bear runs in fear. The warrior stands tall against a circle of light.

"There are countless ways to undertake the journey." Desjardins was coming out of his trance. "Some stumble upon it on their own, others need to be shown the way." As the fur trader spoke, he pushed the amulet across the table. "Here. It's for you. Perhaps it will prove useful one day."

Quebec City, on this Monday the 14th day of October 1734.
Another appointment to discuss new issues based on what I've learned...

The notary's office was not far. As Montigny stopped to gaze out at the river's endless span of blue-gray, he heard voices and stifled laughter. A large group was marching past. Montigny watched. Several Indians—he counted nine—and three black men were moving in single file toward a large church near *rue de Buade*. They were all either approaching their twentieth year or had just seen its passing. A nun and Jesuit priest were leading them. A very young woman wearing the habit of a novice was at the rear. As the cortege reached the parvis and entered, a streak of lightening cut its way across the sky. There was a clap of thunder and it began to pour. Montigny ran inside to wait out what he hoped would be a passing cloudburst. He was in the Basilica of Notre Dame.

Beggars had positioned themselves at strategic points in the church. Two flanked the main portal. A third stood near the entry to the crypt. Montigny tossed a coin into one of their baskets. The dry refuge was well worth the small admission fee.

The smell of frankincense and melting beeswax would have alerted even a blind man to his surroundings. An occasional chord could be heard as the tuner adjusted the pipe organ, creating disjointed harmony and disorienting echoes. A few parishioners were scattered here and there. The low, uncomfortable wooden chairs with rush seats were much like the ones Montigny had to endure at weddings and baptisms back home. The Indians and black men were bunched together up front on the right. The priest stood at the helm of the troupe. His voice resounded through the vast enclosure, forming a distant counterpoint to Montigny's footsteps as he wandered about the nave, admiring the work of the artisans who had created the edifice under what must have been daunting conditions.

The paintings of the Stations of the Cross were extraordinarily fine in their execution, two in particular: the scourging at the pillar and the crucifixion. What unknown artist had so skillfully succeeded in conveying such suffering? At a side altar, the Virgin was mourning her dead son. Montigny pondered the marble pietà. What was it about the lustrous stone figures that captured his attention? He remembered his recurring dream and saw himself holding a woman against his chest. Looking away, he fought to keep the nightmare from playing itself out yet again in his mind.

He walked toward the main altar and the class at the front of the nave, sat on the opposite side, and pretended not to watch. One of the Indians, a Cree, was reading a religious text with obvious difficulty.

"So God created man in his own image. Male and female he created them. And God blessed them, and God said to them, be fruitful and multiply, and fill the earth and subdue it."

"Thank you, Georges." The Jesuit's voice detonated as he addressed the Cree. "Your reading skills have greatly improved. And now it's Victor's turn. Come to the front of the class, Victor, and tell us the lesson of Genesis in your own words."

The Indian took his place next to the Jesuit and began: "Great Spirit mix earth and water to make man. Put in sun to bake. Great Spirit return. Man black. Great Spirit say, 'Too much cooked.' "

The class snickered. The priest was clearly annoyed, but didn't intervene.

"Great Spirit make other clay man. Put in sun to bake. Great Spirit return. Man white. Great Spirit say, 'Too little cooked.' "

There was more laughter. The priest tapped his right

forefinger nervously on his left arm while silently biting his lower lip. He was not pleased, but must have been as curious as the rest of them to hear the end of the tale.

"Great Spirit try again. Man red. Great Spirit say, 'Cooked just right.' And so Great Spirit make black, white, and red man."

The conclusion elicited approving nods from the class.

"That was not the version of creation I asked you to learn, Victor." With a downward wave of the hand, the Jesuit dismissed the Indian and signaled him to go back to his seat. "Sister Marguerite will work with you this week."

"Now, Antoine," continued the Jesuit, "tell us about baptism. What does it mean?"

One of the three young black men in the group went to the front.

"Means I be like you."

"That's right, Antoine. You will become like us." The Jesuit was noticeably relieved. Antoine was making more sense than Victor.

"But Father, I be afraid."

"Why, Antoine?"

"'Cause it'll hurt real bad."

"Why do you think that?"

"For me to be like the white man, you got to pull off my skin."

"What on earth are you talking about? You know we would never do that," said the Jesuit in a paternalistic tone.

The whole class was laughing now. The nuns exchanged powerless glances. Antoine raised his eyes upward, lifted his hands in the air and exclaimed, "Hallelujah!" When he went back to his seat, he shook his head and mumbled, "They so serious. Don't knows a joke when they hears one!"

The heavy spire bell reverberated eleven times. Passing the pietà again, Montigny quickened his pace until he had pushed open the Basilica's large deeply carved oak doors and was outside. The storm had diminished to a light mist.

Quebec City, on this Tuesday the 15th day of October 1734.

Swords and daggers pierce my being at every turn. The blood I shed is not visible to the world, yet it flows profusely.

Unbearable is the pain I endure.

Thank God the innkeeper stores white spirits in his back pantry. It is a palliative that is not accessible to all. He agreed to share it with me—for a reasonable price, he said. How laughable. Any price would be reasonable for a liquid that might provide relief at this moment and attenuate the agony. Eau-de-vie. I want its fire to burn my heart and mind. Consume the grief. Extinguish the suffering.

Montigny filled his glass a fourth time. Madame Seguin and Pierre were fast asleep in the adjacent quarters. Perhaps his son would find tranquility. Perhaps his son's governess had derived comfort from the book of letters she kept by her bedside. Now, in his profound solitude, deep in the silent darkness, the third room he had rented for the season was a shelter from the tempest. But his storm was not outside. Seated in an armchair by the mantle, he pulled the locket from its velvet case and opened the silver front piece that hid the miniature painted on smooth, white ivory. It was the work of an itinerant Spanish artist passing through Bordeaux on his way to Holland. Montigny had forgotten his name, but the image the artist had rendered was there for him to ponder. Fine, precise brushstrokes, a palette of blues, golds, and reds. Hair that glowed like the sun, eyes with the shimmer of moonlight, magenta lips barely parted. The fairness of her countenance reflected the beauty that lay within. A generous heart, a soul both genuine and pure.

He closed the locket's cover and reached for the book by his side. Would its pages sooth his spirit? Would the words appease his aching soul? *Good nurse, come draw me the choicest wine from the jars you set aside in the hope that the ill-fated man will one day return to Ithaca, safe from death and doom...*

Resist as he might, his thoughts invariably returned to the image of the woman who had been his reason for living, given his existence meaning and, through no fault of her own, destroyed it. The hearth's blaze was turbulent. He riveted his eyes on the empty chair across from him. She was there with him, silently watching—a shadow as fragile and wavering as a candle's flame. Should he welcome her or cast her out into the night? No, he could not send her away, could not dismiss her so cruelly. He wanted to take her hand, reach across the divide that now separated them, and tell her what he had never said before. She looked on. Her lips did not move, yet she was speaking to him. Was this a visitation or was it a dream? He knew not which. When her utterances ceased, his lips formed words she understood but did not hear, for his voice had forevermore been forbidden to her. The strange harmony of their conversation continued until dawn.

Quebec City, on this Wednesday the 16th day of October 1734.
I thought in coming here I would be far from the superstitions that plague France and deride human reason.

The sound of yelling from the street woke Montigny. He didn't know where he was. He was not in his bed, not in his room. Still seated in the chair by the fireplace, his eyes fell on the empty bottle by his side. Vague recollections of nocturnal visions filled his mind as he faltered to the window. Unconnected words from below reached his ears. "Cemetery." "Outrageous." "Consecrated hosts." "Orgy." "Satan."

He ran down to the street to join one of the groups of men and women in animated discussion. Emotions were high. There was no thread of logic to the discourse.

"They don't know if it's human blood. Could have been an animal or a person that was sacrificed. No one's sure."

"And they didn't find a body? No remains?

"Not in the graveyard. Just blood."

"They found the infant's body on *rue de la Fabrique*."

"Them hosts was stolen from the convent chapel a few weeks ago."

"Madame André saw a fiery canoe fly through the sky that night, right over the city."

"Devils haunt the convent, ya know. They run up and down the stairs and throw things in the middle of the night."

"One of the nuns saw a demon. Came into her room, he did, and sat on her bed, and..."

"If women of God aren't spared, then..."

"This ain't the first time hosts've been stolen. 'Member last spring? And they never found out who done it."

"It was the devil."

"A black mass, that's what it was. No doubt about it. The

stuff in the graveyard proves it."

"There weren't no bruises on the infant's body. They don't think it was used in the ceremony."

Montigny's biles were agitated. He was afraid he might say something that would anger them all. He was so incensed he could not have spoken coherently even if he had wanted to.

"Well all these things is connected in some way."

"I bet those two are in on it. They cast spells, some say. And look at the kind of man the younger one married. Courted the devil, he did."

Montigny went back to his room in dismay. He had taken part in clinical analyses of potions used in cult ceremonies in France. Arsenic, sulfur, semen, menstrual blood, toads, hair, bats, such were the ingredients. As a student of medicine, he had studied at length the *Chambre Ardente* affair, an intrigue at the royal court some forty years earlier involving priests performing black masses over naked women and placentas. Poisonings, bribery, sacrifices of newborns and young children had been reported. The king's edict did not put an end to the madness. Montigny and many of his colleagues maintained, or at least hoped, that some of the crimes never really occurred. And indeed, uncertainty shrouded the atrocities since the most extravagant confessions had been made under torture.

In the colony, it was common knowledge that the earthquake that rocked Quebec and Tadoussac in 1663 was caused by four devils shaking the earth to turn it upside down. The Mother Superior of the Ursuline convent had seen them in the sky with her own eyes and townspeople corroborated her story. The tremors were divine punishment for the colonists' commerce of alcohol with the natives. A fair share of young girls had been possessed by spirits, even Satan himself. By order of the Bishop, the servant girl Barbe Hallé was treated for possession at the Hôtel Dieu. The miller responsible for inducing the demonic apparitions was a Huguenot, an outsider newly converted to Catholicism. He never confessed to witchcraft, despite the inquisitor's efforts, but he was executed just the same, some say for selling brandy to Indians, other claim for blasphemy.

Reason is unknown to us... Not only do we not have principles that lead to truth, but those we have adapt quite well to what is false. Fontenelle's words seemed just as applicable as the day they were written, thought Montigny. Wasn't sorcery a type of intellectual capitulation in the face of the unknown, an easy choice compared to having to make moral or ethical decisions?

I see the radiance of her deep green eyes before me. They are the ocean. I count the hours that separate me from her...

Quebec City, on this Thursday the 17th day of October 1734.

It is late now, but I cannot sleep. May this night never end. She brings me fire in the winter of my despair. Another kind of flame...

He longed to continue the conversation he had begun with her the day of her accident. Before he arrived, her sister had set up the folding maple wood table in the main room and put out four place settings. There would be three adults and one child— past and future assembled together. Four—the symbol of the totality of creation. Medicine men in the Algonquin tribe underwent four stages of initiation in the attainment of the highest degree of wisdom. Four officiants presided over the mysteries in honor of Demeter and Persephone at Eleusis. Yet it was Marie Claire's ceremony, the celebration of her life before her time of mourning that interested Montigny. But first, there was the communal meal, the banalities of supper. It was not what he wanted, not what he wished for.

Marie Claire spent most of the evening helping Suzanne eat. Anne did nearly all the talking. The acrid smell of lye was ever present.

"How are you holding up with the cold, Doctor?"

Trivial discourse, idle table talk, he thought. It was not that he didn't enjoy Anne's company or conversing about inconsequential matters. He'd been raised to understand that these were the elementary ingredients of social intercourse. He was always happy to have exchanges with genuine people not bound by the artificiality of grand etiquette that often bred hypocrisy. And he had learned what a grave error it was to view others with condescension merely because they may be ignorant of things he had come to know over the course of his life. Often such people had their own wisdom to share. But at that moment, he wanted to be transported back to Acadia, that zone he had entered so briefly when he was last with Marie Claire.

"Please call me Jean Luc." It was a spontaneous break from the aristocratic decorum ingrained in him since he could walk, an unpremeditated negation of the class distinctions that were the cornerstone of his world. He hadn't the slightest inkling why the words had come forth or why he had pronounced them.

"Does it get this cold in France?"

Before he could answer Anne's question, Marie Claire stood and went to the pail of water near the hearth. She wet a rag, came back to the table, wiped Suzanne's face, and cleaned the surface around the child's plate.

"Well, I can see your sister's ankle has healed quite nicely." He was addressing Anne but watching Marie Claire. "No, the temperature never dips this low, not even in the mountains. I think the worst thing here though is the wind. The port has nothing to shield it from the gusts coming over the river. But you know that better than I."

"Well that's true. I was born here, in this very house."

"Really? So this house belonged to your parents?"

Marie Claire discreetly reached for a few pieces of untouched bread and placed them in the deep pockets of her skirt.

"It did. Marie Claire was born here, too. This is where we both grew up. Then she went off to Acadia. The outbreak of small pox was after that. Mother and Father soon died of it. And so here I am. Or I should say, here we are—Marie Claire, Suzanne, and me."

The silence was uncomfortable.

"Let me clear the table," Anne sputtered. "Did you like the pork and beans, Doctor?"

"His name is Jean Luc," corrected Marie Claire.

Anne had already removed the plates and gone to the back to get the dessert. "He'll always be Doctor to me," she shouted into the front room. "He's the one who brought you home and mended your ankle." Marie Claire simply shrugged to Jean Luc in recognition of her sister's obstinacy.

A knock at the door echoed in the room. Anne told her sister to stay put and went to answer. Standing in the doorframe was a girl of thirteen or fourteen. She was wearing the common attire of servants, a white bonnet and apron, and was holding a jar of preserves. She did not smile and made what Jean Luc perceived as odd sounds and gestures. He heard only Anne's words as she ushered the girl directly into the back room. The noises that reached the dinner table were like long moans.

"That's Sophie Boudreau, the servant girl from across the street," Marie Claire explained. "She's deaf, poor thing. She was born that way."

Had Anne not introduced the young domestic because she didn't want to disrupt supper and knew that communication would have been too difficult? The sounds grew increasingly agitated. "Rooo...rooo...rooom. Bbbb...bbbed." Finally, Anne showed the girl out and brought the dessert to the table. She appeared distracted. She was not herself.

"Now, Doctor, have you ever tasted sugar pie?" she asked, barely looking in Jean Luc's direction. He had the impression she was addressing her question to someone else.

"No, can't say I have, Anne."

She continued, absent-mindedly at first, but gradually focused on the here and now. "The sugar's really maple syrup. It's a standard sweet around here. Nothing like the fancy tarts and cakes you're used to, I'm sure, but it's good just the same."

Anne seemed to be a kind-hearted woman. Up to that point, Jean Luc had thought that if she had a secret side like her sister, she succeeded in hiding it far better. Now he was uncertain. She cut a wide slice of pie and slipped it onto the plate in front of him.

"You're spoiling me."

"Not at all, Doctor," she replied as she cut three smaller wedges.

"It must be hard for you and Marie Claire to manage all by yourselves," he remarked in an attempt to draw Anne back into the discussion.

"You mean without a man around. Yes, it is. But if something needs fixing or there are heavy chores to be done, I hire a soldier for a few hours, sometimes even for the whole day. They're glad to get the work. It helps them round out their wages. It's a little extra drinking money for them. And they

don't ask as much as journeymen do. I'm just thankful I haven't
had to house one."

"House a soldier?"

"There aren't enough barracks, so they lodge a good
number of the recruits with the townspeople. There's no choice
in the matter. A cooking pot, a ladle, spoon and fork, that's what
we're supposed to provide. And a straw mattress. We can't
refuse. But they haven't assigned one to this house yet. Perhaps
that's because I'm a woman and have been living alone all these
years."

Upon Jean Luc's arrival, the cat had banished itself to one
of its hiding spots. Now that they were finishing dessert it made
an appearance. Sensing the possibility of scavenging for scraps,
it jumped onto a chair and eyed the pie dish. As Jean Luc
watched the creature, he remembered a small painting he'd seen
of a feline ogling a fish on a plate. The artist's name escaped
him, but he remembered the work's clever title: "The Lucky
Thief."

"Colberte! Get down this minute." Anne's roar sent a black
streak speeding across the room and into some far corner of the
house.

"Colberte. That's a rather odd name, isn't it?"

"Well, yes, I guess so. I named her Colbert first, thinking
she was a he, but after a few days, I saw I was wrong. And so
Colbert turned into Colberte."

Had Anne chosen the name in deference to the cardinal who
had administered much of the government's business during the
Sun King's reign? If that was the case, his reputation must have
been considerable even here across the Atlantic and so many
years after his death. His restructuring of the colony's
administrative hierarchy had not been completely in vain. After
all, it earned him the somewhat dubious honor that Anne had
bestowed upon him. But how would the old cardinal have liked
the unanticipated feminization of his name? Jean Luc laughed to
himself at the thought. He quickly learned that Marie Claire's
sister doted on her cat, as old maids often do. The mere mention
of it unleashed a flood of details that were of little consequence
to anyone but herself.

"Colberte actually adopted me. I came home one winter's

day a few years ago and found her on my doorstep. She was just a kitten. As soon as she saw me, she started running circles around my feet to keep me from moving. She was afraid I'd go inside and leave her out in the cold. I felt sorry for her so I gave her some milk, but I didn't bring her in. I didn't want the trouble and fuss of caring for an animal. Three days later, she was still at my door and I hadn't the heart to send her away. She's been with me ever since."

I could tell the conversation had become little more than lifeless noise for Marie Claire. She seemed to be watching Anne and me as if in a dream. Had she retreated from her surroundings to seek sanctuary elsewhere? Perhaps she was making the journey on her own.

Without knowing it, he too had ceased to play his part. Anne understood. It was time. Time to clear the table. Time to put Suzanne to bed. Time to make herself scarce.

Jean Luc and Marie Claire were now alone. "Anne is such a dear. I can't imagine what I'd do without her. She never married, never had any children. That's probably why she's so good with my daughter. She even lets Suzanne sleep in her room. There are times when I can't face anybody, not even my own child. She'll always have Anne to depend on. Anne will always be here—if I'm not."

Will she bar me entry? Not invite me into the warmth of her distant night? Not share with me that which she so preciously guards within?

How might he venture his way into unmapped regions? He asked what conditions were like elsewhere in the colony. She understood the intent of his question. Looking down, she began:

"Things got steadily worse. Suzanne was already three and Thomas was going on five. He was such a beautiful child. So big for his age. His eyes were the same color as mine. The day it all began, Thomas was on the floor playing with a toy ship his father had carved for him. I was lulling Suzanne to sleep in the rocking chair. I could feel Jacques's helplessness, sense his distress when I asked him what he was going to do."

"What's my choice?"

"But is that what you want? We can find some other way to get money. You don't have to go through with it if you don't think it's right."

"I still don't like the way the trial went. I got the feeling there wasn't enough evidence. They just wanted to prove him guilty, no matter what."

"But everyone here knows what happens if they get caught—especially at night."

"Well if a man's desperate, what's he supposed to do? Listen, Marie Claire, you know those times we were out of money and there was no food in the house? The captain didn't give me an advance like I told you. I stole the bread and eggs. I'm guilty of practically the same thing."

She wanted to speak but hesitated. The law had no mercy. They were both aware of that. Then the words came to her. "But you were only thinking of the children. How can that be wrong?"

Had his avowal changed her love for him in some way? Could it truly be changed? Or had she embraced his guilt, accepted the burden of blame? "If you feel that strongly about it, just refuse." It was almost a whisper, as if she feared someone else might hear. "Tell them you're quitting. Let them find someone else."

"And how will we survive? How will we feed Thomas and Suzanne? The only time I get work on the boats now is when there's no one else. I'm at the bottom of the list. They barely talk to me ever since I had to put the baker's son in the pillory. But you can be sure they'll all be out there bright and early. They won't want to miss a second of it. Hypocrites, that's what they are."

"You have to do what you think is right."

"I wish I could. If I go through with it, at least we'll have some money coming in."

Marie Claire put Suzanne to bed. Thomas had fallen asleep on the floor, curled around his toy boats. She woke him, took him by the hand, and helped him under the covers. Jacques was still at the table lost in his thoughts. She pulled him to his feet, led him to their bed, and drew the alcove's curtains shut. She unlaced his shirt, ran her lips across his chest, and took hold of his hand as it moved down her breast.

Jean Luc listened. His life had intertwined with hers. He could no longer differentiate between them. His upper body arched in pleasure as her pelvis brushed against his again and again. Beaded prisms of sweat covered their bodies, glistening in the candlelight as they found release. He held her head, encircled her face with his hands, and gazed into the eyes of time.

The ground was covered with snow that early morning as Jacques watched his hands, wet from a cold sweat, place the noose over the head of the young Pawnee. He had checked the slipknot more than once. It had to pull tight under pressure.

The Indian showed little emotion. Jacques led him up to the platform, threw the rope's other end over the beam of the gallows—a wooden structure constructed expressly for the event. Jacques positioned himself by the lever. The Pawnee looked out above the heads in the crowd to view the sky one final time. It was gray, almost colorless, yet infinitely beautiful. The trap door opened and the Indian's descent was abruptly cut short. The sky yanked upward. The slipknot had done its work. The body jerked and dangled in space. Deep red, then blue, colored the Pawnee's face. His tongue protruded. His bowels released the last of their contents. The kicking continued a while, and then there was calm, no sound except for the creaking of the beam from the weight of the corpse swaying in the wind.

Jacques gave the body a forceful blow with his knee to ensure no air was left in the lungs, as the magistrate had instructed him to do. Monsieur Belivau the baker, Jerome the blacksmith, Collard the general store owner, Martin, and how many others were there, fascinated by the spectacle, awed by the encounter with the unknown.

"It happened about a week later," continued Marie Claire. "Winter was almost over, but there was still some snow on the ground—mostly dirty brown slush."

She was walking down the town's main street with Thomas. A steady midafternoon wind was pushing the light freezing rain in shifting directions. She greeted some of the passersby but they ignored her. Eyes were peering out from everywhere. The children might do it again. The general store was a block away. It seemed like the other side of the universe. Would she ever get there? When she finally passed through the door to safety, Monsieur Collard was behind the counter waiting on two women buying lamp oil and candles. Other customers were milling about. The talking turned to dead silence. The hangman's woman had entered.

She tried to show no fear and act as if everything were normal.

"Good afternoon, Monsieur Collard."

He did not respond. She pretended not to notice, lifted Thomas onto a stool by the door, and walked to the counter. The women with Collard quickly gathered their parcels and left. He looked down at his ledger and began writing.

"I have a list of a few things we need. Let me see—three pounds of flour, two pounds of red beans..."

No reaction.

"A pound and a half of buckwheat and a small box of tea. Oh, I almost forgot, some molasses."

Still nothing.

"Excuse me, but..."

"We don't have any," Collard interrupted.

"You don't have any what?"

"We don't have any anything. We're plumb out of everything you asked for, Madame Lambert. Sorry, you might want to try another store."

"But there is no other store."

"I mean in another town."

She leaned over the counter, almost pleading, her voice low but firm. "Monsieur Collard, the children are hungry. I have almost nothing left to feed them."

"I feel bad about this, Madame Lambert," he whispered back, "but what can I do? They've all made a pact. Even old Belivau is in on it, and he's the one who laid charges against the Pawnee in the first place. If I take your money, the whole town'll be on my back and I can't afford that." Collard could see the customers were staring. He had to prove he was with them, say what they wanted to hear. Loudly. He cleared his throat. "Sorry, Madame Lambert, your money's no good here. We know where it came from."

All eyes converged on the intruder, penetrating her. Seconds passed—an eternity. Thomas looked at his mother in bewilderment as she approached him empty-handed and pulled him down from the stool. Once outside the store, they began retracing their steps.

A few shops down, Thomas spied a boy scrutinizing them from behind a barrel. Several more on both sides of the street were hiding and watching. Suddenly unafraid to show himself, one of them packed a handful of wet snow into an icy ball and hurled it at the midpoint between Thomas's shoulder blades. A few more replicated their leader. Some reached for stones. There was a volley of ice and rocks.

As Marie Claire and her son began to run, a sharp chunk of flint struck Thomas just above his left ear. A thin red line trickled down his neck. Marie Claire grabbed him by the hand and dragged him with all her strength. As she did, she lost her balance and fell headlong into the mud, into a sea of ridicule, an ocean of embarrassment stirred by gales of impish laughter. Filth covered her face and clothes. The barrage of snow and stones stopped, but no sooner had she made it to her feet than the demons attacked once more. It was only after the biting pain of stones hitting her back and legs subsided that she knew she was out of their reach. Yet she could not slow her pace. She had to protect her only son, pull him from danger. The wood cottage never seemed so distant. Thomas's feet barely touched the ground until they were home.

Jacques was feeding Suzanne porridge when they burst in sobbing. He put the girl down. Rushing to them, he saw the mud on Marie Claire's hands, face, and clothes, and realized that Thomas was bleeding. He took the cloth that had served as Suzanne's bib and wiped the blood from Thomas's wound, then held Marie Claire in his arms. Thomas stood as close as he could, wrapping his arms around Jacques's legs. Solid ground. Shelter. The boy never let go as his father rocked his mother back and forth.

Evening came in silence, the disquieting uneasiness of outcasts.

"Tomorrow, it will just seem like a bad dream." Marie Claire gently stroked her son's cheek with the back of her hand. "I'm here. And papa's here to protect you. Close your eyes now and go to sleep. Sleep my little angel."

Jacques poured boiling water over the leaves Marie Claire had placed in the tin pot and sat in front of the fire. When she joined him, he filled her cup, handed it to her, and filled one for himself. Both stared expressionless into the steam rising in front of them. She needed to say something, purge herself of the day's events, and claim control of her existence once more.

"I was so worried about Thomas this time."

"There were more of them, weren't there?"

"At least ten. Up to now, it's just been snow and ice. Today it was rocks. What will it be next?"

"We've got to get out of here. It's too dangerous for you and the children. I don't care much about what happens to me. I brought it on myself."

"Don't say that. You were caught in the middle."

"They all used to look the other way when they saw me taking a little food. Now they never lift their eyes off me. They watch every move I make. They want to get me and they'll find a way. It's just a matter of time."

"It's been hard enough since the British took over, but what happened today wasn't the work of the British. It was our own kind that did it. There's nothing left for us here anymore."

"I always hoped to do better."

"We'll start over somewhere else. We can go to my sister's in Quebec City till we figure out what to do. You'll see, things will be different."

Marie Claire and Jacques watched the flames dance before them and dreamed of a life that could offer hope to their children.

I was living the experiences with her as she spoke. The flames in the hearth blazed high for a moment before beginning to die out. The surge of brightness caused her to pause. Only then did I realize how late the hour had become.

"I've stayed too long. I'm keeping you up."

They both stood. She felt the words forming on her lips. "It's made the anguish more bearable."

"Marie Claire... I'd like to see you again." His voice was halting. She looked away, unsure how to receive this stranger who'd come ashore to her island of loneliness. She nodded, almost imperceptibly, then broke the uneasiness with a distraction as she handed him his things. "You know, you really should get yourself a warmer hat. The ones they sell in Paris are just for fashion. You need a fur hat, one like the trappers wear."

She opened the door. The air was sharp and clean. Its coldness entered their lungs as he placed his hands on her shoulders and kissed her on the forehead. In the night sky, on the celestial equator near Taurus, Orion gazed down at the small terrestrial figures framed by the open doorway. She pulled his scarf up tighter around his neck. "Stay warm."

Heedless of the cold, she looked on as he made his way in the moonlight against the shimmer of the few remaining streaks of color on the trees.

If I believed in such things, I might think her sister blended drops of some potion into my drink like the servant Brangwain in the old tale of Tristan and Iseult. Was it not the magic philter that united the lovers against all obstacles, all of society's proscriptions? Perhaps I would think she herself to be the sorceress. It is not unlikely that the Indians have versed her in the art of preparing elixirs from herbs and plants. Whatever the cause of my fascination, I am completely under her spell. Surely the story of her life in Acadia is part of the web she weaves.

Quebec City, on this Friday the 18th day of October 1734.

Bourville sent a messenger by with a note early this morning. It was a matter of urgency, he insisted... So many digressions on my road to nowhere, foolish excuses of purposefulness. But all paths have some destination, do they not?

"Someone is contesting Louis's will," blared Bourville. Jean Luc had barely taken a seat and was at a loss for words.

"Do you have any knowledge of a Monsieur Philippe Boisvert?" the notary asked. "I received a visit from him yesterday."

"The name means nothing to me."

"He claims to be the son of Emma's brother. Boisvert was her maiden name. He came here with a letter signed by your uncle that could nullify the entire testament—supersede it and bequeath everything to him."

"I can't believe..."

"Nor can I. But if the letter is authentic, and that remains to be determined, it would be difficult to deny its legality, given the date inscribed upon it."

"Perhaps my uncle had a change of heart and decided it

would be in the best interest of the estate to leave it to this Boisvert fellow."

"That's possible but not likely. I knew Louis. This is not like him. Still, I'm baffled by the letter. The handwriting appears to be his."

Jean Luc could not inspect the document since Boisvert refused to let it out of his possession. He saw only a copy made by one of Bourville's clerks and the notary's written attestation to having seen the original. Reading it, Jean Luc felt a burden had been lifted from him. The estate, the slaves, none of that was his responsibility anymore. Yet as his discussion with Bourville continued, something compelled him to authorize the notary to make preliminary inquiries to confirm the legitimacy of the letter. He had come such a distance to meet an uncle who died two weeks before his arrival, discovered he'd been willed an estate with over two dozen slaves but could only take possession of it—and them—by adhering to outlandish stipulations, and now he might find himself embroiled in a legal battle. His long winter was only beginning.

That evening, in the course of their conversation in the tavern, Desjardins told Jean Luc that Louis had never spoken to him about Boisvert. Although the fur trader seemed to know about everyone and everything in the colony, strangely he wasn't sharing any information concerning the man's identity or financial activities. Jean Luc could see there was no point in pursuing the topic.

"On my way to the upper city the other day, I got caught in the rain and decided to wait it out in the large church at the top of the hill. While I was there, a priest was giving some Indians and young African men a catechism class."

"Or language lesson. Call it what you like, I call it hostage-taking. This place is teeming with missionaries who think it their duty to save the soul of every savage they can wrap their rosaries around. Slavery serves their purposes. It gives them a captive audience. But their goal is not always easily achieved. The Hurons have proven to be a real challenge, especially where the sixth commandment is concerned. Their culture is totally incompatible with it. It seems that chastity is not considered a virtue by either males or females of the tribe."

Savages. It wasn't just the settlers who called them that. Even the enlightened thinkers whose works Jean Luc had selected for his library had adopted the term. Montaigne's essays and the more recent writings of Voltaire came to mind. The noble savage was used to illustrate the superiority of nature over the corrupting influences of civilization. Jean Luc's mental digression had caused him to lose track of the topic, but he recalled that the subject had something to do with sexual behavior as he heard Desjardins ramble on.

"Temptation among the settlers is curbed by offering bounties for early marriages. It's known as the King's Gift, an incentive for procreating young to help populate the colony. It's not a huge amount—twenty pounds—but it lends a patriotic note to getting beneath the covers."

Jean Luc's internal drama was not visible to Desjardins, the struggle between the man who wanted to live and the one who wanted to die. He was being pulled back into a jungle of unwanted responsibilities by his dead uncle and at the same time pushed forward to clear life's path for his son. There was no respite from the charade. He had to continue the travesty and feign interest. Finally, Jean Luc made a comment about the colony's social inequities, perhaps to test the waters and feel out the fur trader's true sentiments.

"Right now, slavery exists," answered Desjardins, "and there's not much you or I can do to alter that. In every culture, there are some who are ready and willing to act as go-betweens. Without them, the slave trade wouldn't be prospering the way it is."

How much did the newly arrived Frenchman already know about the phenomenon? Perhaps he had read the accounts of European sea captains describing African tribes capturing their ships, enslaving entire crews, and subjugating them for years. Did he know of the slavery in the Islamic East African states that existed well before the transatlantic slave trade? The castration of slaves to ready them for sale? The white military slaves taken from Russia and Eastern Europe? The black military slaves taken from Nubia and Sudan? The slavery practiced by powerful monarchs in West and Central Africa?

"Mark my words," continued Desjardins, "slavery will die

out here. Not in my lifetime. Perhaps not in yours. But die out it will."

Quebec City, on this Saturday the 19th day of October 1734.

Surely such thoughts and desires are not blameless. In the half-light of my consciousness, I cannot tell if her hair is gold or auburn. I no longer know who stands before me in my dreams. Are they not the same? Do they not speak to me with one voice?

Quebec City, on this Tuesday the 22nd day of October 1734.

I met with Monsieur Langlois today. He is an amicable man who received me quite cordially. His dwelling is impressive by colonial standards. Not only does he possess the resources necessary for rendering me service, but he is also a refined gentleman, and a knowledgeable one at that. He gave me the impression—whether genuine or not is difficult to surmise—that any financial gain our dealings might afford him will be of little consequence.

Langlois greeted Jean Luc in the yellow drawing room. His attire—the fine Rouen linen shirt, the exquisitely embroidered silk cravat—were testimony to the fact that he enjoyed his prosperity. The furnishings he had imported from France were reminiscent of those Jean Luc had acquired for Loublanc. The gracefully curved lines of the rosewood marquetry pieces were familiar and pleasing to him. It was a style that bespoke stateliness without austerity, elegant yet comfortable. The low marble-topped chests, the Chinese porcelains and Beauvais tapestries conveyed more a *joie de vivre* than an intent to impress.

Langlois skimmed the notary's message, then turned to Jean Luc. "My dear sir, a man of your means and ancestry hardly needs a letter of introduction, but I'm touched that you've taken the trouble. Needless to say, I'll be honored to facilitate your financial transactions while you are here. I would ask but a small percentage on the total amount you might require. A mere token, really." The transaction was not usury in Langlois's view. He was simply providing assistance to a gentleman. Sending for funds from France was, after all, out of the question. It would take too long and there were risks. "As for the date of reimbursement, I leave that entirely up to you. At your convenience."

Like Jean Luc, Langlois believed that personal surroundings could constitute a haven from the world's barbarity, an embellishment of life that transcended the purely biological. His profits, it seemed, would come largely from the social aspect of the agreement—discourse with someone who shared his love of finely crafted objects.

In addition to granting momentary release from the confines of what Pascal had described as the human condition, art was a way of questioning it. Products of the creative imagination constituted one of Langlois's more recent interests, but they had played a significant role in Jean Luc's life ever since he could remember. It was in Paris, on visits to his Aunt Clothilde, the Duchesse de Nanteuil, that he had been introduced to works by most of the artists he had come to admire with such passion. He once had the occasion to visit the studio of Noël Nicolas Coypel, where several canvases by an apprentice named Jean Baptiste Chardin caught his eye. On a subsequent trip to the capital in 1728, he learned that the young painter's works were being exhibited at the *Place Dauphine* and went to see the still lifes and genre compositions. The artist's intimate depictions, his ability to take simple objects to a sublime level of spatial harmony and render the innermost beauty of what others would view as ordinary and prosaic, both obsessed and comforted Jean Luc in his hours of tribulation.

Chardin had joined Antoine Watteau at the summit of his favored contemporary painters. He developed a particular admiration for Watteau's style after seeing *A Pilgrimage to Cythera* in which couples pay tribute to Venus on the island of love. It was a bold transgression of artistic norms. In order to accept the painting and admit the artist into its fold, the Academy of Art was obliged to create a new category, the *fêtes galantes*. Watteau portrayed the elegance of life that Jean Luc continually sought. And there was an element of mystery in his work, a blurring of the real and the illusionary. The ornate furnishings of the man whose services Jean Luc was soliciting briefly transported him out of the common realm in a similar manner.

"Come, Monsieur le Baron, let's sit by the fire."

Above the carved marble mantle hung a guilt trumeau

mirror, enlivened by two bronze doré sconces—one on either side. At the mantle's center stood a tall, elaborately fashioned clock. More than the clockmaker, it was the goldsmith and bronze chaser who had brought the piece to life by shaping the instrument's case into an allegorical representation of its soul. The soft ticking of the small interior pendulum, which could be heard but not seen, was in essence its heart. The pose of the figures adorning it was a visual commentary on the transience of human beauty and the permanence of artistic ideals: a golden cherub perched above the clock's face, chiseling away at the sculpted head of a beautiful woman—time leaving its mark on art and mortals.

"Let me offer you some port. You do like port, Monsieur de Montigny?"

"Yes, but please don't inconvenience yourself on my account."

"It's no inconvenience at all. A man my age needs to take advantage of every opportunity to savor the pleasures of life. My supplier's stock is generally decent enough, and I suppose if we must do business with the British, we may as well enjoy their intoxicants, don't you think? The king of England will stop at nothing to keep his subjects from drinking French claret, so I suppose I shouldn't be surprised that they've managed to take complete control of Portugal's wine commerce."

As the amber liquid flowed from its crystal decanter into the etched short-stemmed glasses, Jean Luc realized why he felt so at ease with his host. The man reminded him of his father. Not physically, but by his outlook and comportment.

"I must warn you to be wary of card money, Monsieur de Montigny. You've probably noticed how eager our merchants are to take your silver and gold as payment. If you can, avoid accepting cards in return as change, but if you have no alternative, inspect their quality. The situation has gotten so bad that there's leverage for bargaining based on the condition of the cards."

"What do you mean?" The Baron de Montigny was not accustomed to bargaining.

"It's a recent phenomenon. Intact, a card is worth the full value inscribed upon it but a missing corner will diminish its value by one half. With a larger portion gone, its worth is only one fourth the amount indicated."

"Incredible. Using playing cards as money."

"Yes, it is and it's unhealthy for the economy because it encourages bartering. People prefer exchanging goods directly instead of taking payment. Here, let me refill your glass." Langlois removed the stopper from the decanter. Their glasses were still almost full, yet the topic exasperated him so, he knew he would need more port to calm his nerves. "You see, each year, a new budget is set for the colony and in the fall, a ship arrives with the funds. But that arrangement started to fail about fifty years ago. There simply wasn't enough tender to go around. The first measure they tried was to decree that all coins were worth one fourth more in the colonies than in France. Not long after that, the king authorized the West Indies Company to issue coins valid only in the colonies."

Jean Luc sipped his port as Langlois expounded on the failings of the investment enterprise that Colbert had persuaded Louis XIV to establish. Running at a deficit more often than not, it was dissolved after ten years. Among its assignments was the trafficking of slaves. A similar company was set up again, in 1719, but lasted only three years. Nobles had been allowed to hold shares in the venture without infringement on their rank. One of Jean Luc's great uncles had bought heavily into it. The existence and demise of the company had subsequently been a frequent topic of family conversation when Jean Luc was a very young man.

"Now, suppose you have the same money worth more here than in France," continued Langlois. "And you have the West Indies Company minting its own currency for trade solely in the colonies. What do you think the outcome would be?"

"Total disaster."

"And total disaster it was. How could importers here pay their creditors in France without taking a loss? That's when the Intendant decided to try yet another scheme: a system of credit based on playing cards."

"But why playing cards of all things?"

"Necessity, my dear Montigny. Paper is an expensive commodity here. It's all imported."

Bourville's fine stationary came to Jean Luc's mind as he listened to Langlois.

"Cards are readily available, relatively sturdy, and simply need a stamp to give them the look of authority so coveted by those who govern. They're supposed to be redeemable for coinage once the king's vessel arrives, but more cards were issued than there were funds to cover them. It's a recurring problem that directly affects my business, as you might imagine. I've kept records over the years."

Langlois went to his bureau plat, pulled open the right drawer, rummaged through a stack of papers, and returned with an air of satisfaction. He held a loupe over the document he'd pulled from the pile. "Listen to this. At one point, there were two million pounds worth of cards in circulation. That was seven times the annual budget sent to the colony by the king. Seven times! The king's ministers advised him to get rid of the cards by buying them up at half their value. Now wasn't that a clever trick?"

Jean Luc thought back to his first night at the tavern and remembered how swiftly the innkeeper's palm slapped the table and produced the worn paper rectangles as if by sleight of hand. Now he understood that it wasn't the innkeeper who was performing magic tricks, it was the king working his own hocus pocus to double his profits.

The document Langlois was scrutinizing had become a blueprint for the colony, a colony whose very existence was as tenuous as life itself, and he was lost in the details of it. "Last year alone another 200,000 pounds worth of cards were issued. There's no end to it! Prices for goods and services are fluctuating drastically. We're going through a critical period. Anything could happen."

"Well now that you've explained it, I suppose playing cards are an appropriate choice for such high stake gambling," quipped Jean Luc.

"You're right on that. You never know how much—or how little—your money is worth. I only hope this nightmare will end soon. But enough of all this money talk. We do engage in frivolity here from time to time, thank God!"

Having traveled himself, Langlois knew the difficulty of

penetrating the closed circles of a foreign city's high society. Before their conversation came to an end, he assured the baron that he would put him in touch with some of the municipality's more prominent families who frequently hosted pleasurable events in the afternoon or early evening—musical recitals, literary salons, or informal gatherings where politics were discussed and gossip exchanged over liqueurs and pastries.

Social herdings, that's all they were as far as Jean Luc was concerned. Langlois did not know his new business acquaintance had become indifferent to such functions, did not realize that very little interested him anymore. The house of cards that was his life had already crumbled and he was not ready yet to try to piece it together again.

Quebec City, on this Monday the 28th day of October 1734.
There is new information concerning the contestation. Bourville asked me to pass by before noon today.

"Philippe Boisvert is indeed the man he claims to be."

"Then it's settled. The estate is his, and I'll go back to Bordeaux." The words stuck in his throat. He didn't know if he could ever return to that place, ever return to where it happened.

"I wouldn't be that hasty. There appears to be some ambiguity as to his motives for being in the colony—something to do with his situation in France before coming here. Many a man has been known to put an ocean between himself and some shady deed. I suggest we investigate further. Do I have your permission to do so?"

"If you believe this is what my uncle would have wanted."

"I do. And in the interim, I suggest you visit the property again. Get to know it and the people living there. Until the will has been invalidated by the courts, or until we decide to acknowledge the legal weight of the letter in Boisvert's possession, it's the only reasonable course of action."

I must write to her. Tell her I'm leaving for the estate and taking Madame Seguin and Pierre along. The inn is not the best place for a child his age. They're both feeling penned in. Madame Seguin is running out of fairytales for him, and there's not much reading left to keep her occupied.

I will rent a carriage again from Monsieur Ferdinand.

Marie Claire, I do not wish to leave you.

Beau Val, on this Saturday the 2nd day of November 1734.
   *Pierre has been tired and listless ever since our arrival late
Thursday. I fear he may be falling ill. William and Jeanne have
been as helpful as anyone could. Their devotion is extraordinary.*
   William, the estate's majordomo, was a black man who
looked to be in his fifties. His severe limp did not detract from
his natural dignity. His wife, Jeanne, a Montagnais, was a
heavyset, hardworking woman who was not quick to smile, but
whose loyalty to her husband and her masters was
unquestionable. Louis de Montigny had acquired her about a
year after William. Both were intended to be house slaves.
Within months they obtained their owner's permission to marry.
Because they enjoyed the privilege of living under the same roof
as the master, they were at the top of the hierarchy, the pinnacle
of the estate's bonded workers. The children born of their union
likewise worked in the house. Leon served and cleared the table,
and performed a multitude of household tasks. Lucille assisted
her mother with the kitchen and laundry chores.
   William and Jeanne knew all too well the risks of illnesses
and their potentially devastating consequences. They had lost
their oldest son, Aloysius, during an influenza epidemic. Jean
Luc was perplexed by their attentiveness to Pierre. He had
always assumed that friendship and affection were not possible
between individuals held in servitude and those who subjugated
them. But the human spirit is not as easily constrained as the
body. The heart often follows paths that reason cannot fathom.
Apparently, such was the case with Jean Luc's uncle and his two
house servants. Not long after Louis purchased Jeanne, he
learned she had a daughter who had been sold separately to a
ship owner in Montreal. For years, Louis tried unsuccessfully to
buy the girl so that she might be reunited with her mother—a
gesture that showed to what extent social and emotional relations
in the colony formed a tangled web, one that was spun with the
threads of sincere human attachment, but also those of ambition,
need, and mutual dependency. Had Louis left France because he
felt overshadowed by his brother and needed to prove himself at
whatever cost? Had he made moral concessions to achieve his

goal? Was his benevolence toward the slaves driven by self-interest, a means to appease his own guilt?

Beau Val, on this Sunday the 3rd day of November 1734.
  Pierre shows no improvement. We must return to the city.

Quebec City, on this Monday the 4th day of November 1734.
  We arrived late this afternoon. Travel was difficult.

Quebec City, on this Wednesday the 5th day of November 1734.
  His eyes have reddened. He has a dry cough and high fever. He is discharging mucus. I cannot leave his side.

Quebec City, on this Friday the 8th day of November 1734.
  The fever has fallen but small white spots have appeared on the inside of his mouth. They are becoming larger. The light pains his eyes. We keep the curtains drawn. I am sure it is measles. I fear complications—pneumonia or head fever. I have asked the innkeeper for extra blankets.

Jean Luc requested a pitcher of warm spiced wine for Madame Seguin. The innkeeper was indulgent enough to ignore the law prohibiting alcoholic beverages in guestrooms as a favor to the baron. Now Jean Luc understood why the man had been so secretive when he'd sold him the *eau-de-vie* a few weeks earlier, why he'd instructed him to tell no one of the transaction that had transpired well after the closing bell.

Quebec City, on this Sunday the 10th day of November 1734.
  The fever returned yesterday. The rash on his forehead has begun to spread to his chest. The hour is late. Though I am overtaken with exhaustion I do not wish to rest, but I must. Madame Seguin has promised to wake me if there is any change. Tomorrow, I will go to the Hôtel Dieu. I should not have waited this long.
  Why have I taken my son so far from home and put his life in peril by coming to a savage land that holds its own dark secrets? Typhoid, smallpox, measles, influenza. So many small wooden crosses in the city's cemetery. Children, like Pierre. I cannot allow it to happen.

He reached for the thick worn volume on the nightstand. He had read the epic poem in his youth under the watchful eye of his tutor. Even then, he was sensitive to the beauty of the verses and lamented the fact that his command of Greek was not sufficient to allow him to fully appreciate them. Now he had come back to the ancient account of the warrior's wanderings to re-explore the work in his own language. The French version in his hands was a gift from Etienne, his oldest friend. Lying in bed, he clung to the book as if it were a life raft.

Book eleven: The Land of the Dead. The house of Hades is inhabited by so many unknown and known souls. My trusty oarsman requests to be buried and mourned, and that a monument be erected for future generations to remember him. My dead mother also roams in this kingdom of shadows, having died of a broken heart due to my long absence. She wonders why I am here and remarks that the awful sights of the somber gloom are not for the eyes of the living. Her being, a mere shadow, dissipates at my touch. Nevermore will I hold her in my arms. She bids me to return to the light. So many more spirits of the dead and gone assembled here speak their words of truth to me. Among them, the soothsayer, who predicts a difficult return fraught with dangers and even death at sea...

The soft changing hues of the pages in the flickering candlelight slowly carried Jean Luc away. He dropped the heavy book.

Swirling shadows cast ever increasing darkness over the waves as they rise and fall, rise and fall. They are immense and so violent that they surge up like walls, so high that their crests are not visible. Menacing swells are poised like monsters to engulf the craft and take it down to the ocean floor or even lower. Pierre, where are you? My son, my only son. He is by my side. My relief is immeasurable. I must hold him tightly. It would be easy for the child to fall overboard. The open boat is moving rapidly, too rapidly. Surely such speed is not possible. No manmade vessel, large or small, can advance this quickly. The tall figure at the helm does not respond to my pleas. The incessant jolts do no affect him. What is propelling the vessel? There are no sails, no rowers. Behind the spectral form at the rudder I see reefs and a huge opening in the rocks—a mouth waiting to swallow us up. At last, the boat is slowing down, coasting. Pale rays emanate from the cavernous void. Against the light, a woman and girl are standing on the rocks, their arms outstretched. Who are they, beckoning to me with such laments, pleading, entreating me not to enter? I try to grasp the hands of the veiled figures as the boat draws near but they are merely hazy forms, masses of fog, ever smaller as the craft moves through the craggy archway of the water-filled grotto. The vessel floats deeper into the rocky chamber. I can no longer hear the wails and pleas. Winged creatures await, perched in each dark recess of the barren silence. One swoops down to latch onto Pierre and carry him away in its giant claws. More follow. Their attack is relentless. I must fight them off, but there are thousands. The boat has turned a bend and the birds have retreated. I cannot hold Pierre tight enough to stop his tiny body from trembling.

A thunderous crash. The boat has rammed against jagged rocks. Pierre is gone, vanished into the black waters! How can this be? I plunge to save him. Pierre, my child, where are you? What force is tearing at me, pulling me down? Tentacles as strong as chains take me ever deeper. The night fills my lungs. Suffocating darkness. I cannot breathe...

He awoke suddenly. The bell in the church spire tolled four times, its resonance carrying over the city and far into the wilderness.

Quebec City, on this Monday the 11th day of November 1734.

I have spent all morning and the early part of the afternoon with Pierre. He is so innocent yet so miserable. I am apprehensive about leaving him. He is always afraid I will not return, that he will never see me again. As it happened with them...

There has to be something more I can do. I must try everything, no matter how unorthodox. If I do not, and Pierre dies, I will be guilty of sacrificing my son on the altar of my beliefs.

He has finally fallen asleep. The time has come to head to the Hôtel Dieu.

The austere architecture, a reflection of the rigid Jansenist perspective that had filtered its way into practically every aspect of French thought even in the colonial territories, only heightened Jean Luc's anxiety as he passed through the hospital's entry on *rue Charlevoix*. His request to consult Doctor Sarrazin was met with surprise. The chief surgeon had died a few months earlier. His reputation extended beyond the borders of the New World, yet the news of his passing still had not reached France before Jean Luc set sail. Michel Sarrazin had been appointed the King's Physician to the colony toward the end of the previous century and, for a while, was its only certified doctor. Jean Luc's disappointment was tempered by the fact that he was allowed to confer with the great man's successor, Timothé Sylvain, an Irishman who had wholly adopted the language and customs of the colony, down to his very name.

The focal point of the room that served as Sylvain's office was a heavy walnut table in the Louis XIII style. A few armchairs were unceremoniously scattered about. Three leaded windows looked onto a low, wooded hill. Movement outside caught Jean Luc's attention the moment he entered. Squirrels were chasing each other around the massive trunk of an oak tree, darting in every direction, like his thoughts. As he watched the animals scurry through the layer of crisp brown leaves blanketing the ground, lone snowflakes began to whirl through the glacial air against the graying sky. His mind was muddled when he extended his hand to Doctor Sylvain.

Jean Luc wasted no time in describing the symptoms of his son's illness and the therapy he was administering: no bright light, liquids for hydration, complete rest, isolation from everyone except Madame Seguin and himself. He performed daily analyses of the boy's stools and gave him elixirs to regulate his yellow and black biles and expel the contaminated humours. He categorically refused to induce bleeding, even to reduce the fever.

But the care seemed inadequate. What if it did not cure the boy's ailment? Sylvain reassured him but Jean Luc remained unconvinced. His principles and certitudes were in chaos. He could not leave. To prolong the consultation, he queried Sylvain about his predecessor, the great Doctor Sarrazin, and his dedication to the advancement of science. It was a means of keeping at bay the demons dancing in his mind. Their incursions were ever more furious since Pierre had fallen ill. Might he even broach the topic that had been gnawing at the very foundation of his beliefs?

He listened absentmindedly to Sylvain's anecdotes about how Sarrazin had spent over thirty years collecting plants and minerals of the New World, regularly dispatching reports on his findings to the Royal Academy in Paris and sending hundreds of specimens to scientists at the *Jardin des Plantes*.

"The only indigenous animal he did not dissect was the skunk, the reason ostensibly being the malodorous consequences that would ensue."

Jean Luc found it difficult to display amusement at Sylvain's attempt at humor, but a personal detail Sylvain mentioned almost in passing struck a chord. In order to devote all his time to his work, Sarrazin had entrusted the daily tasks of his household to his three slaves—two Indian women from different tribes, and the son of one of them. The great Sarrazin was a brilliant mind, a man as successful in his field as Jean Luc's uncle had been in his own; yet they both must have found legally sanctioned human bondage perfectly normal. On what basis? What kind of natural law, what kind of spiritual dogma could allow one segment of a given population to subjugate another?

Sylvain's verbal meandering had become a distant drone to Jean Luc until he heard him say, "Wouldn't you agree, Doctor de Montigny, that philosophically speaking, it's a form of empowerment? That's what witchcraft is."

The word the baron had been afraid to utter had been spoken. Now he listened attentively. Over the past week, as his concern for his son mounted, a part of him surfaced that he had never before encountered, one that contemplated the effectiveness of occult practices in situations where science failed. Could there be a ritual in the sorcerer's book that might render the venom in his son's body harmless or at least hold the disease in check? It was Jean Luc the distraught father, not Montigny the doctor, who was suddenly giving Sylvain his full attention.

"Whether real or imagined, it's a form of empowerment for

people with little other recourse at their disposal. It can be innocuous, as in attempting to resolve a conflict or obtain a wish, or dangerous, as when it is used as a weapon of manipulation."

Jean Luc had no interest in the sorcery to which Sylvain was referring. It did not offer promise for his son. Yet he controlled his edginess as he listened to the colonial physician go on. "Just this past summer, the bishop annulled a marriage on the basis that the couple's infertility was the result of bewitchment. The blacksmith suspected of casting the spell was banished from the city."

More than one peasant in the villages surrounding Loublanc had learned the spell as well: tie a piece of cord or strip of cloth into three knots while reciting a verse of the *Miserere* backwards. But there were antidotes—wear your shirt inside out, hold a wooden cross, put a ring under your spouse's foot, urinate into the keyhole of the church where you were wed. Jean Luc cared little about such irrelevant nonsense. He needed something more, something to help Pierre. But Sylvain went on relentlessly.

"Even nuns have been known to concoct potions. They mix brews spiked with a finely ground powder—supposedly the bones of saints—and administer the blend to the ailing, especially British settlers and Huguenot sailors. The nuns believe the combination of prayers and just the right dose of saintly bones will prompt their unsuspecting victims to convert. If that isn't witchcraft, what is? The irony is that the Church puts sorcerers in the same category of undesirables as thespians and prostitutes."

A strategy to preserve its authority, thought Jean Luc. Men of the cloth would never relinquish their control over supernatural forces to individuals outside their ranks. If such forces did exist, should he not avail himself of them for his son? Could so many people be mistaken?

~~~

A flood of emotions filled Pierre's being. Some were distinct, others vague and elusive. He had long forgotten his illness in New France, his father's tireless efforts to care for him, the countless hours he had spent at his bedside. He had no knowledge of the pain the man suffered at not being able to expel the disease from his body and never imagined his father considering the use of sorcery and potions.

Pierre remembered the day he had to draw the sheet over his father's face, over eyes that had turned away from this world and cast their gaze inward in the direction of paths not yet taken. For hours Pierre remained in the bedroom. He could not separate himself from the one who had always been there by his side, from the life that had given him life. But with the passing of time, perhaps to lessen the pain of his absence, the memory of his father dissolved into a confused blur, an indescribable sensation of nostalgia.

As Pierre looked up at the vaulting overhead, he felt something brush against the back of his neck. Soon they would come to cut his hair, bare the nape. He imagined that the blade had already done its work and released his spirit from his body, freed it from the confines of the prison cell to float through space toward the house of his youth where existence seemed to have meaning. He could see his father writing at his desk in the library at Loublanc. He often sat by the fire there, an open book or gazette on his lap. More than once Pierre had caught him lost in his thoughts. Each time, he wondered if the words on the page had triggered an imaginary journey or if his father's musings were in answer to a distant call to which only he was privy. It used to baffle Pierre that he was so interested in seemingly inconsequential news from New France. He recalled his father's fascination upon reading that one Timothé Sylvain, alias Timothy O'Sullivan, was involved in a legal dispute with the widow Youville of Montreal over the ownership of a Pawnee slave. And he had no idea why his father was amused when the Swedish botanist Carl von Linné presented the Sarracinea purpurea to the scientific world. Was it because his father had known that its discoverer, Sarrazin, had given the plant the unscientific name *oreille de cochon*? Had he known that Sarrazin learned about it from the native Indians who used it to treat syphilis, one of Europe's less celebrated imports to the New World? Sarrazin. Sylvain. Names from an almost forgotten past.

~~~

Jean Luc's mind was in a fog, his thoughts trapped in a labyrinth illuminated only by the dull sulfuric light of doubt and anguish. He could barely hear Sylvain's voice.

"At least we haven't gone as far as they did in Massachusetts."

Jean Luc had read about the hysteria in Salem. Medicine had not been able to account for the disturbances, even well after emotions had quieted. Science was deficient, fragmentary. That realization only exacerbated his distress.

"When the intellect encounters occurrences beyond its comprehension, it seeks explanations and grasps at solutions. Fear tends to take over," he heard Sylvain say. "We haven't as yet found scientific causes for such phenomena, but I'm confident that one day we'll be able to furnish medical reasons for the aberrant behavior presently attributed to demonic possession. Who knows? We might discover that a good many of those poor souls they burned alive were simply suffering from some sort of ailment caused, say, by a fungus in something they ate. Something as commonplace as potatoes, or perhaps wheat."

The light in Sylvain's office was growing dimmer and taking on slate tones. Jean Luc turned to the window. A thick mantle of white had replaced the cloak of brown leaves he'd seen upon his arrival. Flakes were spiraling like small tornadoes in the sudden squall that was bringing in yet more of the snows of winter.

Heading down the corridor to the main door, Jean Luc knew there was no more he could do for Pierre, no miraculous solution.

Once outside the hospital's sheltering stone enclave, he was overtaken by a powerful blast of wind. As he held his cloak tightly, he felt his body slowly mummify. Swirling bandages of white enveloped him. Razors of ice slashed his face. He was advancing alone along a wavering path on foreign soil. He rounded the corner of *rue Saint Stanislas* and heard the bells of the Ursuline convent pursuing him from behind. Suspended between heaven and hell, the huge clappers were sounding the evening Angelus—the signal for all demons to abandon the witches they were transporting to their Sabbat and flee to their lairs.

Quebec City, on this Saturday the 16th day of November 1734.
      Five days, five endless days and nights, constantly with
Pierre. Though the illness is subsiding, I must keep him confined
to his room for yet another week. He had trouble sleeping last
night, so Madame Seguin entertained us both with her own
version of an ancient legend she had perhaps learned as a child
or come across in a book. She adapted the classical tale to fit
Pierre's world with great skill. Yet I must wonder if her story of
King Nacleus was truly intended for my son.

~~~

      Once more, Pierre stopped reading. Nacleus. The governess
had told him the tale again and again. He never tired of it. Never
tired of her gentle voice lulling him to sleep. Now, in the
darkened cell, he heard it for the last time. In the confines of his
solitude, the story took on another layer of meaning, spoke
beyond the boundaries of childhood.
      Long, long ago in a far-off land, there lived a very rich king
named Nacleus. His queen was the fairest lady in the kingdom.
They lived in a magnificent palace surrounded by wonderful
gardens and had many, many servants. Each morning, they
awoke to the strains of lovely music performed by their very
own lute players and pipers. Only the best wines and finest foods
were fit for his table. He was the happiest of men, yet feared that
everything he loved would be taken from him—his little dog,
Flash, his beautiful white palfrey, Moonbeam, and, of course, the
fair queen.
      One day, King Nacleus was walking through his gardens at
dusk when he spied something moving in the juniper bushes.
"Come here, Flash, you rascal!" he said, thinking it was his
faithful companion. But Flash ran up from behind, barking
happily. "What could be making my juniper bushes rustle so?"
thought King Nacleus. He was just about to push the branches
aside to investigate when out popped a funny little man with a
pointed nose. His feet looked more like those of a donkey, and
there were two small horns growing on his head. If the creature
had turned around, King Nacleus would have seen that he had a
tail as well! "But...but...whoever...whatever are you?" exclaimed

the king.

"Why, Your Majesty, I'm a wood sprite. I live in the forest among the tall trees and take great delight in frolicking in your garden. How odd we've never met before!"

King Nacleus was dumbfounded. His eyes were as big as two gold ecus.

"Have no fear, Your Majesty. I'll not harm you. In fact, I'm pleased to make your acquaintance at last. My name is Willowisp. How do you do?"

King Nacleus sighed. "Oh, well enough."

"But, Your Majesty, you have everything a man could hope for. Whatever could be making you so melancholy?"

"Yes, my friend, I am the most fortunate man in the kingdom, but I would be even happier if everything could stay as it is forever and ever. If only I could protect everything and everyone I touch from the ravages of time."

"Are you certain you desire such a gift?" asked Willowisp.

"What difference does it make? Such power is not given to mortals."

"Ah, but you are mistaken, Your Majesty. In payment for the pleasure I've had romping through your garden, I'll bestow upon you the very gift you desire."

"Can this be true?" exclaimed King Nacleus gleefully.

"If you don't believe me, see for yourself. Why don't you pick a flower?"

The king plucked a fragrant blossom from his favorite gardenia plant. No sooner were the snowy white petals in his hand than they turned from soft to hard.

"There, Sire. The flower will be yours forever. It will never change.

"May the gods be praised! Thank you, oh thank you, Willowisp."

"No, no, it is I who thank you. Now if you'll excuse me, I must be going. Good evening, Your Majesty."

The sprite vanished before the king could bid him adieu. King Nacleus touched all manner of trees and flowers on his way back to the palace. They would never alter, never wilt, never fade. They would remain forever beautiful, as they were at that moment. The king was beside himself with joy but his laughter soon changed to tears. His servants spread a feast before him. As he took a bite of roast pheasant, the cooked bird hardened like the gardenia. So did the wine from his goblet as it touched his lips.

King Nacleus was worried indeed. With his new power, how would he ever be able to eat again? He threw down his fork and shook his head in woe. The queen and little Flash saw the king was forlorn and ran to console him. Without thinking, he leaned down to scratch Flash's ear. The poor little dog's thick black fur became stiff and cold, preserved for all eternity. Looking in horror at the statue that had once been his dear little friend, King Nacleus understood the great mistake he had made. He would never be able to touch the queen again, never kiss her ruby lips, never feel her arms around him.

He picked Flash up and ran into the garden. "Willowisp, oh Willowisp. Take back my gift. I want it no longer!"

"So you've changed your mind, Your Majesty?" asked the wood sprite.

"Yes, yes, I was wrong!"

Willowisp could see King Nacleus had learned his lesson. Removing a tiny pouch from his pocket, the wood sprite sprinkled some of the blue powder it contained on the king and threw the rest into the air. To the king's great joy, Flash was a real dog again, his feast was warm and savory, the flowers soft and fragrant. He could hold the queen's hand.

"There you have it," said Willowisp as he scampered toward the forest, "but don't ever forget what you have learned."

"Oh no, I never will," shouted King Nacleus, bending down to take Flash in his arms. "The world is full of many treasures. We must enjoy them in the moment, for the course of time cannot be halted. Without change, there is no life."

~~~

Quebec City, on this Wednesday the 27th day of November 1734.

The son of night, brother of sleep, has abandoned his struggle. He no longer seeks to pull Pierre from the living. I may now call on her. She has been constantly in my thoughts. Her emerald green eyes haunt me. Does she know my absence has not been deliberate?

Snow drifts rendered the streets nearly impassable. It was late morning by the time Jean Luc knocked at the door of unfinished tales and unfulfilled desires. He did not remember the features of the woman who answered as being so drawn. Her figure was gaunt, her eyes tired. Perhaps it was the harsh daylight that accentuated her haggard appearance. This time, there was no soft candlelight in the main room to spread an ennobling veil over the commonplace or transfigure the sparse surroundings and the mortals who inhabited them. He had idealized her in his mind. Like her sister, she had become a part of the private world of esthetics that made reality bearable for him. Yet as she prattled on so earnestly about a variety of trivialities, the goodness of her soul effaced her physical imperfections and she took her place once more on the sublimated canvas of his imagination.

Anne went to inform Marie Claire of the visit before continuing to tend to the mounds of clothing and linens in the back room. She knew she was not destined to be in the foreground of life's picture. As her iron smoothed the embroidered pillowcases, she embroidered the lives of the women who rested their heads upon them, imagining they resided in palatial mansions. She envisioned garments befitting ladies receiving gentlemen callers in richly furnished gilded salons—*robes à la française*, sleeves embellished with bobbin lace and silk brocade engageantes, Mechlin lace lappets streaming from a cap or bonnet.

Marie Claire appeared. The fairness and grace he remembered were enhanced by her plain, dark attire. Her confinement to black's varying tones would continue for another six months, possibly longer. She had not decided. Perhaps she would be buried in black. She welcomed the rigid code imposed upon her since she was not ready to forget those for whom she wore cloth the color of ebony.

His time of mourning was over. The brown breeches and gold buttons were proof of that.

She showed great concern for Pierre and relief to hear he was out of danger. Yet I know not what invisible cortege traversed her mind when I told her I would again be absent. I let her know I needed to make another trip to Beau Val, explaining that, because of Pierre's illness, I had not been able to explore the property as I had intended. And now that Boisvert has laid claim, I must comprehend fully what is at stake.

Marie Claire's tenderness was enveloped in a cloak of detachment. He did not shake it from her and quelled his desire to kiss her by brushing his hand over hers. Her touch would be with him every moment over the long days, perhaps weeks, ahead.

He was barely out the door when Anne brought a basket of warm, freshly ironed laundry from the back room. Like Anne, Marie Claire knew her role. She never refused, never complained. She and her daughter were an imposition, an added burden. Draping her heavy wool wrap over her shoulders and securing it tightly to keep the cold gusts from blowing it open, she kissed Suzanne goodbye, pulled the hood over her head, and went out, basket in hand. Anne watched sadly as her sister disappeared from view, erased by the swirling snow.

She turned left just before the *Place Royale* and knocked at the door of the Hertel household. When the door opened, she pulled the top stack from the basket and handed it to the servant girl.

Trudging through the snowy market square, she felt a tug at her arm. As soon as she saw the gestures the shabbily dressed man who'd grabbed her was making, she pulled herself from his grip and clutched the basket tightly. His laughter and the syncopated cadence of her gait sent a rush of disquieting images through her mind. She needed to dissipate them and not sink into the mire of regret and grief. As she passed by Daniel in front of the church of *Notre Dame des Victoires*, she reached into her pocket, retrieved the pieces of bread she'd put there the night before after supper, and placed them in his hands. He smiled in thanks. "*Que dieu vous bénisse, ma fille!*" Light had long left the beggar's eyes, but he recognized her warm touch.

Beau Val, on this Thursday the 5th day of December 1734.

What more evidence could there possibly be? This is most surely my last sojourn here. I must tell Bourville as soon as I can...

Jean Luc had seen the master bedroom during his first visit to the estate, but only briefly. He had not wanted to disturb the memories it held so soon after his uncle's passing. His second stay had been cut short by Pierre's illness. Now, on this third visit, the urge to feel the presence of his father's brother took hold of him. Before entering, he paused in front of Emma's portrait hanging at the end of the corridor by the bedroom door, as if to ask her permission—or her forgiveness—for intruding. Sitting in the beige watered silk bergere, he sensed for a moment that the woman in the portrait was there beside him. Her dressing table was as she had left it more than two years earlier. The crystal perfume flask was half full. The summer riding gloves had not been put away. He contemplated the bed where Louis, Viscomte de Montigny, had expired. On the marble-topped gueridon next to it lay a copy of LaRochefoucauld's *Maximes*. Jean Luc picked up the volume and opened it at random. "Our virtues are for the most part nothing but our vices in disguise." He turned the page. "Weakness is more the opposite of virtue than is vice." LaRochefoucauld had no illusions where human nature was concerned. Had Louis de Montigny shared the same enlightened pessimism?

As he pondered what sort of man his uncle might have been, what passions had driven him, what convictions he had harbored, Jean Luc felt a small bulge between the book's back cover and last page. A pressed flower? A lock of her hair? Were LaRochefoucauld still alive, he would have seized the occasion to write an aphorism on curiosity. Romantic thoughts quickly vanished as Jean Luc unfolded the first of the two letters he discovered tucked inside the *Maximes*. It was from Boisvert, a dithyramb to Louis's kindness and generosity. The effusive verbiage peaked at the letter's closing.

My gratitude is without end. I remain forever your loyal and loving nephew.
Devotedly,
Philippe

Of more interest to Jean Luc was the second letter, signed by his uncle only days before his death. Unlike the first, it was written on fine vellum.

Beau Val, September 9th, 1734.

    My dear Philippe,

    Please excuse the clumsiness of my script. I grow weaker with each passing day. Having at last made your acquaintance has brought me such joy. Your father often wrote to my dear Emma about you and your exceptional goodness. You are a fine son. He was justly proud of you. And now, I am only too happy to assist you in your time of need. As I wrote you in my previous letter, I shall make arrangements with a notary here in Beau Val to prepare legal documents retracting my original will and making you the recipient of all my worldly goods and possessions. I would far rather pass this estate on to you, whom I have come to know and love, than to a man I have never met. Do with it what you must in order to pay your debts and set your finances straight. This is my desire and intent. I shall inform you as soon as all is ready.

    My warmest regards,

    Louis

It was over. How could the legitimacy of Boisvert's claim be disputed? Louis de Montigny must not have had time to send this last letter to Boisvert, let alone change his will, but his desire to do so was clearly indicated, just as it was in the letter Boisvert had shown Bourville. A sense of relief passed over Jean Luc, as it had when Boisvert first surfaced. There would be no more decisions to make, no more battles with his conscience—at least about the estate.

Quebec City, on this Sunday the 8th day of December 1734.

    We attended a social gathering this afternoon at the residence of the Marquis and Marquise LeMoyne de Chatel. It was not where I cared to go, not where I wished to be.

Jean Luc assumed the invitation waiting for him at the inn on his return from Beau Val was due to Monsieur Langlois. The LeMoyne name was associated with a long line of Canadian noblesse. Its progenitor, Charles LeMoyne, had arrived in the colony virtually penniless nearly a century earlier and subsequently made his fortune in the fur trade. He purchased a seigneury and was elevated to the rank of nobleman after distinguishing himself in

various military exploits. Such social advancement was far from the
norm, even in the colony, where the caste system could occasionally
be less rigid than in France. All of Charles LeMoyne's twelve sons
likewise pursued military careers. It was a well-known fact,
however, that the host of the afternoon social was at best a distant
relative of the illustrious family.

A procession of horse-drawn sleighs filed past the stately
upper city home. Some pulled off once their passengers had
disembarked, others remained close by in wait of their masters'
return.

Servants approached with incredible swiftness to take the
wraps of Monsieur le Baron de Montigny, his son, and the
unidentified dowager accompanying them. The threesome was
ushered into the drawing room where the marquis and marquise
were receiving their *invités*. The waistcoat and jacket of the
marquis's green cut velvet *habit à la française* were embroidered
with polychrome threads, enlivened by touches of gold and
silver. The jacket's high standing collar offset what seemed to be
an infinite number of buttons. A Brussels appliquéd lace jabot
covered the marquis's throat. His shoe buckles were quite large
and his hairpiece was of a style Jean Luc cared little for—a bag
wig, tied in a black silk pouch at the neck to keep the white
powder from falling onto the marquis's coat. He clasped his
pocket watch in his left hand as he greeted his guests. The hem
of the yellow Lyon silk brocade dress the marquise was wearing
was just high enough to reveal her satin court shoes. Its most
elaborate features were double-flounced cuffs and a tailored red
stomacher made of linen bands with corded scrolling. The bell-
shaped panniers that gave volume to her skirts prevented her
from standing in close proximity to her husband, which did not
entirely displease her. She had taken great care to enhance the
whiteness of her complexion by placing a tiny black satin
mouche on her left cheek. The fan she carried, a superfluous
accent given the season, was made of carved ivory with chicken
skin overlay. She made certain to open it periodically to display
the colorful pastoral scene painted on one side.

After exchanging the conventional formalities of etiquette,
the callers were left to fend for themselves. Almost immediately,
Jean Luc detected laughter above the confused chatter in the

formal salon. Wandering through the double doors, he discovered over half a dozen children running about under the supervision of an amiable matron designated by the hosts to oversee the youngest guests' entertainment. Her presence relieved Madame Seguin of her duties for the afternoon, to the governess's immense joy. Her greatest fear upon entering the mansion was that a moment of inattention on her part would result in catastrophe—the breaking of a vase or some other precious object.

Madame Seguin took full advantage of her newly found freedom, which she knew was to be short-lived, and buzzed from cluster to cluster of colonial status seekers, gathering whatever conversational pollen she could. If the other guests had been aware that she was merely a governess, they would have dismissed her as a social nonentity. As it was, rumor quickly spread throughout the rank and file quaffing punch in the parlor that she was a relative of the Baron de Montigny—an aunt or cousin. Over the previous weeks, the local gossips had circulated the word that some terrible event had marred the baron's past. Despite the rampant curiosity, it was tacitly agreed by all that, out of tact, no questions would be asked about the Baronne de Montigny, whose absence only added to the mystery surrounding Madame Seguin's identity. Consequently, she was treated with the utmost civility. More than twice she took a glass of port from one of the silver trays that passed through the room in the steady white-gloved grip of domestics adroitly weaving their way about the small assemblages.

The governess incognita conversed intelligently on virtually every subject broached. The marquise's great aunt, Madame Perron, told her the Ursuline convent housed a substantial library that might be of interest to her during her stay in the city and offered to write a letter of introduction on her behalf to facilitate access to the convent's reading room. Whether she would have done so had she known Madame Seguin's real social rank is anyone's guess. In any case, the governess was elated.

Jean Luc, on the other hand, suspected that the guests were more interested in impressing their peers than listening to, let alone taking interest in, the conversation. The afternoon was one of infinite boredom for him, a sensation only heightened by the monologue to which he was subjected by the master of the house. During that brief but seemingly eternal encounter, the baron learned that the LeMoyne residence was heated by a wood burning stove imported from France and that few families in the colony could boast such a luxury. The apparatus gave off four times more heat than an ordinary fireplace and, indeed, the drawing room was quite comfortable despite the glacial temperature outside. The warmth offered the younger ladies the occasion to remove their wraps and display the décolleté of their dresses. Some of the older female guests had quickly learned on previous visits that in order to avoid embarrassment it was imperative to keep a safe distance from the contraption. The intensity of the heat could easily cause the wax that camouflaged the pockmarks on their cheeks to melt through their face powder.

The host also found a roundabout way to make it clear to his captive that the domestic help in the household had been culled from the city's small pool of professional servants. "Madame LeMoyne refuses to have any other kind. She will not be bothered putting up with the clumsiness of young, untrained girls whose parents cannot afford to keep them at home. Professional domestics cost more, but they're well worth it. And there are appearances to think of."

Such trifles were of little concern or interest to the Baron de Montigny. As he politely pulled away from his host, he saw that card tables had been set up at the far end of the drawing room where some of the guests were engaged in games of *pharaon*. The clock in the drawing room chimed six times. Of an older style popular in the previous century, its lines were straight and it was decorated with a multitude of miniature columns and pinnacles. Watching the afternoon hostages stifle their yawns, Jean Luc decided it was time to leave and collected his son from his temporary governess. Prying Madame Seguin from her freedom was more difficult.

Despite the insipidness of the excursion, I was glad to give Pierre the occasion to go out after his long confinement. The activity did him a world of good and Madame Seguin thoroughly enjoyed herself. At least the afternoon has not been a total disaster.

If only she could have been there with me...

Quebec City, on this Monday the 9th day of December 1734.
    I called on Bourville first thing this morning to show him the letters and instruct him to concede the estate to Boisvert, but...

Bourville put on his spectacles and looked the documents over carefully. He went back and forth from one to the other and held them up to the light. He had not been able to examine the first letter Boisvert had shown him, not at his leisure as he had wanted. After a long pause, the notary turned to Jean Luc and pointed to the letter signed by Louis de Montigny.

"It's a forgery."

It was a crushing verdict. If Bourville's allegation was true, Jean Luc was now once again responsible for the fate of his uncle's estate. He could not let the property, the fruits of half a century's work, fall into the hands of a charlatan. He pressed the notary to explain what it was that had led him to such a conclusion. Bourville's reasons were fourfold. Firstly, he was absolutely certain that Louis did not want the estate to be divided or sold. Secondly, Louis would not have considered engaging the services of a notary other than himself, his lifelong friend. Thirdly, the handwriting, despite its shakiness, more resembled Louis's penmanship of some twenty years earlier. Bourville had documents on file to show it. And finally, even though the paper was of superior quality compared to that of Boisvert's letter, it was not Louis's usual stationary.

"We're dealing with a clever scoundrel," said the notary in exasperation. "He realized the existence of several letters would lend further credence to his claim. Who knows if others are privy to some of them? He's probably already thought of that. If we attempt to conceal these, we might end up falling deeper into the trap he has set. And there is considerable circumstantial evidence on his side. He has seemingly settled permanently in the colony and, from what I've gathered, he is the only living nephew Louis actually met. Ostensibly, Louis died before he could have the documents notarized. A court could very likely rule in Boisvert's favor."

There had to be more proof. Bourville apprised Jean Luc of his intention to carry out any inquiries he deemed appropriate. Jean Luc wanted to take a closer look at the estate's finances.

*We went over the farm ledgers and the records for the
sawmill's overhead costs and income. In addition to the slaves,
there are a fair number of day laborers. Most work at the mill. I
shall return to Beau Val to further inspect the operations of the
estate, but only after the holidays—unless my presence there is
absolutely necessary before then. Pierre and Madame Seguin
will derive more pleasure from the festivities in the city, as will I.*

*I miss her smile. Its sadness. When will I see the first tear of
happiness in her eyes?*

Midnight was approaching. It would be hours before the
others emerged from the cloud of slumber that had descended
over them, but she had not given in to unconsciousness. She
needed to know for sure. Some said it was possible. She dressed
quietly, closed the door to her bedroom, and slipped out into the
night. The moon's reflection on the snow made it easier for her
to find her way. He would not think her nocturnal visit odd.
That's what they told her. He was accustomed to receiving
people with requests such as hers at all hours—especially after
darkness had fallen and before the light of dawn. No one wanted
to be seen going there.

Following the path deep into the woods, she felt uneasy.
Turn back, she thought. Go home before they awake. Tell no
one. Pretend you never went. No. She had to go through with it.

She had only seen him once, in the market. A shadow in the
daylight. But that was long ago. Mathieu. Besides his name,
what did she know about him? She had heard much. There were
many rumors, each different. Which were true and which were
imagined? According to some, he was a sorcerer not of woman
born, the child of a witch impregnated during a Sabbat in the
lower city's graveyard not far from *rue de Meulles*. Others said
the Sioux abducted him when he was a boy. The medicine men
taught him their secrets—potions, herbs, powders, all were
known to him. But when Mathieu's spells and philters proved
powerless in curing the chieftain's youngest son, he was driven
from the tribe. Now he lived apart, rejected—at least by day. The
death of the chieftain's son remained a mystery, since those who
had recourse to Mathieu's remedies reputed them to be effective.
He had powders to make sterile couples fertile and potions that
could shrink the belly of any pregnant woman. There were

concoctions for removing the breath of life and still more for communicating with the dead.

A faint light was visible in the distance. Sheltered as it was by dense tree growth, the cabin would have been impossible to find without precise instructions. The directions Madame Guiton had given were accurate.

She knocked on the wooden door, well worn by time and use. The wait was long. The hooting of a gray owl guiding the soul of an Algonquin brave to the land beyond the sun broke the night's stillness. The creaking of hinges accompanied the appearance of a black silhouette against a column of uncertain light. She stepped on the long thin shadow the hermit's figure cast over the snow's pale silver and entered. The door of good and evil closed onto the night. It was not until shortly before dawn that she returned home.

Quebec City, on this Thursday the 12th day of December 1734.

The Sovereign Tribunal has accepted Boisvert's grievance. The case will be heard.

I am thankful Uncle Louis made financial arrangements for what he must have known would be the long period following his death and the eventual transfer of the deed to my name—or someone else's. The funds Bourville distributes monthly to William allow him to tend to the property and the needs of the slaves. The winter is harsh. The wind and snow here are like nowhere else on earth. I am heartened to know they are sheltered, that they will have the means to feed themselves and keep warm without my intervention.

Were this the Rome of old, the mid-December feasts of the Saturnalia would be upon us and the social order would be broken—slaves on equal footing with their masters, if only for a time. Slaves... It is difficult for me to write the word and far more so to say it.

She left the house in the early morning hours. Numbing cold, drifts, and uneven terrain did not stop her from forging her way toward the river. The only sounds she heard were the wind whisking over the tops of the tall pines and her own gasping as she tried to catch her breath. She had to reach the river no matter what. Finally, she could hear the rushing currents, see the dark course wend its way eternally, timelessly, through a landscape of primeval vegetation. The river's force was such that it was always the last body of water to freeze. She remained immobile—a statue on the edge of the large boulder jutting out over the surging foam. She had only to step forward a few inches and everything would change. The pain would be brief, and then the suffering would be over. She heard utterances from the river's depths telling her to go back, or perhaps to join them. She pulled the small leather pouch of finely ground powders from her sleeve and breathed deeply their acrid scents, as he had instructed. Then she poured the contents of the pouch into the river and recited the chant he had made her memorize. Three times, her voice swirled into the white crests appearing and disappearing before her eyes. Embrace the cold arms that summon.

Quebec City, on this Friday the 13th day of December 1734.
Her sister sent a message this morning imploring me to come. I had not seen her since my hurried visit almost two weeks ago. Countless obstacles had prevented me. I did not know what to expect. But I knew it was urgent. When I arrived she was...

Lost in a low point of the forest, surrounded by sharp rocky embankments covered with fir trees, she knows she has to keep moving. The black horse is not far behind. She has seen its flaming eyes, blazing mane, enormous hooves. The beast is gigantic. She cannot tell if it is acting on its own or if a rider is spurring it on, following her every turn. If there is a horseman, he must be covered in black, as dark as night, like the stallion. How could a horse be so colossal?

She pushes through the brush. The hawks overhead obscure the light by their sheer number. She can barely see but has to keep running. The ground is shaking from the pounding of the galloping black stallion. It is hard to move forward, hard to climb up. The incline is steep, so steep. And the horse is getting nearer, ever nearer. Yes, there is a rider. His cloak blows furiously in the wind. The huge beast is approaching. There is no way to escape. If only she could hide, become small. She crouches behind a curtain of trees and brush. The horse and rider race by and stop by a stone formation at the center of the hollow.

For what demonic purpose? The rider throws a large black bag onto the ground. The earth is silenced. She dares not move, dares not make a sound. The horseman jumps down as the monster gallops up into the colorless sky and disappears over the horizon, its fiery eyes and mane illuminating the dull light of dusk.

The rider places the bag on the sacrificial stone and traces a circle around it with a stick. At the snap of his fingers, the circle bursts into flames. He takes two skulls from the bag and places them on the altar.

He turns in her direction and emerges from the circle of fire, for he has heard her scream. He advances with long steps that make no sound, determined movements. There is no one to help her. And who could protect her from the forces of hell? He is running after her now. She tries to move. Her legs will not carry her. Her motions are slow. She will never get away, never. Soon he'll be on her...

...delirious and yelling incoherently, her bed soaked from the vapors of her body. I touched her and was certain my hand had been burned.

Jean Luc ordered Anne to fetch a pail of snow. They took turns preparing cold compresses made of rags wrapped around fistfuls of snow and placing them on Marie Claire's forehead and chest. The fever worsened during the night but by dawn, the hallucinations stopped. Marie Claire was able to eat a few spoonfuls of warm broth and later some wheat bread.

The deaf servant girl from across the street and Anne have devised a rudimentary system of gestures that allows them to communicate. Sophie has been going to the market, doing the wash, and preparing the meals so Anne can tend to her sister. The girl's assistance is a comfort to us despite her sullen disposition and distant manner. She is truly an unhappy child.

Jean Luc sent word to Madame Seguin to let her know he would not return to the inn for a day or two, and to request that she send him fresh garments. In the interim, she could dispatch a messenger if she needed him. He worried about Pierre and hoped he would not feel forsaken.

Jean Luc slept in the main room on a pallet by the hearth. Anne prepared a cot in Marie Claire's room where she kept watch and took charge of heating the bricks and placing them in the iron pots by the bed for warmth.

"That trapper who saw her fall into the river had more courage than he realized," Anne told Jean Luc during one of their evening vigils. "Thank God he was strong enough to fight the currents and drag her to shore. He was lucky he didn't lose his own life."

Quebec City, on this Sunday the 15th day of December 1734.

With reluctance, Sophie had to return to her employer today. Monsieur Charbonneau has not been pleased by her prolonged absences over the past days. He made it clear she is not to sneak off again regardless of how crucial she might think her services are elsewhere. I sat with Marie Claire while Anne washed the supper dishes. We said little. There seemed to be no need to voice our thoughts. I took her hand and held it in mine. It was then that she attempted to describe the battle raging inside her.

"I left the world of the living once again. I thought this time I wouldn't come back. I wasn't alone. Others were there with me. Beings that were familiar yet...unnatural. Their nearness terrified me, but somehow reassured me at the same time. I still feel their cold hands pulling at me. I imagine it's because of Suzanne that I continue the struggle. The demons will not let go. I do not know if I will ever free myself from their hold, or if I should even try."

Something stirred deep within Jean Luc. His voice was somber. "The light you carry inside you is precious. It can never be replaced. Do not allow it to go out. Make it grow brighter to illuminate the path for others, but be wary. Do not share it with everyone. Some are not worthy."

Quebec City, late evening on this Wednesday the 25th day of December 1734.

She looked resplendent last night. Anne has forced her to rest these last two weeks.

The *Place Royale. Notre Dame des Victoires.* Madame Seguin, Pierre, and Jean Luc were seated at the rear of the congregation. Suzanne, Marie Claire, and Anne were further up on the opposite side of the main aisle. Suzanne smiled and waved to Pierre. He looked away bashfully and buried his face in his father's coat, but peeked out every so often to see if Suzanne was still watching him. And she was.

"I wash my hands in innocence..." The alter boy poured water over the hands extended in front of him—the *lavabo*. Gazing steadfastly at the priest's white vestments, Jean Luc felt anguish. When would he be cleansed of his own guilt? He could not escape the day of reckoning forever. It would ultimately come. He saw her once more in the barren landscape of his imagination, her features less distinct now, so different from those of the woman there in the church. Both stood before him against an empty sky—the then and now of his existence. The faint ringing of a small bell dissolved the images as a pebble cast into water turns reflections into ripples. The elevation of the host. The elevation of the chalice. A second chime. The celestial and earthly kingdoms in conversation.

Bells always signaled important moments, perhaps because, along with clocks, hourglasses, and sundials, they were instruments for measuring time and were directly linked to political, religious, and economic power—symbols of control that set the city's daily pace. Bells were a call to obedience. They pealed whenever there was a change of command and a new governor arrived. Jean Luc pictured the exquisite chiming clocks he'd seen in the homes of Langlois and LeMoyne—outward signs of their respective owners' status since such timepieces were a rarity in the colony. Bells were a reminder not only of time passing, but also of human subjugation to it—the joyous sound of carillons at weddings, the lonely tolling for the dead. The thought paralyzed Jean Luc's mind. His game of mental wandering was a dangerous one, leading him down paths he did not wish to take.

Jean Luc was detached from the parishioners. Watching them as he would performers in a pageant, he was struck by the discernable distinction between social and personal continuance. He looked at the woman seated next to her child a few rows up. Like himself, she was caught between opposing and irreconcilable truths—the timelessness of emotions and the call of rigid social duties. For weeks before her confrontation with the shadows of Hades, he had been unable to see her, unable to continue the journey with her back to Acadia. Pierre's illness had taken all his time, all his strength. And now, this night, would she care to see him or prefer to remain forever bound to a passion that would not cease even in death?

The priest droned on. The mass seemed endless. Jean Luc began to ponder the city he had come to know over the past months—the Basilica, churches and convents, the hospital, the Jesuit college. His mind roamed up and down the steeply sloping streets past the ecclesiastical edifices. There was an overabundance of them. A fine line separated judicial matters from matters of faith. Blasphemy could be punished by burning the transgressor's lip with a hot iron or severing his tongue.

"*Agnus dei.*" Lamb of God. The suffering of the innocent, thought Jean Luc. During his consultation with Sylvain at the Hôtel Dieu, the head surgeon had described how he had been forced to cut open the breast of a nun to remove a malignant growth with nothing to ease her misery but brandy. He wasn't allowed to administer narcotics. The Church forbade them.

Finally came the three words everyone had been waiting for—"*Ite misa est.*" The doors swung open onto the starlit night and a rippling cascade of a thousand bells as the small choir's song accompanied the congregation's exit. *Il est né le divin enfant! Jouez hautbois, résonnez musettes.*

The *Place Royale* overflowed with talk and laughter. Jean Luc, Madame Seguin, and Pierre kept moving about in a vain attempt to stay warm. They were envious of the locals, seemingly unperturbed by the cold. Heavy gusts whirled the dry powdery snow up into the air like so many sparkling gems in the moonlight. He wanted to give them to her. Offer her the diamonds of the night. But would she want his gifts?

She passed through the archway, draped in the black of her solitude, pulling the cape's ample hood over the lace coif covering her hair. Before he had time to greet her, she was surrounded by parishioners—more barriers separating him from her. He was making his way through the moving blockade when he saw the silver-tipped cane poised in front of him. "Monsieur de Montigny! Madame Seguin! Joyeux Noël! And could this be Pierre?" Desjardins tilted his hat. "Yes, yes, even I attend Christmas mass," laughed the fur trader. Jean Luc's disbelief must have been visible. He never expected to see the man anywhere near a church. But before Jean Luc could respond, Desjardins had disappeared into the crowd.

"Joyeux Noël, Marie Claire." Jean Luc's turn had come at last. He kissed her on both cheeks. "I was hoping you could join us for Christmas supper at the inn...along with Anne and Suzanne, of course." He'd almost forgotten to include them.

Her smile was cryptic. Regret or relief, he wondered, as she pronounced her devastating response. "Monsieur and Madame Caron have invited us to spend the day with them. I'm afraid we've already accepted."

"In that case, perhaps we could get together for New Year's."

"We won't all be here. I've talked Anne into taking Suzanne down to Trois Rivieres for a visit with our cousin, Aurelien. That's him over there. He's spending the week in town to buy provisions. Anne needs a rest. And I want some time alone. It was hard to convince her, but I promised her Madame Caron would check in on me every day."

A star had fallen on the horizon of Jean Luc's hopes.

"Doctor, I think my niece fancies your little boy."

Anne was watching Suzanne and Pierre, each timidly peering out from behind an adult shield. Her remark pulled Jean Luc from his brooding. As he looked at both children in their long, skirted garments, he remembered himself at three or four wearing what he could only think of that night as a dress. A flush of embarrassment warmed his cheeks. He had never questioned the practice. And had he clothed his son any other way, people would have stared. As the social code dictated, Pierre would need to wait at least three more years before he could go through his rite of passage and begin wearing male attire. In the interim, he and Suzanne looked like two angels. Christmas cherubs. Creatures of innocence.

"Doctor, has Pierre had the occasion to see the countryside yet?"

"Not much. We've made a few trips to my uncle's estate, but..."

"Then why not let me take him to Trois Rivieres with Suzanne? He'll be able to play with other children and see something new."

"Anne, they might already have plans for New Year's day," interjected Marie Claire.

Madame Seguin listened inconspicuously to the exchange, knowing the outcome would affect her directly. Jean Luc weighed the suggestion. For so long, even before their arrival in the colony, his son had been isolated. "You know, perhaps he would enjoy it. And Madame Seguin could have a bit of freedom."

The governess struggled to repress the smile forcing its way onto her lips. In her excitement, she barely heard Anne say, "We're leaving the morning of the thirtieth and should be back the following Monday, the sixth. Just a week."

Jean Luc had imagined a day trip or an overnight excursion at most. He had no idea where Trois Rivieres was, how close or far away it might be, how long it would take to get there. He camouflaged his apprehension behind a facade of concern for Anne's peace of mind. "Are you sure you want to put up with Pierre all that time? Won't it be an inconvenience?"

"Not in the least."

"Would you be my guest for supper New Year's Eve?"

Marie Claire's question caught Jean Luc by surprise.

Quebec City, on this Monday the 30th day of December 1734.

It snowed hard throughout the night. The winds had still not subsided when we set out this morning. I had second thoughts about letting Pierre go.

All along rue de Meulles, men were attempting to clear the passages in front of their dwellings—a task equal to that of Sisyphus under these conditions. Desjardins told me Quebec gets enormous amounts of snow each year, as much as ten feet. Drifts are occasionally twice that high.

Despite its plainness, the abode was an oasis in a desert of stark white.

Anne's father had built the first house of wood, but it burned to the ground before she was born. Before Marie Claire. Before Jean Luc. He built the second one in stone, using slate for the roof instead of cedar shingles, and roughcast the outside walls to reduce the effects of repeated freezing and thawing. The roof was steep, to allow the snow to slide off. There were few windows, none on the northeast side where the winds were strongest. The artisans and shopkeepers who lived nearby had larger, more comfortable quarters with two stories, plus an attic and cellar for storing grains or furs and controlling moisture. That afforded them the luxury of reserving the ground floor for business. Anne had to make do with less.

When the sleigh pulled to a halt, a man shoveling snow stopped his work and extended his hand to Jean Luc. Aurelien had arrived early that morning in preparation for the trip back home, glad to have the company of Anne and the children for the long expedition. The harsh weather would not dampen his determination.

He reassured me more than once there would be no danger. His confidence convinced me not to deprive Pierre of a playful week with other children his age. Arrangements have already been made for their return with one of the neighbors.

Quebec City, on this Wednesday the 1st day of January 1735.
Her smile greeted me last night, auguring unanticipated beginnings and long desired endings—perhaps.

He prolonged the warmth of their embrace. The wine he brought was the color of her lips. She set one bottle on the table and the other on the sideboard, next to the wax nativity.

He presented her with a green paper cone filled with confections and a small gift wrapped in blue cloth before brushing the snow from his clothes and removing his hat.

"I see you took my advice and got yourself a real hat."

"Glad I did. I bought it from Monsieur Coton. He has a nice shop."

"He hasn't been in business long. Let me set your things by the fire."

"I hope Anne and the children made it to your cousin's safely."

"It's not that far, especially now with the new road. Aurelien knows his way with his eyes closed, and I couldn't think of a better person than Anne to accompany them. Saint Anne is the patron of travelers, you know."

He said nothing.

"But if they should encounter difficulty, there are inns every twenty miles or so, and people in the countryside are used to showing hospitality at all hours of the day and night. That's how they get news from the towns."

The odor of lye was barely detectable. Her hands were not as red and chaffed as usual. There was less work between the holidays. She tried to conceal the awkwardness she felt. "Come, I've prepared supper."

Two tapers, each set in a low pewter holder, illuminated the place settings. Filtered through his esthetic prism, the scene before him became a tableau: a Chardin, cast in the soft ambers of La Tour.

He removed a silver blade from his coat pocket and placed it by the ironstone plate. By now, he knew to bring his own knife. It was customary for both gentlemen and ladies to do so. He purchased his in a shop in the upper city a few weeks after his arrival, and was especially fond of the intricate design on the mother of pearl handle.

He uncorked the wine from Haut Pomadour and poured himself a taster's portion. Twirling the goblet that her parents had brought with them when they left Normandy decades before, he sniffed the tiny ruby whirlpool in the manner shown him by his father and took a sip. "1728 was a good harvest. We hold the better yields longer. We've found it improves the flavor."

He filled her goblet, and then his own.

She had not been initiated to the mysteries of wine. Her sister considered it beyond her means and reserved it for select occasions. She raised her goblet and tilted her head. "Bon appétit!"

How could she have been so bold as to invite a man to supper? She, a woman in mourning. And why had this stranger accepted? Suddenly the social chasm that separated him from her became acutely apparent—his education and worldliness, his wealth and title. She had never been alone with him before. Anne and Suzanne were always close at hand. Their presence defused her self-consciousness. But now she was the one who needed to keep the conversion going as they ate their soup, even at the risk of revealing her ignorance. "How were the benefits of holding the wine longer discovered?"

Whenever it was a question of art or oenology, he could be just as talkative as Desjardins. That evening, though, he would have graced her company with any topic she wished.

"It was the result of human negligence, you might say. People had always assumed wine soured after a year, but every now and then, someone would find a bottle they'd forgotten about, blow off the dust, and hope it might still be worth drinking. After a while, someone realized that aging wine changes its flavor for the better. And so, what was once a fluke is now becoming standard practice."

He had told the story countless times before but still enjoyed it as much as she, as if it were the first time.

She removed the emptied soup bowls, brought a deep cast iron casserole from the fire to the table, and returned for the remaining platters. He looked quizzically at the yellow object on his plate.

"That's a cob of corn. Some people call it maize. We prefer to call it Indian wheat. You're going to have to forget your European manners for once and eat with your hands, like the natives."

She blushed once the words had been spoken, suddenly remembering that the man she was addressing was an aristocrat—and at her table, simple as it was. The hint of a smile on his lips suggested he found her frankness pleasing.

Cheese, nuts, candied blueberries, the ordinary had become extraordinary. It was a banquet. The fire cast ever-shifting reflections on the ceiling. The moving shadows were like spirits there with them, the silhouettes of two others. Marie Claire and Jean Luc watched in silence as these glimpses of the past took them back and forth across the Atlantic. Outside, snow spun in the wind against the night sky.

She began to speak of their departure from Acadia and the events preceding the calamity. The players in her story were waiting for my return to resume the performance, but it was not a play that was unfolding...

"Anne took us in without asking any questions, without imposing restrictions or making demands. She was good to us. We didn't want to make her life harder. She was getting by doing laundering, but that didn't bring in enough to feed extra mouths. We were just going to stay long enough for Jacques to find work, but we gradually realized we had come to another dead end."

Supper was long finished. Marie Claire and Jean Luc were huddled atop the bearskin in front of the hearth. Colberte had appropriated a warm spot near the fire. The cat's eyes were two flames glowing against the blackness.

"One morning stands out in my mind. Suzanne had begun to stir. Jacques could hear her soft, happy babbling. He pulled off the quilts, went to her cot, gently took her in his arms, and set her down on the bed next to me. The commotion had awakened Thomas. Jacques helped him dress while I played hand games with Suzanne. I could tell Jacques was not himself."

Frustration was carrying Jacques down into obscure valleys. Something was going to happen. Something had to happen. He would make it happen.

"Today's the day," he suddenly announced with false assurance.

"What do you mean?"

"I'm going to get work. I've got to. We've stayed with your sister long enough. It's time to move out and have a place of our own. To make sure things go my way, I'm bringing Thomas along for good luck."

The desperation in his voice worried her. Her words would have little effect, that she knew, but she needed at least to try to prevent the volcano from erupting, abate his growing sense of worthlessness. "You'll find something. Be patient. You're right. Things will change today. I have that feeling, too," she replied, not realizing her words were a prophecy.

After breakfast, they gathered in the front room. Marie Claire bundled up Thomas while Jacques put on his coat. Winter was practically over. There was very little snow left on the ground, but it was still chilly, especially at night and at daybreak. Jacques led his son by the hand as they walked down the street together in the morning sunshine that would cause the day to grow warmer as the hours went by. Marie Claire stood in the doorway with Suzanne in her arms.

Father and son headed toward the port, unaware they were being observed. The Pawnee's features were rough. A long scar etched the left side of his face, just missing the corner of his eye. It was the mark of a difficult past. Some claimed he was a métis, which explained his partially European attire and facility with the white man's language. He was a slave on the run. Secretive yet smooth talking, he had a knack for slipping in and out of crowds unnoticed. He studied people, spied on their conversations, scrutinized their movements, virtually heard their most private thoughts. He was practicing his dark alchemy on Jacques and Thomas that day as he watched them approach a man giving orders to workers on one of the docked ships. It would not be long before the start of the new sailing season. The port was slowly waking from its long hibernation. Jacques wanted to be part of it, part of life. The ship's foreman only shook his head and returned to his work. Jacques grabbed Thomas by the hand and went down along the wharves to talk to someone else, but got the same curt response.

During the course of the morning, Jacques spoke to every boat captain and dock foreman in the port to no avail. Tired and hungry, he and Thomas found a spot to sit near a heap of old kegs. Jacques unwrapped the bread and salt pork Marie Claire had prepared for them. They ate in silence. Jacques seemed far away. His stare was hollow. Thomas knew it was better not to say anything, even though he was still hungry, even though he was shivering. Finally, Jacques got up. Thomas followed him into a shop. The clerk was busy restocking the shelves. Jacques offered his services. Without paying much attention, the man made it clear he didn't appreciate being disturbed and went on with his business. The scene repeated itself in almost every store in the lower city. Penetrating the upper city was out of the question, Jacques knew that. It was late afternoon by the time he and Thomas plodded back to Anne's house.

Marie Claire was ironing when she heard the front latch. The distress in Jacques's eyes spoke to her. He barely looked her way before going off to sulk in a corner.

Anne had heard the latch, too. When she entered the room, Suzanne was yelling and jumping about. Thomas was sprawled out on the bearskin, exhausted from the long ordeal. The tension in the air was palpable.

"Now children, how about going for a nice walk?"

Thomas was not enthused, but Suzanne was restless. The prospect excited her. "Oh yes. Please, please, let's."

Anne knew she had to make the offer more enticing for Thomas. "We can go to the bakery and buy some sweets." Suzanne clapped in merriment as Thomas affected reluctance, then acquiesced.

As soon as they were out the door, Jacques broke his silence. "I thought finding work here would be easy. It's a big city and there's a lot going on, but every time I talk to someone about a job, I get the feeling they've been told. They know I used to take stuff. They know about the rest, too. Even the few times they've said yes, they come up to me the next day and tell me things changed. Now nobody'll even hire me for a day. There's a curse on me."

"Oh Jacques, you don't really believe that, do you?"

"All I know is we can't stay here. We didn't move far away enough. We've got to keep going. As far as we can. Head south. Down to the British territories. They won't know about me there. Or what I did."

Marie Claire looked around her at everything she would have to abandon—the house where she was born, the street where she grew up. Jacques was right. They would never have the life they wanted unless they completely severed themselves from their past—if they could. It was an absurd situation. The political instability in the colonies was an extension of the turmoil that characterized their own existence. Or was it the other way around? When Acadia fell to the British, everyone there became subjects of King George. But the Acadians refused to swear allegiance to him, refused to renounce their language and religion. They were looked upon with suspicion by the French if they traded with the English colonies and considered untrustworthy by the British if they traded with Quebec. When Marie Claire and Jacques went to live with Anne, they became King Louis's subjects again. Now they were making plans to leave and settle somewhere in the southern English colonies. Were they French? Acadian? Canadian? They certainly weren't British, yet destiny was pushing them to the settlements of the French king's rival.

A few days passed. The *Auberge du Roy* was not as busy as usual that early spring afternoon. Jacques had been drinking for some time. His eyes were fixed on his hands resting on the wooden surface in front of him. They were strong young hands, hands that could work long days. Jacques was a man who expressed his essence through action, but he had been reduced to taking odd jobs at best. He gulped the last swig of beer and gazed into the empty mug, his faculties numbed. Without warning, another hand came into view, one that did not resemble his. The hand plunked a full tankard on the table. Jacques peered up.

"Looks like ya could use another." The Pawnee was holding a second mug for himself.

Jacques lifted the tankard and started to drink. The Indian pulled up a chair. "Ya seem kinda lost. Like ya don't wanta be here."

Jacques had no desire to speak, no interest in what this stranger had to say. But the Pawnee persevered. "Kinda feel that way myself. That's why I'm leavin' these parts. Goin' south."

"South?" The word piqued Jacques's interest.

"Yep. South. Leavin' jist as soon as I git what I need."

"I'm heading south, too."

"Well ain't that a coincidence?"

"Taking my family. We're not welcome here."

"I know that feelin'... So which are ya? A hunter or a trapper?"

"Neither. I've done some hunting in my time, but I mostly work on the docks when I can. I'm a fisherman."

A fine mist sprayed Jacques's hands as the Pawnee spit out his beer with a laugh. "A fisherman! You won't make it south on yer own."

"Why not?" Jacques bellowed. He could feel his anger rising. Heads in the tavern turned to see the cause of the commotion.

The Pawnee was careful to replace the arrogance in his voice with solicitude. "It's pretty rough in spots. There ain't no roads... D'ya know how ta cross a river safely? Ya gotta know when and where. I ain't talkin' fishin'. D'ya know the tribes? Which is at peace, an' which is fightin'? Which is friendly, an' which ain't? And who's gonna make sure yer kids git up an' down them steep cliffs without fallin' ta their deaths?"

The tight feeling in Jacques's chest returned. It was another failed plan—before it even began. Mounting confusion and rage overcame his senses.

The Pawnee took advantage of the moment. "Look, you wanta go south an' so do I. You don't know the woods an' tribes. I do. I'll make a deal with ya. When I said I was leavin' as soon as I got everythin' I need, I meant a certain sum of money and some equipment."

"Equipment?"

"Yeah. Gear. Ya know, ropes, hatchets, knives. The stuff ya need ta survive in the wilderness."

"Oh, yeah," replied Jacques, still capable of feeling embarrassment, despite his drunken state.

"So, what d'ya think? Kin we do business? You git me what I need, an' I git you where you wanta go."

"Let me think it over. What's your name, anyway?"

"Nicolas."

"Mine's Jacques."

"Well, my friend, I'll tell ya some more things that'll help ya make up yer mind."

Hours passed. Sylvie refilled the tankards over and over again. Nicolas did most of the talking. Jacques was ready to sell his soul.

"So that's my price. A new set of clothes, the gear we talked about, two bottles a rum, an' seventy-five pounds cash. An' I don't want none of that card money neither."

"And when would we leave?" Jacques slurred.

"In a coupla weeks. Winter's jist about over now. Mosta the snow's melted..."

The two men were staring at each other. Silent. Each with a mission. Each with a secret. Finally, the Pawnee's gruff voice broke the stalemate. "So, is it a deal?"

The call to action demanded a response. A decision had to be made. But Jacques had already left the colony a hundred times in his mind. "Yeah, you got yourself a deal."

They sealed the pact with a handshake.

Jacques was gone most of the time after that. He never told Marie Claire where he was going or what he was doing, only that he was getting things ready for their departure.

One night, in the darkened stillness reigning over the lower part of town, a hand pushed a blanket up against the glass of the general store's rear window to muffle the sound of the pane shattering. Reaching in, the hand unlocked the window and pushed it open. The intruder threw the piece of wood he'd used to break the glass into the store and crawled through the window. He had to work in the dark. A candle or lantern would draw attention. His eyes slowly adjusted to the obscurity.

He'd gone over the list countless times. Most of the expensive merchandise was stored behind the counter. Moving quickly, he began pulling what he needed from the shelves and piling it together: three eight-inch knives, a hatchet, three spools of rope, sheets of waxed canvas, a musket, two flintlock pistols, a box of ammunition for each firearm, tin cups and plates, three woolen blankets, pouches and cloth bags. The pile on the counter was growing. He checked to make sure he hadn't forgotten anything. Then he remembered and started ransacking the premises.

A deafening noise sent a chill of fear through his body. He'd knocked over the ladder used for getting items down from the top shelves. A dog began to bark. He knew he had to hurry now, but waited until silence returned before resuming his search. Soon he found it, wedged behind a stack of ledgers under the counter. His hands forced the lockbox open. He counted out seventy-five pounds in coins, put back the rest, paused, and then took a few cards. Bolting to the front of the counter, he quickly loaded the supplies into the burlap bags. As he was sliding the last of the ammunition into one of them, light illuminated the panes of the front door. A jangling of keys made him freeze. He grabbed the piece of wood, dragged the bags behind the counter, and crouched down. He didn't dare breathe. He knew better than anyone the consequences of getting caught at night.

The door opened. Brightness filled the store. The shopkeeper raised his lantern to eye level. He had barely taken a few steps when he saw the disorder. He turned to run for help, but stopped instinctively when he heard a sound and twisted his head to see what had caused it. Numbing blackness overcame him, as if he had crashed into a wall of stone. The thief threw down the heavy strip of wood, grabbed the bulging bags, and pulled them out into the night.

Marie Claire stopped talking. The second bottle of Chateau Haut Pomadour 1728 was almost empty. Jean Luc poured the last drops into her glass. The fire's yellow-gold had died down to a blue-orange.

"Do we have to wait till midnight to open the presents?" Her voice faltered as she asked.

"No. Let's go ahead."

Marie Claire had placed the gifts by the hearth. She picked up the cone of candies and loosened the knot of the grosgrain trimming. "This ribbon is beautiful. I'll use it to tie Suzanne's hair back. Now I know you didn't bring this maple sugar all the way from France."

"No, I thought it was time I took advantage of the local specialties. And I wanted to sweeten the New Year."

Marie Claire chose a piece of the grainy delicacy before offering the green cone to Jean Luc. "I must admit," he confessed, taking it from her hand, "when I saw these in the shop, my intentions were not entirely magnanimous. I was half thinking of myself."

Feigned disapproval was her response. "I see."

"Maple sugar is not easily procured in France. It's considered exotic. My Aunt Clothilde told me about it, but I never had occasion to taste any until Anne's sugar pie. So I will remain forever grateful to you, Madame, for giving me yet another opportunity." As the granules slowly dissolved on his tongue, he hesitated for a moment, pretending to be judging the merits of a fine wine. "Fit for a king. For the whole of Versailles!"

"I'm glad it's to Your Majesty's liking." She reached for another piece. "It certainly is to mine."

He handed her the second gift. A look of playful suspense illuminated her face as she pulled the ribbon from the blue cloth. Beneath the lustrous moiré was a small white porcelain box with a hinged cover. Painted roses of pink and yellow adorned each side. Along the rim and lid were decorative bronze bands to prevent chipping and secure the two pieces together at the back. A brightly colored peacock embellished the lid's surface. The object's underside bore the French porcelain maker's insignia. She was not accustomed to such finery and would not have recognized even the most well-known makers' marks. Yet she was sensitive to the object's beauty. Her hands had never held anything like it before. "Oh, Jean Luc! It's lovely."

"That's just the box. Why don't you open it?"

She pulled back the lid. Nestled in the shallow base was a delicately crafted pendant with a brilliant gray-black stone mounted in gold.

"It's hematite. The jeweler told me the dark color is typical of this region. All the hematite I've seen back home is reddish brown. That's where the name comes from: *hema*. It's Greek for blood."

She could not speak. He realized too late what he had said. Both of them remained silent a moment, unable to think of anything short of insipid to dispel the anguish aroused by the word he had uttered. Finally, he reached for the pendant. "Let me help you put it on," he whispered.

Taking one end of the filigree chain between the thumb and forefinger of each hand, he braced his palms against the back of her neck and fastened the clasp. Without a word, she rose to her feet and went to her room. He would not blame her if she never spoke to him again. But suddenly she reappeared, holding a tiny oval mirror with a wooden backing mounted in forged metal. It had belonged to her grandmother. The handle showed careful workmanship, as did the boudoir scene painted on the wood surface. She sat down again next to him and admired the reflection of the pendant framed by the mirror's metal mount.

"It's exquisite... Thank you."

The wavering of her voice betrayed the pain she was striving to conceal. The phantoms still hovered over the abyss. She had to elude them. She wasn't ready to descend into hell again. Not her hell in any case.

She handed him the third gift. It was noticeably larger than the others and wrapped in crimson cloth, trimmed with white cord. She was eager to see his reaction. Pulling off the cord and fabric, he discovered an uncommonly long green scarf. A pattern of yellow arrows ran down the center.

"What do you think?"

"It's... I love it." His reply was unconvincing. Looping the band of wool around his neck, he wondered how he would keep from tripping over it. It seemed more suitable for a Titan.

"That's not the way you wear it!" His awkwardness enchanted her. "It's not a scarf. It's a *ceinture fléchée*. It goes around your waist to prevent the wind from getting under your clothing. It should keep you warm for the rest of the winter. I'm sure none of your friends in France have one."

"Thank you." His words took on a significance he could neither understand nor explain. He leaned toward her and gently touched his lips to hers. She did not pull away but lingered in his warmth. Then, slowly, she unwrapped the scarf from around his neck. He didn't want her to stop, wished she would bare him completely and press her body against his.

She moved the gifts to one side. "You've told me almost nothing of yourself."

He stared blankly into the fire, as if he hadn't heard. He had thought, had hoped she would not require this of him. He'd been confident the dazzle of the gifts would be enough to fill her imagination. But he was wrong.

He had to ready himself. Set the stage first. Sketch the background before painting the drama in the foreground.

He explained how, as a young man, his father had planted a small vineyard on the grounds of Haut Pomadour, one of the family estates, and started making wine as a pastime. His intellectual curiosity prompted him to learn everything he could about the vintner's art. His efforts, coupled with the energy of youth, proved successful well beyond his modest expectations.

The wine he produced and served at his table was of such superior quality that friends and supper guests began to remark upon it, hoping they would be fortunate enough to receive a bottle or two to take home with them. Little by little its reputation grew, and the elder Montigny entered into what became an extremely lucrative enterprise. Cultivating the vine was, along with medicine, one of the few commercial pursuits in which the monarch permitted nobility to indulge. Jean Luc's father soon gained royal approval not only of the pursuit, but of the product as well. Despite the court's longstanding preference for the more easily obtainable Burgundies, the aging Louis XIV, followed by the ever-dissolute regent, regularly placed orders with the Haut Pomadour estate.

"My father was able to ensure financial stability for the

family without forfeiting the respect of his peers. The properties that had been ours for generations have remained in our possession thanks to him. The chateau my grandparents intended to pass on to me became mine when I came of age."

"It must be beautiful. I can't even imagine. What's it like?"

Loublanc had been built over a hundred years earlier. Jean Luc began making changes soon after he acquired it. The lighter, airier look he was so fond of had come into fashion with the regent. Philippe d'Orleans wanted to break from the austerity of the Sun King's last years. He hadn't cared much for severity and rigid surroundings, and in fact neither did the young king now on the throne. France's fifteenth Louis may have only been in his early twenties when Jean Luc undertook the refurbishment of Loublanc, but he had already left his mark where style was concerned.

"What kinds of changes have you made?"

There was a moment's pause. "I've replaced some of the heavy old chandeliers with crystal ones...had the wood paneling in the reception rooms painted and gilded...added some bronze ornamentation and commissioned new furniture. But it all takes time."

He did not tell her that nothing more had been done since last May—since the day time stood still. That need not be explained to her, he concluded. She would ultimately deduce it, he was certain. "One thing I decided not to change is the layout of the grounds. I've always been partial to the formality of them."

"Listening to you makes me feel as if I'm in a dream, a fairy tale."

And I am King Nacleus, he thought.

"The first time I saw her was at Loublanc." His voice was distant. "I had organized a recital."

The tall paned double doors and windows giving onto the gardens were open that evening at Loublanc. The summer air carried with it the scents of roses, lilies, and irises, each trying to overpower the other, blending in an ever-changing perfume. The servants had set up a few rows of chairs on one side, facing the chamber ensemble. The musicians were tuning up.

He was with his friend, Etienne, and Etienne's sister,

Charlotte, when he noticed her across the room, standing by one of
the windows, talking and laughing with a group of guests. She
must have arrived late, since he didn't remember having greeted
her with the others. He couldn't take his eyes off her. Etienne
could tell he wasn't paying attention to his prattle. "Well, it
appears I'm merely talking to exercise my vocal chords. What's
put you in such a trance?"

"Over there, by the window. In the blue dress. She's ravishing."

Peering in the direction of the casement windows, Etienne
saw the slender figure in flowing blue satin against the red velvet
drapes. "The blue dress? Oh, that's my cousin, Madeleine. From
Nantes. She's visiting us for a few days. I knew you wouldn't
mind if I brought her along. Actually she had to take another
carriage. I got tired of waiting for her to finish primping. I never
thought of her as ravishing, but that's probably because she's my
cousin. In any case, now that I think about it, I guess you're
right. Would you like me to introduce you?"

"If you don't, I'll never speak to you again."

Charlotte giggled into her fan in anticipation of what she
knew would be her brother's equally sarcastic remark.

"Oh, this does sound serious. Come on then. After all, what
would life be without the melodious cackle of your chatter
ringing in my ears?" He paused before adding, almost as an
aside, "Then again, perhaps I should refuse."

Jean Luc's exasperation was apparent. He was in no mood
for his friend's cheeky humor.

"Just teasing," Etienne reassured. "Alright, here we go."

The trio wended its way to the circle of guests conversing
with the woman in blue. Jean Luc bowed slightly and brought
Madeleine's soft, delicate fingers nearly to his lips. She felt his
breath float over her hand.

"*Mesdames et messieurs, s'il vous plaît.*" The voice cut
their interlude short. "Your attention please. We're about to
begin. Kindly be seated."

"May I invite you to sit next to me?"

As Jean Luc turned to give Madeleine his arm, his eye
caught the reflection in the mirror behind her of the painting by
Lancret that hung on the opposite wall. In the mirror's polished
image, he and Madeleine had joined the imaginary *fête*

champêtre depicted by the artist. They took their places in the
front row. Etienne and Charlotte sat to their left. The three
musicians were poised with their instruments, ready to play,
waiting until there was complete silence. With a nod from the
lead violinist, chords broke the stillness, transforming the opening
bars of the composition from ink on paper to sound. The music of
Couperin's grand trio sonata that filled the room told the story in
harmonic terms of Corelli's ascent to Parnassus. The continuo's
resonance gave depth to the melody defined by the two violins.
Jean Luc gently nudged the edge of Madeleine's beaded blue
satin slipper with the polished tip of his shoe. Without taking her
eyes off the chamber ensemble, she smiled and moved her foot
within closer reach.

He could still hear the melody, still see the musicians, still
imagine Corelli drinking from the Hypocrene Spring and the
muses waking him to lead him to Apollo. Jean Luc was next to
Madeleine once again. Nothing had changed. And then the
vision faded into the hearth's ashes.

~~~

Gazing at the pages before him, Pierre began to hear music,
a concerto for strings or perhaps a *symphonie concertante*. The
vigorous bow work and quick fingering carried the soloist's hand
up and down the lacquered neck, taking Pierre to a time filled
with optimism and hope, far from the cell where he now found
himself. He remembered the piece. It had been written by Joseph
Boulogne, better known as the Chevalier de Saint-Georges—one
of Europe's best swordsmen. The son of a slave woman and a
French plantation owner, he was a Free Mason, like Mozart. It
was said that when the young Austrian composer visited Paris in
1778, he could not hide his envy of Saint-Georges's talent. Many
envied it. A master of virtuosity, he had made a stunning debut
performing a violin concerto of his own composition, gone on to
direct several orchestral groups, and was appointed head of the
Royal Academy of Music by Louis XVI. To Pierre, the public
and royal recognition of Saint-Georges's achievements served as
an example of the new social equality that was gaining
momentum.

But the recognition was short-lived and the appointment withdrawn. The Academy's divas had seen to that. They balked at the thought of taking orders from a "mulatto." Everyone knew no one else possessed Saint-Georges's genius. And so, the position was never filled. His works touched the soul, knew no boundaries of class, rank, or race. Yet, despite his father's aristocratic lineage, the man had never been fully accepted within the circles of nobility, could never wed, and was thus condemned to fleeting affairs with married women. His most heart-rending composition had been written following the death of his infant son, left to starve at the orders of an enraged, cuckolded husband. The last Pierre had heard, Saint-Georges was serving the revolutionary cause, heading a contingent of some one thousand men.

His hope was that the tides would not turn against Saint-Georges again. This time, the stakes were too high. Pierre more than anyone was aware of the dangers of fanaticism. The extermination of his own family was testimony to that. His one consolation was that his father was not alive to witness the savagery. Turgot, Malesherbes, and Vergennes had been capable ministers, determined to bring about significant reforms. But their initiatives had been blocked by parliament on too many occasions. And now radicalism had triumphed. The social order had been destroyed, with nothing in position to replace it. Would Saint-Georges, like Pierre, become a victim? Would his musical compositions be swept away, along with so many other hallmarks of civilization, and lost for generations? Would the pages of harmony and refinement be dispersed to the four winds, blown to the shores of oblivion?

Such confusion and suffering. Pierre tried to let the music continue to play in his mind but it was nothing more—yet nothing less—than a memory, a cool stream on a hot summer's day.

~~~

"It's past midnight and we haven't toasted the New Year. I heard the bells, but..."

"It doesn't matter. Let's go on. Tell me more."

"Are you sure?"

Marie Claire nodded. Her presence gave Jean Luc strength.

"It wasn't long before Madeleine and I were married. Helene was born within the year. Helene. We named her after Madeleine's mother. Such bliss. We were oblivious to almost everything, not conscious of time passing. But it was, as it is tonight."

Madeleine was sitting across the room from Jean Luc, gently gliding her hand over Helene's blond curls. It was the slow circular movement of Marie Claire's wrist as she ran her fingers through her hair distractedly that had called forth the image in his mind and he captured it as if it were a moth flying out of the flames.

"We were in the room where we'd first met at the recital. Sun was streaming through the windows. Helene was leaning on the armrest of her mother's chair."

The gilded paneled doors on either end were closed.

"I know you don't approve, Jean Luc, but..."

"It takes you away from me. And I worry about you."

"You really shouldn't, *mon chéri*. Father Gilles is truly grateful whenever I help with handing out the food. There are people literally starving just beyond your father's vineyards. It's scandalous."

"You have a kind heart. That's one of the reasons I married you."

"Now don't try to flatter me just so I'll forget you're unhappy with what I'm doing."

"I'm not unhappy. Well, no, that's not true. Actually, I'm very unhappy whenever you're not here."

"But Jean Luc, my dear, you're a doctor. You help people. It's your contribution to society. You don't have to do it, but you do. Let me make my contribution, too."

"Perhaps you're right. It's selfish of me. And unjust to both you and those you tend to. But you've got to be careful. Promise me you'll never go alone. Promise me you'll always go with Marthe or one of the other servants."

"Oh come now," she laughed.

"Madeleine, I'm serious," he snapped.

A knock at the double doors interrupted the argument.

Hardly had Madeleine's "Come in" been completed when Marthe entered and gave each of them her usual reserved nod. "Monsieur. Madame. It's time for Mademoiselle's afternoon nap."

"Already? I had no idea it was so late. My little darling, let Marthe put you to bed."

"But I'm not tired." Helene rubbed her eyes sleepily. "I don't want to. I want to stay here with you and papa."

"Mama will be in later to make sure you're having wonderful dreams."

"But tomorrow, I'll stay up all day long. I won't need to take a nap."

"Yes, *ma petite puce*. We'll see about that tomorrow. Now give me a big hug."

Marthe took Helene by the hand, but the girl pulled away and ran to her father. Squeezing her tightly, he whispered in her ear, "Sweet dreams, *mon ange*."

Marthe led Helene out and closed the doors behind her.

"Now what were we talking about? Oh, yes, we were solving all the world's problems."

Jean Luc rose from his brocade fauteuil, stood behind Madeleine, and rested his hands on her shoulders. "I've heard unsettling stories. People have been attacked not far from here. That's how bad it's gotten. The poor have no fear of the law anymore. To them, people like us are the culprits, the ones responsible for their misery. And I suppose they're partially right."

"Not really, Jean Luc. You're born to a social rank and there's little you can do to change it. That's just how it is."

"But so many have given in to despair and turned to crime." As he spoke, he gently rubbed Madeleine's shoulders.

"I know. Poaching and thieving are on the rise. And deporting criminals to the colonies certainly doesn't solve the problem."

"Not everyone starting over in the colonies was forced to leave here. Take my Uncle Louis, for example..."

"Well from what I've heard, things aren't that easy over there. Think of what happened to Gerard. He was back within a year."

"My dear, you know as well as I that your cousin was not

cut out for plantation life. Or tropical heat. Most aren't. That's
why they'd rather deal with the devil they know at home than
one they don't somewhere else. Just look at all the women of no
rank or means who miraculously find themselves with titles,
annual pensions, and even a chateau or two. Courtesans, that's
all they are..."

"I hope you don't think men are any better. Why do you
suppose so many turn to the church? It's not out of saintliness, I
assure you. Have you noticed the number of royal ministers who
happen to be bishops or cardinals?"

"Well, you have to admit Fleury is an exception. He may be
a cardinal, but he's an excellent Minister of State. Our currency
is stronger, trade and commerce are improving..."

"You're beginning to sound like a statesman!"

"Is that a compliment, darling? Do you think I missed my
calling? It's still not too late."

"Your medical duties will keep you busy enough, *Monsieur
le docteur.*"

"You mean if we want to have time for more important
things?"

"And what might those more important things be?"

"Oh..." He searched for his response, then bellowed like an
orator addressing a crowd. "Taking afternoon naps."

"Oh yes, I see," she replied in mock seriousness.

He extended his arm. "Madame, may I escort you to the
formal napping room?"

"The formal napping room? Why certainly, Monsieur. With
pleasure." She stood and put her arm through his, lifting her *robe
volante* slightly with her other hand.

"The pleasure will be mine, I assure you, Madame."

As if hosting a grand ball, they paraded past the pier mirrors
and family portraits toward the doors at the opposite end of the
room. The figures in the Lancret painting watched, as they had
on the night of the recital. With affected concern, Jean Luc
turned to Madeleine. "Madame, we need not tell the young
Mademoiselle Helene that we did not truly nap."

"Oh, Monsieur, I would never dream of telling her such a
thing." Then with a teasing grin, she added, "But if we will not
be napping, pray tell, what will we be doing?"

Laughter echoed in the halls as he opened the double doors and smiled in her direction. But she was gone. Marie Claire, silent beside him, was staring into the smoldering embers. The only sound was the howling wind outside.

"I really have stayed too long." His voice had changed. He remembered where he was.

Marie Claire could not face the emptiness. She wanted the escape to last, wanted to remain at Loublanc. Wanted to hear him laugh again, wanted to laugh with him.

"Listen to it out there. With all the wind and blowing snow, you won't be able to see two feet in front of you," she murmured. But she knew what was expected of her and had to adhere to the protocol for living out her grief. She stood and took hold of his hands, as if to pull him up. "I'll get your things," she heard herself say.

They walked to the threshold. Their long kiss transgressed social rules formulated well before they were born, transported them elsewhere—both to the past and far from it. With the slowed motion of a hazy dream, she opened the door. Immediately, the warmth was swept away. Wind raced through the house. In front of them was a swirling wall. No light. No moon. Only grayness. Everywhere. She watched his silhouette become progressively indistinct, enveloped in a cloud of icy fog, until there was nothing. She did not wish to shut him out, send him into exile.

"It's too dangerous," she yelled. "You'll never make it."

Too late. He had vanished. She leaned against the solitude of the closed door, the tomblike cold of the wood planks. For whom did she mourn?

She heard a sound. Faint at first, then louder. Knocking. Yes, she would be rescued. She lifted the latch. He was there. The sweet call of tenderness had overpowered the unyielding code that stood between them. They kissed once more. The conventions of this world could not have authority over them.

"Madame?"

She put her arm through his.

"Monsieur."

I was walking with Madeleine again, heading to our private apartments at Loublanc. No. Suppress the thought. Banish it forever. It is an injustice to both of them. Or is it, my love? My loves. I know not anymore.

The room was cold. She reached for the Prussian blue curtains surrounding her bed and pulled them shut. He embraced her slowly, gently. A look of pain came over her face. He stopped. His fingertips delicately inspected the jagged lines on her thigh and arm, the rough gash on her left side just above her pelvis. How had she survived? He kissed her scars, then her entire body. She responded to his caresses.

Her bed was a ship, a magical vessel. Had I become Jacques? Was she Madeleine? And what difference does it make in the sphere we have entered?

Quebec City, on this Thursday the 2nd day of January 1735.

A second day with her, priceless hours of serenity. Pulling back the bed drapes, we were greeted by Apollo's chariot, an almost blinding luminosity above the eastern horizon.

The bricks in the iron pot by the bed had turned cold during the night and the fire in the main room's hearth went out on its own before the first light of day. I brought it back to life. She heated milk in a small caldron over the flames and stirred in the chocolate and sugar. A dark potion like no other.

I visited the port this afternoon. She could not accompany me. The burden of mourning would not permit it. She is condemned to the prison of her grief. Anne is not here to satisfy society's expectations.

The river was white with a fleece-like cover of ice and snow. It has completely frozen over, making it possible to cross to the other side on foot. Vapors rising from the surface transformed the waterscape into a wondrous spectacle. A few lone skaters circled about through the mist. One, with a large satchel strapped to his back, moved with more determination than the rest—a messenger, no doubt, carrying official papers to points up river. Mercury gliding to Trois Rivieres or Montreal with unchallenged speed and grace.

As he walked through the streets on his way back, bells and carillons resounded at almost every corner adding an acoustic accent to the visual display surrounding him.

Late last night, she brought me still further into her past.

In the darkness of the room, she did not recoil from the pain his touch awakened in her wounds. Her agony would allow her to participate in her lost husband's suffering.

The passion of the moment might quell an anterior desire. The hunger in need of fulfillment had to be satiated the only way possible. Temporarily. Jean Luc looked deep into her eyes at the figures dancing there, people he had never known but who were closer to him than the air he breathed. He now knew her story was his own. He had become dependent on it, like a drug that simultaneously harms and heals.

"Go on. Tell me more." It was a plea of desperation.

"This was the last bed we slept in together. In this very room. It used to be my parents'. Anne has always preferred the room we had as children. That's where she sleeps to this day." Jean Luc turned and kissed her, as Jacques had done before him less than a year earlier in the same room. In the same bed. She was somewhere between then and now. Who was the man beside her? Didn't he already know what she was about to tell him? Or was it her words that formed the bond uniting them, uniting her to the stranger? And to Jacques. She tried to focus on what no longer was. Call it back. Bring it out of hiding.

"Jacques never told me how he got the supplies and I was afraid to ask. The morning of our departure finally came. The snow had completely melted. We'd be walking for the first leg of the trip, so we couldn't bring much—tools and a basket of food, a change of clothes for each of us. It was very little, really, for a family starting over, but still the load was heavy. The Pawnee's things took up most of the weight.

"Anne held me in her arms for a long time. We thought we might never see each other again. Jacques opened the door. The sun had barely risen. The streets were deserted. Anne waved as the four of us walked away. I kept looking back until the house was out of sight. Soon the woods came into view."

Jacques spied Nicolas at the edge of the forest. He gestured to Marie Claire to wait with the children and walked toward the Pawnee with two of the bags. As soon as Jacques was within earshot, Nicolas grunted, "Got everythin'?"

"Everything you asked for."

"Let's see."

Jacques reached inside his coat, pulled out a soft leather coin pouch, loosened the drawstring with his right hand, and poured some of the gold and silver pieces it contained onto his left palm. The Pawnee tried to grab them, but Jacques quickly closed his hand into a fist and yanked it back. "Not so fast. You'll get your money." Placing the pouch securely in his pocket, he opened one of the bags and pointed to a new set of clothes: shirt, breeches, belt, scarf, jacket, cloak, hat. Nicolas picked up the shirt and breeches, and nodded approvingly as he looked them over.

"What about the gear?"

Jacques tilted his head in the direction of the other bag. Nicolas thrust his hand inside and took the hatchet. With meticulous precision, he held it up and ran his thumb lightly across the blade. The sharp edge glistened. For a second, it was the focal point of his universe. He inspected the implement's thick oak handle, expertly carved in the European manner, and then slid the hatchet through his belt.

"Good. Real good. An' the liquor?"

"Two bottles, like you said. See for yourself."

Nicolas snatched one of the bottles from the second bag and took a few gulps to make sure the alcohol had not been diluted. "One thing the white man's good at."

Jacques turned and signaled to Marie Claire and the children. As soon as the Pawnee saw the way they were carrying their bags and the food, he shook his head and smirked, "I told ya ya'd never make it without me. That ain't no way ta go trekkin' through the woods. We gotta divvy all this stuff up an' pack it better. You an' me'll take the heavy gear." Nicolas kept the musket and one of the pistols for himself, then parceled out the remaining items, and rearranged them. He unrolled a long piece of rope from one of the spools, cut it, and tied it to a bag. He crisscrossed the rope several times over the burlap to secure it, then formed two large loops, cut another piece of rope, and wove it in and out of the interlacing. His swift movements were like wizardry.

"Hoist 'er up on my back," the Pawnee told Jacques. "Watch this. Ya slip yer arms through the loops so all the weight rests on yer shoulders." He adjusted the position of the loops. Next, pulling the ends of the second rope around to the front of his waist, he joined them with an intricate knot. "See? This way the bag can't shift none." Nicolas was not a man prone to small talk unless his words were meant to achieve a specific purpose. "Now I'll tie yers the same," he said to Jacques without flinching. "That way ya kin carry the girl. She'll balance the load. Yer woman'll hafta take yer bag a clothes. I'll fix 'er a shoulder strap. Kin she hold on ta the boy an' the basket, too? She strong enough fer that?"

"Don't worry about me. I'll take care of Thomas and whatever I have to." Her response satisfied the Pawnee. She and Jacques were determined to bear the weight of their possessions. Perhaps the hardship would redeem them.

The slow descent had begun. They walked single file, with Nicolas in the lead. Jacques was at the rear, holding Suzanne in his arms. Marie Claire kept an eye on her son, taking him by the hand when the inclines were steep. After they had made some headway, it was Marie Claire's turn to carry Suzanne. She gave Jacques the bag of clothes, picked up the little girl, and locked her hands together so as not to lose her grip on the child. Jacques watched over Thomas. Their children. Their lives.

Hours passed. Everyone except Nicolas was exhausted. His body conserved energy by minimizing its movements. He was accustomed to hauling gear over difficult terrain. His manner of walking reinforced his stamina. It was more like coasting over the earth's surface than taking steps, his torso not rising and falling with each stride, but advancing in a smooth, even motion like the mast of a ship on a calm sea.

Nicolas stayed further ahead, using the hatchet to chop branches and clear the way. Finally he paused at the top of a slope, untied the knot at his waist, and set his backpack on the ground. The others remained behind, waiting for his signal. He looked at the river in the distance, and then gazed up at the sky. The sun would soon be setting. Without warning, he reached for his bow and arrow, swerved, and took aim in Jacques's direction. Too stunned to move, Jacques closed his eyes, anticipating the pain of the shaft penetrating his chest. Marie Claire watched in horror. The arrow seemed to be moving in slow motion, following a path no mortal could dodge. The laws of nature had been abolished. Any attempt to flee its course would have been senseless. When it whisked past him and struck a rabbit, Jacques caught his breath and laughed nervously, "I thought you were aiming at me." Nicolas went to collect his kill. "If I'd been aimin' atcha, ya'd be dead now. I never miss." He held his prey up proudly. "Now we got the beginnin's fer supper."

Soon after, Nicolas decided they'd stop by the river and set up camp for the night. The men mounted two makeshift tents with the sheets of canvas. Nicolas cut fir branches and demonstrated how his tribe used them to create a soft surface for sleeping. "It ain't like them straw mattresses yer used ta, but it's better than nothin'." The Pawnee was to sleep in the smaller tent, the rest of them in the other.

The light grew progressively dimmer. Nicolas told Jacques and Marie Claire to build a campfire. In no time, he skinned the rabbit, skewered the carcass onto a long branch and set it over the flames. The aroma of the slowly roasting meat was comforting—one reassuring certitude in the face of the unknown. A few of the provisions Anne had packed for them helped make the small amount of meat suffice.

Once everyone had finished eating, Jacques and Nicolas stretched out to rest by the campfire while Marie Claire gathered the tin plates and washed them in the river's icy currents. It was only May and the land had not yet forgotten the long winter's penetrating cold. She hastily bathed Suzanne and got her ready for bed. The little girl sat on the ground, watching her mother help Thomas wash up, but soon fell asleep under the starlit sky. Marie Claire could barely hear the men's voices, muffled by the rippling of the rushing water.

"So, what ya runnin' away from?"

"I'm not running away. I'm trying to make a better life for me and my family. There's not much opportunity here."

"Ya goin' down ta Gloucester or New Bedford? Lotsa fishin' down there."

"Could be. What about you?"

"I got some business ta settle. Looks like I gotta go south ta do it."

"What kind of business?"

"Nasty business. A man killed my brother."

"Sorry to hear that."

"Story's kinda complicated. The killer got off free 'cause a the laws—white man's laws. Never hadta go ta trial nor nothin'."

"Why did he do it? Did your brother try to hurt him?"

"Nope. Didn't even know each other."

"Sounds strange."

"Yep. Told ya it was complicated. An' it's up ta me ta set things straight. But I'm on the right track now."

Neither of them had any more to say to each other. Finally, Jacques broke the uneasy stillness. "It should be clear tomorrow. Fishermen are pretty good at predicting the weather. That's one thing I can do. We'll be able to cover a fair distance."

"The weather's jist part of it. The woods is another. We got steep crags ta cross. It's tricky. Dangerous, too. We'll need ta use the ropes."

"Why not go further down river till we find a spot where the terrain's not as rough?"

"We'll save lotsa walkin'. Even if it takes a little time, it's worth it."

Marie Claire didn't want to hear more. She lifted Suzanne and brought her into the tent. Thomas followed wearily.

"So, have I earned yer trust yet? Am I livin' up ta yer expectations? Ready ta give me my money?"

"We're barely south of Quebec City. You know I've got the money to pay you."

Jacques stood and made his way to the tent. An enormous shadow hovered over him like a beast readying to attack. Was it simply his own silhouette cast by the flickering light of the dying campfire on the brush and trees? Or was it something else? When he pushed open the flap, Marie Claire was lying near the center with Suzanne. Thomas was huddled alongside one of the canvas walls. There was barely room enough for Jacques. He eased himself next to Marie Claire. As he struggled to remove his boots, he heard her whisper, "There's something odd about him. I have an eerie feeling."

"Why? Because of what happened today?"

"I really thought he was going to kill you."

Jacques tried to downplay his own apprehension. "Well, you see? You were wrong. And that rabbit sure did taste good."

"But...there's something..."

"He's got problems, too. His brother was murdered. He's looking for the killer."

"Do you think he's out for revenge? Does he intend to slay the man with his own hands?"

"He didn't say that. I don't know what he's planning to do."

Jacques pulled aside the canvas flap and looked out at the moon. The distant howling of wolves filled the night air with sustained, lonely echoes, laments of incomparable feral beauty. Jacques silently pondered the infinite blackness above until he realized Nicolas was watching him. He gave the Pawnee a nod and pulled the flap shut.

Nicolas was now sure the others were settled in for the night. He grabbed one of the bags and dragged it into his tent, then gathered a few maple branches—the straightest he could find. In the seclusion of his canvas shelter, he retrieved a bottle of rum from the bag and uncorked it. The dark liquid ignited his throat with its familiar, penetrating force. Using his sharpest hunting knife, he began whittling the branches into shafts for arrows, drinking more and more as the night wore on. After he'd carved a half dozen or so, he reached into the bag for one of the spools of rope and made a series of small slits on a long piece— first in one spot, then another.

They broke camp early the next morning. The air was brisk. After an hour's hike, Nicolas stopped. When the rest of them caught up with him, he was looking down. Jacques and Marie Claire followed his gaze. Inches in front of them was a drop of at least thirty feet. Marie Claire shrunk back.

"Here's where we're goin' down," grunted Nicolas. Was he annoyed by her fear or taking delight in it? "Ya think there's fancy walkways an' staircases fer ya all the way ta New England?" Then, gaining control of the emotion he had let burst, he took a more conciliatory tone. "Listen. If we go down here, we kin cut through the woods an' catch the river a little ways in. It'll save us 'bout fifteen miles a hikin'. Once we git close ta Trois Rivieres, I know where there's canoes we kin use. It'll go way faster after that. We'll catch the Richelieu River an' go down ta Lake Champlain. That'll bring us inta the British territories."

Jacques and Marie Claire didn't know what to say. Nicolas

was the one who spoke. "It's better ta do this now, in the mornin', when everyone ain't so tired. Here's the plan. You first." He pierced Marie Claire with his eyes. "That way, me an' him kin hold the ropes. An' you'll be there ta help the boy when he gits ta the bottom. Once we lower him, we'll send down the supplies. Then you'll go." The Pawnee was staring at Jacques. "After that, I'll bring the girl. She's too little ta do it by herself. I know how ta work the ropes so I kin slide down with 'er. Don't need no one up top ta lower me." He paused to let them absorb what he'd said.

"Ready?"

The word resounded in their ears.

"I guess so." Jacques's voice was barely audible.

"Now, we gotta be careful how we tie the ropes. The whole secret's in the knots. We make a loop fer one foot an' another fer 'round yer waist. All the weight's on yer foot. If we didn't do it that way, the loop 'round yer waist could slip. An' bang! It'd turn inta a noose. Then it'd all be over." He laughed.

Marie Claire had never heard Nicolas's laughter before. She saw Jacques's uneasiness. Was it because of the odd laughter or the word "noose"?

"Now the other leg ya keep free fer balance an' maneuverin'. Got it?"

Everything was happening so fast. Marie Claire and Jacques had no choice but to comply with the Pawnee's will. He was controlling them. They were without recourse as they watched him take some of the ropes and tie them together, knotting a loop for Marie Claire's right foot and another to slip around her waist exactly as he had explained. He wrapped the opposite end around the trunk of a tree near the edge and checked the ropes over to make sure they were secure. Jacques tried to help, but the Pawnee refused, insisting that fishermen's knots were of no use to him. Jacques did not tell him he had learned to make hangman's knots as well.

"How's it feel?"

"Alright, I guess. I really don't know."

"Looks good to me," Nicolas grumbled, almost as if she hadn't spoken. "You an' me'll lower 'er down easy," he snarled at Jacques. "Now let's go."

Marie Claire looked over the edge. The drop was practically vertical. The rocks along the side were jagged, with sparse bits of greenery growing out of some of the crevices. Her palms were wet as she gazed down. Closing her eyes, she lowered herself and had the sensation her stomach was going to drop out. Was the sky above or below? She slowly got her bearings as Nicolas and Jacques worked together to steadily release the ropes. The wind took her skirts like sheets blowing on a clothesline. It was that uncontrollable flutter of her garments that told her she was no longer on earth, but twirling somewhere in the universe. Perhaps nowhere. Then she felt something jabbing her and pulling at her skirts. She was hooked to a small mass of branches.

"Stop!"

At the sound of her plea, the men immobilized the ropes. Using her free leg, she began to rock from side to side the way Nicolas had told her. Once she'd gained enough momentum and managed to pull her body from the foliage, she called out to them to continue. From then on, her downward journey was smooth. Nicolas was astonished by Jacques's strength as the two of them guided Marie Claire's descent. The Pawnee saw that the fisherman could have managed without his help, but kept the observation to himself.

Once she was on the ground, she removed the ropes with trembling hands so Nicolas could hoist them back up. Without losing a second, he adjusted the loops and tied them the same way around Thomas's waist.

"Now jist do like yer ma. No need ta be scared, kid." Nicolas's dark gaze betrayed no emotion.

Crouching down, Jacques looked his son straight in the eyes. "Think of it as a game. Mama's down there. After you, it will be my turn. Suzanne will play the game, too, and we'll all be together again down below." He sat Thomas on the edge of the precipice, relieved that the boy was surprisingly brave, perhaps because he did not fully comprehend the risks involved. When Marie Claire saw the small body dangling in space, floating between life and death, she had to keep herself from crying out. Her only consolation was that Jacques was holding the ropes. He would never let anything happen to his son. She held out her arms to the boy, grabbed him, and pressed him against her breast.

"Hey! Watcha doin' down there? Hurry up. Take them ropes off the kid!"

The Pawnee's command drew her out of the calm she had entered as she held her child in her arms. Mechanically she obeyed. Nicolas yanked the ropes back up and looked at Jacques. "Now the gear an' supplies."

They attached the basket and two of the bags before pushing them over the edge. As the bundles brushed against the foliage and reached the bottom, Marie Claire untied the knots. Almost instantaneously the ropes disappeared into the sky and another cluster of bags appeared. The operation continued until everything was on the ground around Thomas and Marie Claire. Only the two men and the little girl remained up top.

"It's yer turn." Nicolas's tone was strangely serious. Jacques was too concerned about his daughter to pay attention. He bent down and took Suzanne's small hands in his. "You have to be brave. I'm going to join Mama and Thomas. Nicolas will bring you to us. Don't be afraid."

Jacques kissed his daughter on the forehead and positioned himself at the periphery. He had not noticed Nicolas putting down the ropes and replacing them with others. Coarse shrieking broke the silence. The raven was carrying a few morsels of prey in its beak. Black winged creature. Spirit of a god. The trickster. But Jacques did not know that, as he watched it glide by. He turned to Nicolas and nodded, then slid into the void.

Marie Claire looked up at Jacques swaying far above her. Something was wrong. Even from where she was standing, she could see the rope between his waist and foot was weak in one spot and progressively fraying. She thought her heart would stop. He had to make it down quickly, before the rope broke. Suddenly Jacques dropped about ten feet. The force of the fall caused the rope to snap. His body was abruptly jerked back as the loop around his waist took over the task of supporting him. Marie Claire tried to scream, but no air would come from her lungs. Had Nicolas lost his grip? Or slid on the rocky surface? Jacques was still a good twelve feet in the air. Strangely, he wasn't moving down. Why wasn't Nicolas easing the ropes to get him to the ground? Why was he letting Jacques just hang there?

The loop around Jacques's waist climbed up his body to his shoulder pits and was inching its way to his neck, pulling his arms above his head. It was tightening and pressing on his throat. Where was Nicolas? Jacques grabbed the rope above his head and held onto it with brute strength. He had dropped another four feet and was having trouble breathing. With a sharp snapping sound the second rope broke. Jacques fell to the ground. Was he unconscious? Marie Claire took him in her arms and lifted his head. He opened his eyes and smiled at her.

"I made it." His voice was feeble.

Marie Claire couldn't let go of him, couldn't stop clutching his body against her own.

Now realizing the danger of his own descent, Thomas knelt beside his father, clinging to him like a bear cub to the trunk of a tall pine.

"It's over. Let's forget about it," murmured Jacques.

"But Suzanne is still up there. With him."

Nicolas was crouched at the rocky ledge looking down at them impassively. He soon disappeared. Marie Claire helped Jacques to his feet. Each of them held Thomas by the hand as they watched for signs of movement overhead. Desperate, disconnected thoughts ran through Marie Claire's mind. A few seconds later, a rope fell from the sky. They could see Nicolas. Did he have Suzanne with him? It was impossible to tell. The sun was just coming over the crest of the precipice. The dark figure against the bright light started to descend. Yes, she was in his arms. Everything was so quick now—the Pawnee snaking down the rope, the little girl safe in her mother's arms, the two men face to face.

"So what the hell happened? I thought you knew what you were doing."

"Yep," replied Nicolas with indifference.

"Well then?"

"I put my trust in the gear ya gave me. You put yer trust in the white man's wares. Can't ya see he was sellin' used goods?"

"These are new supplies. The ropes are new."

"Well, the ropes musta got cut by rocks or the like. Don't yer fishin' nets git worn? Don't ya ever hafta mend 'em?"

"We check our nets before we cast them out."

"An' when ya pull 'em in, are they always in the same condition?"

Exasperated, Jacques shrugged his shoulders. "Maybe you're right. I don't know."

They gathered up the supplies and started walking. The Pawnee was a magnet pulling them along. Now that they were in the middle of nowhere, they were more dependent on him than ever. Soon they came to the river once again. Nicolas announced they would stop for lunch. He told them that, to save time, they would finish what was left of the food Anne had prepared. After that, they'd have to fish and kill game. No one had any desire to talk as they ate, not even the children.

"You tell yer sister next time ya see 'er, she makes a mighty fine meat dressin'. Wish we had enough fer the whole trip."

The sullen voice reminded them that there was no escape. After a moment, Marie Claire got up and walked to one of the bags by the river, pretending to look for something. She needed any excuse to get away. She couldn't hold back any longer. The tears flowed. Jacques went to her and put his arm around her. They were out of Nicolas's earshot but still spoke in whispers, convinced he could hear everything they said.

"Come on now. We'll get through this. Then we'll never see him again. Did you see how he just slid right down with Suzanne in his arms? She doesn't seem afraid of him."

Marie Claire turned and rested her head on his shoulder. "I know. I need to be strong. But I don't trust him. I don't believe it was just an accident. There's more to it. I don't know what. Or why he'd want to do anything to us."

"Hey, Jacques," scowled Nicolas from across the camp.

Jacques ignored him.

"I don't know either. But when the rope was tightening around my neck this morning, it made me think. That Indian I hanged. It was my job but I should have refused. I killed a man, and I'll live with that for the rest of my life."

"Hey, Jacques!" shouted the Pawnee still louder.

Jacques turned his head in the direction of the voice. "What do you want?"

"Come 'ere. We need ta talk."

He slowly walked toward Nicolas. "What about?"

"Listen. Sorry 'bout what happened. Maybe I shoulda bin more careful. Maybe. But ya gotta understand. That rope was no good. There was no way fer me or any of us ta know. Let's fergit about it and move on. We got a long way ta go, an' we gotta work together. I know it's hard on yer woman." He paused. Jacques said nothing. Finally, Nicolas continued, "I was thinkin', maybe we should give her an' the kids a break. You and me kin go scout out the best route ta take."

"You mean leave them here? Alone?"

"Yeah. Jist fer an hour. Maybe less. They'll be safe. I know these parts. Ain't no warrin' tribes 'round. No bears neither. And that way, we won't wear 'em out fer nothin'. We'll make better time an' cover more ground jist the two of us."

"I thought you knew every rock and river bend by heart. Isn't that what you told me?"

"Look, sometimes even expert scouts want ta make sure. That's the first thing we learn when we're kids. Don't take no chances. Listen. If it'll make ya feel better, we kin leave a gun with 'em. Kin she use one?"

"She knows what to do. She learned to shoot from her father during the Iroquois raids."

"Oh yeah. She ain't got nothin' to fear then. Won't even needta use it. There ain't no danger."

"I still don't like the idea."

"Look. Are ya gonna trust me or not?"

Jacques was weary and annoyed. "What's my alternative? But I want Thomas to come along."

At the sound of his name, the boy came running.

"He's got to learn how to survive," Jacques said, playfully roughing up his son's hair. "I want him to know things. To be able to make decisions."

"Yeah. Maybe yer right. Maybe he should come, too. So he kin learn." The hint of a grin passed over Nicolas's lips.

Thomas smiled up at them, happy to be included in the men's expedition.

"We'll travel light. Don't need much. We'll be back in no time."

Suddenly the flow of words ceased. The stream of events

stopped and the actors disappeared from before Jean Luc's eyes. All that was left was the fatigue on Marie Claire's face. He knew she should not continue that night.

Quebec City, on this Saturday the 4th day of January 1735.

Like a thief under the cover of darkness, I've attempted to conceal my presence. I do not wish to compromise her reputation or fan the fires of gossip. The woman who looks in on her during the afternoon hours appears content to believe that I come to call each day as well to keep watch over her condition.

Madame Seguin's discretion is charming. When I stopped by yesterday to see how she was doing, she asked me no questions about my comings and goings. She is taking full advantage of Pierre's week in the country, visiting people she met at the LeMoyne social last November and has since befriended, and spending time reading at the convent library. It's peaceful there, she says, like a retreat.

I wish I could find such a haven. And that Marie Claire could, too. Again last night, she made the journey back to the primeval moment of her desolation. And I accompanied her.

Jacques explained to Marie Claire the plan he'd agreed on with the Pawnee.

"You and Suzanne can rest a bit. Afterwards, we'll all set out again and make a little more headway before breaking for the night."

"Suzanne is exhausted. She tore her dress this morning. I'll mend it while you're gone. I think you have a few things that need repair, as well."

"You really should rest."

"Oh, I'll be fine. You had the worst time of all of us today."

Jacques took her in his arms. "We'll be back in under an hour. It'll be good for Thomas. You'll see." He kissed her forehead, her lips. He did not want to release her hand from his, wanted to remain forever illuminated by her gaze.

The Indian, the fisherman, and the boy left the camp and headed south, following the river. It was a disparate caravan moving swiftly into the unknown. As soon as they disappeared from view, Marie Claire spread a woolen blanket on the ground in the shade of a pine tree. She helped Suzanne take off her dress, put her down to sleep on one half of the blanket and covered her with the other. Weary from the morning's events, the child was asleep in a matter of minutes. Marie Claire rummaged through one of the bags until she found her needles and thread. She sat by the dark brown blanket and took a moment to watch it rise and fall with each long inhalation—the protracted breathing induced by slumber. Suzanne was already far from her mother, farther from her than Jacques and Thomas. In what dreamscape had she found refuge? Marie Claire placed the loaded pistol by her side. The sun had passed over the sky's midpoint. It must have been around one o'clock, or perhaps later.

The men walked rapidly. The boy was proud he could keep up with their hurried pace. Nicolas periodically stopped to talk about the terrain and fauna so as to regain Jacques's confidence. And Jacques was eager to learn as much as he could. He did not know they were advancing along the edge of the earth, did not know his guide would soon reveal all the secrets of life and death to him. They reached a clearing and could see that the river split for a short distance, forming two channels that diverged, then converged once more. The wind rushing over the mist ascending from the currents carried with it indistinct sounds from unfathomable regions—voices rising up from the waters which had divided briefly to formulate a tale of woe and a tale of lament only to come together again, for they were one and the same.

Nicolas pointed south. "Jist past that bend, we gotta find out how the river cuts so we kin decide if we should go on followin' it or head inland."

"Then we need to get back. This is taking longer than I thought. By the way, I understood we were traveling light. What's that?" Jacques was staring at the large pouch tied to the Pawnee's belt.

"Never know when yer gonna need a swig er two. Wrapped it in some a the clothes ya got me ta make sure it don't break. Wanna shot?"

"No. That's your pay."

Jacques and Thomas turned to admire the rolling vista before them. The forest was still pale. It would be several weeks before the gentle yellows of the season's new growth would deepen to the rich greens of summer. The woods in the distance were dark and boundless. A cluster of trees on the river's opposite bank captured Jacques's gaze. It seemed to form a gateway, an entrance to a vast and obscure orifice. He thought he spied a wolf circling the strange portal, as if guarding the passage, allowing entry only to those designated to pass into the somber chamber.

While Jacques and his son pondered the expanse, Nicolas untied the pouch from his belt and set it down. His deer skin moccasins made no sound on the nettles beneath his feet.

"The countryside is sure beautiful here. So different from back where I grew up." Jacques was awed by the panorama. The rocky formations intrigued him. The Pawnee had chosen the site well.

Thomas looked behind to see what was causing the large shadow that had appeared on the ground. The boy's screams came too late. The hatchet's heavy blade sunk into his father's head. Jacques collapsed, his eyes frozen, blood gushing forth from the wide gash in his skull and streaming down his face, his body quivering on the ground. Thomas stared, unable to register the horrific images. What was the gelatinous gray substance seeping through his father's hair? Like a machine gone out of control, Nicolas pivoted and struck the child with a quick blow to the front of the neck. He lay on the ground next to his father, his throat now a gaping red hole vomiting a river of red. Nicolas turned again to Jacques and hacked away at his body. The boy witnessed the butchery from beyond. His eyes were open, like his father's.

There was blood everywhere. The ritual went on until the officiant had no more strength left in him to raise his crimson scepter. He unwrapped the bottle of spirits, sat on the ground, and began drinking. As the bottle's contents dwindled, the pitch of his laughter rose. His eyes feasted on the carnage. Inebriated by the liquor and the frenzy of the slaughter, he removed the blood-stained pouch of money from Jacques's coat pocket. As if enacting some occult ceremony comprehensible only to himself, he began to dance around the corpses. Were these the sounds of mystical chanting or simply the groans of drunkenness echoing against the late afternoon sky? Then, following a sinuous path, he disappeared into the woods.

Suzanne's dress, the buttons on Jacques's shirts, Thomas's socks—Marie Claire had long finished her mending. She felt a shiver and looked up. The sun had moved considerably. It was getting late and they weren't back. She woke Suzanne and got her dressed. She hurriedly tied one of Jacques's belts around her waist and slipped the pistol through. She knew that if they hadn't strayed from the river she'd eventually find them.

She had no sense of time as she forged ahead, carrying Suzanne in her arms part of the way, pulling her along by the hand the rest. The sunlight over the open river contrasted sharply with the blackness of the timberline. The forest seemed to harbor an army of creatures, all peering at her as she faltered along the river's bank. She could not move fast enough.

A clearing appeared in the distance ahead. As she drew closer, she saw two forms. She recognized the brown jacket and green pants. But why were the colors now so dark? And what were Jacques and Thomas doing? She advanced with hesitating steps.

Bloody masses. Not human. It wasn't them. It couldn't be them.

She had crossed through hell's gates. Thomas was nearest to her. She turned away, shielding Suzanne's eyes. But there was no way to protect her daughter from the horror. Her legs no longer had the strength to support her. She crumpled to the ground, filling the forest with the double lament of a wife and mother—a thundering wail that rose from the depths of her being. She tugged at the bloody corpse of her husband, rested his torso on her lap. The dark river flowed silently by.

"I don't remember what happened after that. All I know is that Suzanne was lying on the ground, sobbing. Her head was on Thomas's chest. Jacques's blood had penetrated every fiber of my clothing. I believe we would have stayed that way forever had he not returned."

Suzanne saw him stumbling toward them, the instrument of death again raised high above his head, his face disfigured by contempt. Her scream pulled Marie Claire from the well of unconsciousness. She saw the shadow of the hatchet on her arm and swayed back as he swung the blade. It slashed through her clothing—fire in her thigh. Somehow she lifted herself to her feet despite the burning pain. He swiveled and, with an uneven swing, grazed the child's head with the hatchet's blunt edge. She fell to the ground, motionless. Circling around him to grab her daughter, Marie Claire saw the drunken rage in his eyes. He struck once more. The throbbing in her arm was indescribable but she knew she had to act fast, before he had time to lash out. She managed to get hold of Suzanne. That's when she felt the blow to her side push all the oxygen out of her lungs. She began to choke and gasp for air. But the agony was nothing now that she had her daughter back. Laboring for breath, she staggered off, holding Suzanne. The child's body pressed tightly against hers slowed the bleeding from the open wound on her side. He tried to run after them but the rum had sapped the energy from his legs.

"What the hell! Go off on yer own. See how long ya survive in the wilds." Inarticulate snorting punctuated his words.

The killer was alone with the remains of his victims. He fumbled to remove his bloodstained clothes and threw them in the river. His identity was now cast away, lost forever in the rapid currents. Reaching inside the pouch on the ground, he pulled out his new clothes, stepped into the trousers, and passed his arms through the sleeves of the shirt with awkward, drunken movements. There was nothing more to keep him there. He turned one last time to Jacques's mangled corpse, spit on it, and kicked it into the river. A deep red stain colored the water. Slowly, the scarlet dissipated. There was no more blood to give. He looked at Thomas's body, but left it where it was. His strength was spent. No matter, he had accomplished what he'd set out to do. The oath had been kept. He teetered into the wilderness. A macabre laugh permeated the forest.

Jean Luc watched as darkness again encircled Marie Claire. The rhythm of her sobs was cut intermittently by convulsive, hysterical laughter.

"Yes, he was the brother of the man Jacques hanged in Acadia. I can still hear his laugh. The farther I got, the louder it became. I was sure he was catching up with me. But he was nowhere. Everywhere."

She was swaying back and forth like a woman possessed.

Jean Luc feared they'd wandered too far into the forbidden regions. He had to bring her back. He shook her, then held her in his arms. It was a pietà of its own kind, not a mother mourning her child but a man comforting a woman, one wayfarer consoling another. Her low monotone voice echoed in his soul.

"Nicolas was the devil. Nicolas. He destroyed his victims with his magic. Jacques and Thomas had fallen under his spell. I was bleeding. I had no strength left and could barely stand on my feet. I dragged myself through the woods with Suzanne. My dress was soaked with Jacques's blood. Now it was absorbing mine as well. His blood penetrated my wounds. I believe the blending of our blood united us in body and spirit forever. Jacques's blood gave me strength, the force to continue looking for help. Somehow I made it to a clearing where there were a few houses. I looked toward them, wondering if I could go any further. Some farm hands were taking advantage of the last glimmers of sunlight to ready the fields for the spring planting. When they saw us come out of the woods, they stopped their work and stared. It was then that everything started spinning. When I woke up, days had passed. I was at the Hôtel Dieu here in the city."

Jean Luc gently stroked Marie Claire's hair. She was inert, silent. Finally, her lips formed the words. Her vocal chords vibrated. "I haven't talked about all this since it happened. I was in a stupor during the questioning that preceded the trial. I didn't want to come back to this world. It was too much."

As he embraced her, he hoped that reliving the horror might prove cathartic but feared that liberation from such harrowing anguish was not possible.

She has for the moment freed herself. But how long will it be before the shadows haunting her mind come back?

Quebec City, on this Monday the 6th day of January 1735.
    Pierre arrived this evening with Anne. I have been eager for my son's return. It was an occasion of great rejoicing for me, something I cannot explain to anyone. Who could understand my apprehension, my excessive concern, my obsession? So many times this week I asked myself how I had ever agreed to let him go off alone, how I could have allowed him to be away from me

for so long. Whenever I say goodbye to him, the thought that I may never see him again plagues me. The fear is always there. Dearest Madeleine... Sweet Helene... Sparrows fallen from the sky.

He is not the same. He has changed—almost imperceptibly. He is different as a result of the ordinary everyday experiences he has lived on his own. Or am I the one who has undergone some metamorphosis? I, too, have lived events over the past week that cannot possibly be shared with him. Hours and days spent apart transform the relationships between us all. We are forever altered, even when our paths join once again to progress side by side through the continuum of time...

Suzanne crowed with delight when the lucky charm fell from her piece of the galette Marie Claire made to celebrate Epiphany. We placed the paper crown on her head and she designated Pierre as her king. They spent the rest of the evening getting Colberte to chase the piece of yarn that Anne gave them. Seeing such bliss on the children's faces is compensation for life's torments and hardships. At least for a time. It is now past midnight. I was happy to have a key to the inn.

Beau Val, on this Friday the 17th day of January 1735.

Bourville has been gathering facts about Boisvert's past and putting together arguments that he hopes might invalidate his case. I am still not entirely convinced Bourville is right, though. I would hate for my uncle's dying wishes to be foiled by false assumptions. When I asked Jeanne and William about it again, they could do nothing but reconfirm what they told me last October on my first visit. Namely, that Boisvert spent several days as Louis's guest here in late August and that it was, to their knowledge, the one and only time Louis saw him.

Quebec City, on this Sunday the 2nd day of February 1735.

The heavy snows bring with them stagnation. Inertia. Stasis. An existence that neither advances nor completely stops. There is no beginning. No end.

Like Pierre, Suzanne is subject to nightmares and never wants to go to sleep. It's a wonder she didn't go insane following the slaughter of her father and brother, not to mention her own near encounter with death. When I was visiting this evening, Anne took the girl to her room, leaving Marie Claire and me to converse by the fire.

Anne sat on the bed trying to think of some adventure to recite for her niece's benefit, but she needed consolation as much as the child. She wished someone would take her hand, caress, and console her. That would never come to pass, she knew. She thought back to the days of her youth, to her eighteenth birthday—and Laurent. His round, smiling face bespoke his quiet attentiveness. She had loved him so, with a love that was understood, a love that was communicated tacitly through smiles and glances. Before it could be fulfilled, the river took him one spring morning and never returned his body. Michel Joseph was not like Laurent but he was loving in his own way. She said no. She had to. Her parents needed her. They were frail. The work was hard. She could not leave them.

Yet Marie Claire had done precisely that, had done what Anne wanted to do. Marie Claire. The sister she begrudged. The sister she loved. Her only sister. Anne could not tell Marie Claire of her unhappiness, even though her sister was partially to blame for it. After all she had been through, how could Anne hang yet another millstone around her neck? Despite Marie Claire's pain and tragedy, Anne envied her sister's life—her marriage, her children, and now, the Frenchman. Anne wanted to free herself of the secret, tell her story any way possible. But these were things not suitable for the little girl by her side. She would need to weave a tale of her own invention that only she might understand. Unlike all the others she had told Suzanne before, it was not one handed down by her parents.

"Once upon a time, there were two little sisters named Marion and Annette. People always noticed Marion, for she was the prettier of the two. Annette, the older one, spent most of her time helping her parents with chores. Marion was too young to help, and occupied herself for hours each day playing in the woods. The field mice were her friends. Sometimes, when she thought no one was watching, she took pieces of cheese from the supper table and put them in her pocket for them."

Anne hesitated. She had to find words with which to embroider her tale the way she often did while ironing. This time, the adventure would not be about the ladies whose fine garments she pressed. It would be about herself. But what could she say to the child without revealing her unhappiness? Suzanne looked up at her aunt, eager to hear more.

Anne's voice faltered, but slowly strengthened as her story found direction. She remembered the wigmaker, Felicien, and how he loved to chatter with Marie Claire, swaying his cane back and forth. "The old calico cat that lived in the hollow of a tree used to sit on Marion's lap and let her scratch his ears. When he was content, he swished his big furry tail slowly left and right. Later, the mice told her the cat liked to sneak up on them. Even though he was old, he could still run swiftly and silently on his velvet paws. One day, the mice brought Marion a small bell attached to a yellow ribbon, and asked her if she wouldn't tie it around the cat's neck. It would warn them of his approach. But when Marion showed the cat the bell and yellow ribbon, he said it was not proper for an old cat to wear such a fussy thing. So she went to sit by the pond to think of a way to convince him.

" 'Hello, pretty maiden, why are you so serious?' asked a wide-eyed toad sitting on a lily pad.

" 'My friends want me to put a bell around the cat's neck but he doesn't want to wear it.' "

"The toad told Marion what to do. She ran to see the old cat. 'I don't think any other cats in the woods have a bell. It has a fine ring. Whoever wears it will be the most elegant creature in the forest.'

"The vain old cat finally agreed.

"Marion skipped back to tell the toad his trick of flattery had succeeded.

" 'It usually does,' said the toad. 'You know, where I come from, there are trees and flowers you've never seen before. I can take you there if you want.'

"When Marion asked her parents' permission, they thought she was just pretending. They didn't believe in talking toads, so without giving it much thought, they told her she could go. Annette wished she could too...but said nothing.

"The toad cast his traveling spell and all of a sudden, he and Marion were in a canoe of birch bark flying high in the air, sailing through the sky toward the eastern star. When the canoe touched the ground, Marion was in a new and beautiful world. She was sure she would live there happily for the rest of her life. But when the animals nearby discovered she liked the toad, they all abandoned her. One day, a raven swooped down and carried the toad away in his beak. Marion sat under a tree and cried and cried. Finally she decided to try to find her way home. Following the setting sun, she walked for days. When at last she saw her house, she ran inside but her parents were gone and Annette was all alone, except for a black cat with white paws. It had been so long, the two sisters were happy to be together again.

"Marion went down by the pond to think about everything that had happened. Reaching over to pick a floating lily, she lost her balance and fell in the water. 'Help! Help!' she cried. Suddenly, a handsome boy with long dark hair jumped in and pulled her to safety. He had come from a distant land in search of hidden treasure. His uncle had given him a map.

"An arrow on the map pointed to a cave. Marion and the boy went inside. Deeper and deeper they went until they discovered a wooden chest filled with gold coins and jewels of every kind. The boy turned to Marion and said, 'If you like, we can share the treasure.' He took the most beautiful ring from the chest and placed it on her finger. And they lived happily ever more."

Only after Anne finished did she realize the story had not turned out as she had intended. It was not about her, as she had wanted, but about her sister. Again. Anne was barely more than an absence. As in life. As always. Suzanne had fallen asleep, lost in her own imaginary world of truth and fantasy. Anne had carried out her function. As always.

She did not go back to join her sister and the doctor that evening.

Quebec City, on this Saturday the 8th day of February 1735.

The abundance of snow has made travel difficult. It is too treacherous to attempt the journey to Beau Val. Bourville's office is as far as I care to go for the time being. He has learned from various sources that Boisvert incurred serious debts in France before his family deported him to the colony. Having little inclination for work, he tried unsuccessfully to build a rapid fortune in wholesale commerce as soon as he arrived. Not long after it folded, he left Montreal and came to Quebec City with the intention of starting over.

That night, Jean Luc remained with his son and Madame Seguin. He did not venture outside. But others did.

The streets were deserted. They stood by the front window, waiting for the signal. Their dark hooded capes would help them blend into the night. There was hardly any moon. They had taken all the precautions and gathered what was needed. They purchased some twine and asked the baker, Monsieur Arsenault, for an empty flour sack, "To repair the underside of a chair," they told him. They dug up several large stones behind the house because they knew they wouldn't find any in the forest. The snow was too deep and it would take too long. One of them clutched the small wood crucifix in her pocket as they waited. Outside, and in the room, absolute silence prevailed. They dared not speak, listening for the slightest sound, anything that might indicate they should not go, should not do it. Finally, they saw the light of the candle in the window across the street. It was time.

One gave a nod to the other. She could not budge at first, but forced herself to move, telling herself, this time she would not let fear stand in the way. The hooded figures crossed to the other side of the street. The candle disappeared from the second floor window. The door opened and closed. They barely had time to take the small bundle wrapped in a gray blanket. The younger one held it the way she used to hold her children when they were infants. They ran toward the woods, in the direction of the Duchesne River. Afraid they might lose the courage to continue, afraid that by imagining the consequences they would turn back, they tried to drive all thoughts from their minds. Their heavy breathing immersed them in a fog. They could run no longer. Their strength was gone. They had to slow down.

They reached the river's edge. As they were placing the bundle into the empty flour sack, a corner of the blanket unfolded. The older one looked away. The other took the crucifix from her pocket and tried to curl the tiny fingers around it. They shoved the stones in the bag and secured the opening with the twine. They paused, each searching for assent in the other's eyes. They had sworn allegiance to do it together. They would both be guilty. Each grabbed one end of the sack and, with a single sweeping motion, hurled it into the river.

Quebec City, on this Monday the 10th day of February 1735.

I've tried to see them but they are allowed no visitors. They can see no one until they have been thoroughly interrogated. They will remain in the Royal Prison in an underground cell beneath the Intendant's headquarters. The child has been sent to an orphanage and is in the care of the Ursuline nuns. The servant girl has also been accused and is being detained with them.

Witchcraft...or infanticide. Perhaps both. Odysseus, too, encountered witches on his journey.

Quebec City, on this Thursday the 20th day of February 1735.

Each minute is an hour, each hour a day, each day a year. I am haunted by the living and the dead, by faces and voices that will not leave me, that I do not want to leave me. There is no peace for me in this world. Nor will there be in the next. Shadows linger among those who still walk and breathe, cling to those left behind. Or is it the living who cannot accept their own condition of life and the ignominy of continuing. For ignominy it is to go on without those who are dearest and not accompany them in their long journey into infernal night.

Oh, if I could penetrate Hades in search of my Eurydice. Would I fail as Orpheus did?

"I dare say, you look rather sullen this afternoon."

Jean Luc put down his quill, capped the cup of black ink, and looked up. He could not find the strength to respond. Desjardins took a seat at the same table and began to sip slowly and pensively on the wine Sylvie brought him. He knew Louis's nephew would eventually speak, that he would ultimately reveal a corner of the agony tearing at his soul. And he did.

"Do you remember what you told me about shamans? How they view life as a temporary illusion, a constantly changing hallucination?"

"Yes. They have freed themselves from the mirage of physical existence. They are able to enter other states of awareness at will and travel to the underworld or to higher celestial zones. But what brings all this on, Monsieur de Montigny?"

"You said that if the souls of the living escape their bodies, shamans can bring them back. And that they can communicate with the souls of the dead."

"That's true. But the shaman's primary function is to heal, reestablish harmony when physical and spiritual forces are out of balance."

"Take me to one."

Desjardins saw the desperation in the man's eyes. He did not know how to tell him.

"My friend, shamans work within their communities, always among and for their own people...usually at the house of the ailing soul."

They were trapped in painful silence surrounded on all sides by noise. At last, Desjardins spoke. "Shamans never practice their art on someone they do not know. But on occasion they allow outsiders to witness certain ceremonies."

Quebec City, on this Wednesday the 5th day of March 1735.

Great eagle, father of all shamans, carry me to the heavens. I want to climb the sacred tree that holds up the celestial tent and reach the North Star.

I fear I am once more slipping into madness.

Desjardins kept his promise. The ritual was to start after nightfall. The shaman would attempt to cure a brave fallen ill after the death of his brother. Eight members of the brave's family along with the shaman's talker were already present, seated in a circle, when Jean Luc and Desjardins arrived. They had been informed, and paid little heed to the two strangers who took places at the extremity of the large tent. The brave was lying on a pallet, his head facing east. He moved and jostled like someone having a nightmare, and was making inarticulate sounds.

A tall man entered, his face charred with ashes. It was impossible to determine his age. In his right hand, he carried a small drum whose wood rim was covered with dried elk skin on which had been traced several eagles and a bridge leading into a rainbow. The man knelt down next to the brave and with his eyes half closed began tapping a slow rhythm and chanting softly.

The beat, steady and magical, rose above the teepee high into the sky, descended deep into the earth. Would it awaken the shaman's helper spirits? Could it charm them and call them forth? The family and talker joined in, one after the other, imitating the improvised song. The three or four plaintive bars were repeated over and over as they clapped, each to a different beat until finally the chant and cadence found unison. The shaman closed his eyes and went into deep meditation as the others continued chanting. Had he already left his body? Suddenly, he opened his eyes and clapped his hands a single time. All sounds ceased. He began to speak in a loud voice, his monotone words quick and clipped. He was in dialogue with his helping spirits.

He asked for his pipe and began to puff, sending out heavy cascades of smoke. The others lit their pipes and joined him. He spoke through the talker. Desjardins interpreted softly for Jean Luc. "The shaman has seen a bird in a cage, far away. It is the brave's soul. It has been taken from him and carried to a haven of shadows to be with the spirit of his dead brother. The shaman must find his way through the underworld to free the captive bird and bring it back to the land of the living. It is a dangerous undertaking, especially the return journey. But he says other spirits are present among us this evening, spirits from across the great waters that are trying to speak. He cannot understand their tongue and must send them back for they have nothing to do with the brave."

The shaman put down his pipe and tapped on his drum. The chanting began, as before, slowly building. Soon he was traveling on horseback behind his dead father, the tribal shaman before him, to regions inaccessible to mortals. He bent over and put his lips close to the ear of the brave, whose delirious movements stopped soon after the shaman whispered to him words not meant for anyone else.

My head began pounding. I did not know where I was. The chanting grew distant as other voices, incomprehensible utterances, echoed all around. Calm came over the brave. His fidgeting ended. His features were tranquil. He opened his eyes and listened to the words of the shaman. The brave's soul had returned. But my loneliness and pain persist, ever more acute.

They had come, but I could not reach them. Will I ever?

Quebec City, on this Wednesday the 12th day of March 1735.
They were at last released this afternoon. For thirty-one long days they were not permitted to see or speak to anyone. The accusation of sorcery was dropped for all three shortly after the interrogation proceedings began. Lack of evidence. The second accusation was harder to disprove, especially in the servant girl's case. She has been sentenced to six months' confinement.

Is it true they meddle in spells and potions? Have they been willing accomplices to infanticide?

A carriole was waiting at the Royal Prison gate. The driver remained immobile, impervious to the frigid gusts. The passengers seated behind him were silent. The man had nothing to say to the little girl across from him. Their eyes wandered as each looked at anything and everything—except one another. Although the man was the one who had retrieved her from the convent orphanage, the little girl barely knew him. She had no idea why she had been separated from her mother and aunt or why he had come for her and brought her to this strange place.

He would take them home by the back streets. They could not be seen in public. He did not wish them to be exposed to the stares of those who had come to their own conclusions. There had been so many rumors, so many lies. The prison gate swung open. Two women emerged, fragile and hesitating in the brightness of day. They had not felt the sunlight for a full month. When they saw the carriole, they quickened their pace, started to run, but had to stop themselves. They did not want it to be thought that they were escaping.

Both were shaken by the ordeal. Anne the most. Marie Claire's experiences with death and civil authorities have taught her to retreat within herself, be less vulnerable to the chaos around her. She took Suzanne in her arms, embracing a part of herself she might have lost forever. I signaled the driver to pull away.

The stone house finally came into sight, plain and unassuming. Though the eyes of strangers might view it as a dwelling in disrepair, it was a refuge to the carriole's passengers. The women and child quickly entered while Jean Luc paid the driver. Once the sleigh had become nothing more than a distant blur, he closed the door behind him and pulled down the latch. Locked. Barred to intruders. They were protected from the disparaging glances and accusing voices.

"We lied to the magistrate." Marie Claire's voice wavered. How would he accept what she had to tell him? Would he think her evil? A criminal? Anne took Suzanne to her room. She did not want the child to hear what her mother was going to reveal to the man who had brought them home. "We lied to save Sophie."

He said nothing. He would ask no questions, would not subject her to yet another interrogation. She had been through enough of that. He was not even sure he wanted her to lift the veil of secrecy for he might discover a dimension of her he had no desire to see.

"Thank God they didn't torture us." She paused as she struggled to formulate her ideas. She had acted on impulse. Now she needed to use reason to explain her actions, tell him what she could not disclose to the members of the Sovereign Council who had spent so many hours, days, and weeks barraging her with questions.

"Sophie is one of eight children. Her father has always had trouble earning enough to feed them. About a year and a half ago, he heard Monsieur Charbonneau was looking for a servant girl. Charbonneau's wife died giving birth to their fourth child. He needed someone to cook, clean, and launder. Charbonneau and Sophie's father had a notary draw up a contract to make it legal and binding. She was to remain in Charbonneau's employ for three years. His only obligation was to provide food and clothe her. Sophie's father thought it was too good to be true...one less mouth to feed. The girl was frightened. She had never been away from home before and had no one to turn to. That's why she ended up confiding in us—through gestures, drawings, and the few words she could pronounce. She told Anne and me such dreadful things...how he would come to her at night...in her bed..."

Jean Luc could see where the story was leading. Sweet smiles, temptations, an indiscreet hand posed on the young servant's breast, forced caresses, threats. And how could she tell anyone?

Marie Claire was trembling. She felt the tears running down her cheeks and took a moment to regain her composure. "He let her know he'd kill her if anyone found out and made her wear loose garments so it wouldn't show. He didn't allow her to go to the market toward the end. The baby was premature. No one was there to help her. She gave birth standing in the corner of her room, bracing herself against the walls. But the child was stillborn."

Jean Luc knew there was good reason for the servant to want to dissimulate the traces of her illegitimate pregnancy. There were many like Sophie in France and throughout the colony—white slaves.

"Charbonneau panicked. He was afraid the authorities would somehow discover what happened, so he took the first step and went to them instead. He accused Sophie of having smothered the infant and insisted he wasn't the father. She would have never had a chance. They'd have hanged her. That's what they do to girls who hide their pregnancy and kill the baby. But Sophie wanted her child to live. She was going to..."

Marie Claire couldn't continue. Jean Luc held her in his arms. He was angry at himself for having imagined she could have been partisan to infanticide and incensed that society was more concerned with maintaining illusions of order and obedience than protecting human life. He heard Marie Claire's voice once more, felt the words rising from her depths.

"A midwife and a barber-surgeon examined Sophie. Fate was on her side. They were inept and didn't detect that her breasts were producing milk. Or perhaps the midwife took pity on her and concealed the fact. It doesn't matter now, because without the evidence, without the baby's body or a witness, they couldn't execute her. Anne and I took the body of the child. We..."

Jean Luc placed his finger on Marie Claire's lips to hush her words. He did not need to hear any more.

No, they are not Circe and Calypso. They are women of honor, each in her own way. Like Antigone, they have paid dearly for their courage. Doves in a black sky.

~~~

Deep inside death's antechamber, Pierre was prouder of his
father than he had ever been before. The Baron Jean Luc de
Montigny...in the company of laundresses accused of witchcraft
and child killing... Pierre felt comforted knowing his father
remained faithful to those heroic women who challenged unjust
laws to save a young girl's life while putting their own in peril.
Only a man of principle would brave class distinctions and
prejudices to maintain his loyalty to individuals he believed
sincere and righteous. Now Pierre understood why, for as long as
he could remember, his father kept a volume of Sophocles on his
nightstand—the silver filigree bookmark always at the same
page of *Antigone*— "And if you believe my acts are foolishness,
the foolishness may be in the eye of a fool... No, I am not
ashamed."

~~~

*Quebec City, on this Thursday morning the 13th day of March
1735.*
   *I am in the center of hell. A frozen, sterile hole not fit for
humans. Not fit for any living thing. The heavy sky takes my
dreams from me. I look out my window, and everything is gray
and lifeless. I watch the weightless flakes from the last snowfall
swirl aimlessly. Ephemeral crystals. Dead leaves in the wind.
Dust and ashes. My life is a lie. And such cold. Nowhere to seek
warmth. Have I reached the ends of the earth? My heart is
reduced to ruins, like the castles in Saint-Amant's poem.*
   Les sorciers y font leur sabbat
   Les démons follets s'y retirent...
   Là se nichent en mille trous
   Les couleuvres et les hiboux. [*]
   *Desire and will have left me. But it is imperative that I go
forward. For Pierre.*
   Distracted, inattentive, incapable of concentrating on the

---

[*] That is where witches and sorcerers hold their Sabbat. Where flighty demons
retreat. Snakes and owls nest in a thousand crevasses.

business that needed to be concluded—such was Jean Luc's state of mind after almost six months in the colony. He had spent his energy suppressing every portion of his existence in France, driving back the demons inhabiting his memory. Bordeaux had ceased to be a reality, but at what price? He was detached and lethargic. Ever since his arrival, his attention had been turned outward, on Pierre and his illness, on the estate, on Marie Claire and the brutal ordeal she had endured. He had tried to detect the slightest changes in her mood, any hint of sorrow reflected in her features that might be signs of a retrenchment from the world of the living. But there were forces within him demanding to be heard as well. They would make their presence felt any way they could, dragging him down into the dungeons of hallucination and dementia if necessary.

The ditch is deep, the night infinite and filled with incessant, mournful voices. Are the wailing echoes laments or chants? I cannot tell. I look up and see shadowy figures far above at the ditch's edge. There are two, their faces and bodies veiled in black. The sounds of a woman and child weeping seem to be calling out to me. Wolves circle the open pit, slowly moving closer to the figures. Their cavernous mouths are wide open and as deep as the pit. The animals keep circling. In a frenzy, they gash the night stars with their pointed teeth and swallow the light. The darkness is impenetrable. I claw at the gritty clay walls, but the surface crumbles at my touch. There is nothing to grip. I keep falling back, unable to help. I cannot protect the veiled forms. There is something red around the woman's neck. Red against black. So much red. Dark red.

Quebec City, on this Friday the 14th day of March 1735.
   I am nothing but driftwood, carried and tossed aimlessly by the tides. I must see her. When will the messenger return with her reply?
   He was to call on her at four o'clock.
   The black carriole took him through a wasteland of desolation. The city's novelty had worn off. His brooding caused him to see it, perhaps for the first time, as nothing more than a French outpost. The unpaved streets were gaping sewers. A canal

ran down the center to collect rainwater and garbage. Ashes, excrement, and debris of every sort flowed along the open channels. Ordinances requiring the townspeople to dispose of refuse in the river went unheeded. The horses, dogs, and herds of pigs that passed through the city left massive amounts of dung in their wake. Butchers scattered the remnants of their trade in the streets leaving blood and carcasses everywhere. The entire settlement was a murky quagmire from early spring until the first freeze. Odors from the tanneries, slaughterhouses, latrines, and cemeteries filled the air.

The carriole plodded wearily past empty shops and abandoned buildings. The hatter, Monsieur Coton, had been forced to cease operations. Just like Chauffour and Huppé, in Montreal, he had been ordered by royal decree to halt production. This sterile land was a bastard child forced to suckle forever at the aging breast of the mother country, never allowed to grow and flourish.

The driver turned onto *rue de Meulles*.

"Grant me the solace of your company this afternoon. But not here. Somewhere different."

She declined, regretfully, reminding him that she had not completed her year of mourning. Two more months would need to pass before she could be seen with a man, unchaperoned, in public. "Tomorrow, then. I'll ask Madame Seguin to come along. We'll leave Pierre with Anne."

Quebec City, on this Saturday the 15th day of March 1735.

I escorted her to Au Vieux Terroir on rue Montcarmel. It is more secluded than Aux Trois Pigeons or La Croix d'Or, which Desjardins assured me are also respectable cabarets. Not like others here. There are more than forty of them, so I've been told, in this city of six thousand. Many are the haunts of outlaws and whores, harbors for the shattered souls of disheartened recruits. They welcome lonely travelers such as I in search of a fleeting utopia and offer illusions to those desperate enough to believe in them.

The governess knew her function and did her best to be nothing more than a fixture. Passing beneath the spruce branch that had been placed above the door to identify the establishment

to the illiterate, they took a table at the far end. The heavy
curtain at the entrance did little to cut the drafts. Marie Claire
was radiant but reserved. The hematite pendant hung from her
neck, a small breach of the code of mourning, but one she could
not resist. Duchesses and marquises afforded every advantage
could not have conducted themselves with the grace she
displayed naturally.

She drifted in and out of the conversation like a swinging
pendulum.

*Mnemosyne's spell must be broken. How can I help her
reach the gate of Tartarus and drink the waters of forgetfulness?
What means can I use to transport her to Lethe's shores? Only
after they erase all memory of past life are the shades of the
dead who roam the tenebrous underworld allowed to return to
the living. She must likewise erase the pain and suffering from
her mind. As must I.*

She sipped her wine quickly, comforted by the floating
sensation it procured. It was both voluptuous and satisfying. As
their hesitant conversation continued, he drank hastily as well.
He wanted to take her in his arms, travel once again to the outer
reaches of the universe. Each realized the journey that day would
have to be made not with caresses, but with words and images.
Their odyssey would transpire in a public space and they would
be subjected to random glances and judgmental countenances.
She hungered for escape. He could see it in the restrained
desperation of her gestures. He wanted to respond to their mutual
desire, take her far away from the rage and grief. But the only
place he knew well enough was situated in his own forbidden
zone, the one he had consciously avoided. Yet as his thoughts
turned to the joyful days of his youth, he felt a sudden liberation.
Imagining he had taken her hand tightly in his, he began the
pilgrimage, describing the intimate relationship of the soil and
climate with the fertile green vines of Haut Pomadour. He told
her how his father had instilled in him at an early age an
appreciation for the tactile pleasures of producing fine wines—
the delights of the palate, the warmth of the sun.

The family vineyards lay halfway between Bordeaux and
ancient Saint Emilion, where wines had been produced as far
back as the Roman Empire. The proximity of Haut Pomadour to

both the port city and the picturesque hill town made travel to each a frequent event for Jean Luc, even as a child. The red-tiled roofs, the old Cloister of the Cordeliers, and the ninth-century church hewn out of a single solid rock were serenely nestled against the chalky slopes of charming Saint Emilion, as though they had been there since the beginning of time. In contrast, the port of Bordeaux was a gloriously teeming hub of commercial activity, offset by the finesse and polish of the city's wealthy residents.

Astute enough to know that favors at court were contingent upon the whims of the monarch and his consorts, Jean Luc's father had resisted the temptation to desert his lands for the dubious prestige of life at Versailles. While those who had fallen into the trap lived in caged opulence as their properties slowly went to ruin, Haut Pomadour flourished—proof that modest flamboyancy could be had beyond the king's manicured gardens. The chateau had of late lost much of its feudal dankness. The moats had been transformed into water basins stocked with carp, the stables enlarged and rejuvenated, and the old pillories and gibbets pulled down to make way for a pergola in the Chinese style.

Despite his desire to change with the times, Monsieur le Baron François de Montigny had not repudiated his inherited responsibility toward the common people. The success of his vineyards, notwithstanding the devastating winter of 1709, had amplified his natural generosity. His mill was always at the disposal of the villagers, who were exempted from the customary usage fee. Although he could only employ a small number of them year round, a good many took part in the fall harvest. That was the season Jean Luc loved best, when the vines and the ripened fruit they bore became a peaceful rolling sea of blue-green waves. Baskets strapped to the backs of the harvesters navigated through them like tiny pirate ships filled with dark treasures glistening in the sun. Tireless hands loaded the wicker containers with freshly seized booty. Jean Luc and Marie Claire were now floating on the rising crests of the vineyards, the wind's gentle fingers running through their hair, stroking their cheeks. They were free spirits.

When Jean Luc was old enough, his father bestowed upon

him the honor of listening to the vats for the sounds of fermentation. It was more than a scientific phenomenon. It was a voluptuous display of physical transformation. The whole operation seemed to have less to do with botany than with alchemy. It was widely known that the soil of the region was stony and poor, but it produced better grapes than areas of rich earth where the fruit developed too quickly. The process was long and arduous. The roots of the vines needed to penetrate deep—as much as fifty feet—into the under layers to extract what minerals they could. Miraculously, they carried the nutrients up through their stalks to create firm sweet offerings to the gods of light, wind, and rain. Over time, Jean Luc's father cultivated a relationship with the elements that involved great effort, yet allowed the metamorphosis to continue to its logical conclusion. Although the procedure was nearly twice as costly, it was considered well worth the expense. It was, after all, a labor of love.

The cabaret slowly filled, but they were oblivious to the rising noise level, oblivious to the stares directed at her, the widow Lambert. And at him, the stranger who claimed to be of noble birth, but kept company with laundresses, witches, and perhaps child-killers. Regardless of what the gossipmongers said, she was grieving more than they could imagine, the only way she could so as not to go mad. And he was engaged in a battle that they could not even begin to comprehend.

The widow and the baron hadn't the vaguest idea how much they had drunk, how many minutes or hours had passed. Nor did they care. The cabaret was only a port of departure. They were drifting off, hand in hand, to unknown destinations, over an ocean of pleasant sensations, under a cloudless sky. The governess, though invisible to them, had made the journey as well. She felt the warm sun of the vineyards on her shoulders as Jean Luc spoke. The sherry she was sipping took on a different flavor, one filled with the lush bouquet of the fruits of Haut Pomadour.

He recalled crushing the grapes as a boy of four or five with the other children, the sons and daughters of the vineyard laborers. He delighted in the ritual each autumn. Wearing nothing but a loose cotton shirt, he could romp and stamp his feet over the ripened grapes to his content in the huge wooden vats. He still remembered the first time—the new sensations his body experienced, the aromas discharged into the warm fall air as the golden juice spurted forth. It was only later that he came to comprehend to what extent he had been privileged to participate in the process, a ceremony honoring the deities of pleasure, a thanksgiving for the gift of life. They were together in that moment, unwilling and unable to return to the rowdy environment surrounding them.

Quebec City, on this Tuesday the 18th day of March 1735.
They have been damned, rejected by all. The sacrosanct social order has been preserved, at their expense. Why cannot the truth be told? Why must the cracks in the foundation be disguised? Immaculate whiteness covers the mud of this savage land. It hides the blemishes, blankets the black waters, envelops the dark forests and the filth of the streets.

She knocked at the door of the house near the *Place Royale.* Madame Hertel's servant girl told her coldly, "No linens. No garments." There was nothing to be laundered, nor would there ever be. Her services were no longer required. The door closed abruptly. "No longer required." That's what each of them told her. Madame Demers. Madame Jaubert. Madame Massicotte. Madame Legrand. Some doors did not open at all. It was happening again. This would be her fate, for as long as she lived and breathed.

His invitation might pull her from the scorn. Her regret was that she had to leave her sister in the midst of it.

Quebec City, on this Thursday the 20th day of March 1735.
I must flee the city and its false goodness, its pretense of virtue. Tomorrow we will travel to the estate. I cannot remain indifferent to the land my uncle so cherished. The dispute over its ownership has given me a stronger sense of responsibility to ensure its safekeeping.

The carriole clipped through the bright countryside. With runners instead of wheels, it was a carriage perfectly adapted to traveling over snow-covered surfaces and able to attain incredible speeds due to the lightness of its construction. Marie Claire and Jean Luc were seated on one side, Pierre and Madame Seguin on the other. Heated bricks at their feet and bearskin throws kept them warm. Looking out at the thick pristine whiteness that indiscriminately concealed fields and paths, the travelers found it hard to believe winter's end was finally drawing near. The snow grew deeper the further north they proceeded from Quebec City. The driver conceded that it was easy to lose one's way. The road markers were indispensable. Some landowners, he complained, were so stubborn they preferred paying the ten pound fine each year rather than bothering to put up posts in compliance with the law.

The two women kept their hands buried in their long muffs. Jean Luc had offered one made of fox fur to Madame Seguin months earlier, when the climate first proved to be harsher than what she was accustomed to in France. Marie Claire had borrowed hers from Anne. It was made of raccoon and had belonged to their mother. The rabbit fur lining of Pierre's and Jean Luc's gloves protected their fingers from the biting cold. Madame Seguin made no comment about the baron's *ceinture fléchée*, but secretly wished she had one for herself.

"I'm glad you agreed to come. You might be able to help me decide what to do."

"You've been to the property, Madame Seguin. What do you think of it?" asked Marie Claire.

"Oh, it's beautiful. Very beautiful indeed. I don't know if I could take the winters, though. But it's not up to me."

"And how does Pierre like it?" Marie Claire smiled in his direction as she continued, "He hasn't said a word."

The boy turned and hid his face in Madame Seguin's skirts.

"Well, it seems that no one has a clear opinion. I guess I'll have to make up my own mind."

"That's what I was hoping," Jean Luc replied.

As the carriole turned a final bend, the country home appeared. It was made of dressed stone in the Normand style and surrounded by acres of rolling hills. Two men were standing outside ready to greet the visitors. The younger one had seen the carriole making its way to the estate and alerted the household. The men approached as the sleigh came to a halt.

"Welcome back, Monsieur de Montigny."

"Thank you, William."

Jean Luc helped Marie Claire out of the sleigh.

"Marie Claire, this is William. My uncle put absolute trust in him, as do I. William, Madame Lambert will be our guest."

"Pleased to meet you, William."

"If Madame should require anything..."

Gabriel, the Pawnee at William's side, placed a low wooden step next to the carriole. Madame Seguin lifted Pierre onto the small platform before exiting herself with the help of Gabriel's politely extended hand.

"I see Monsieur has purchased a sleigh. Does this mean you'll be staying in Canada?"

"No, William, I've rented it, like the others. The driver will need quarters. Could you see to it that he has proper accommodations? And show him were to put the sleigh, will you?"

"Certainly, Monsieur. Gabriel will take charge of the sleigh and baggage."

The carriole drove past the estate's small chapel and headed for the stables as the guests walked toward the manor. It was a wide building composed of two levels. Its architectural features aimed at comfort and understated sophistication, with a hearth in every room, solid oak floors and polished ceiling beams. The entrance was situated exactly at the facade's halfway point. Inside was a large foyer with spacious rooms on either side. The decor was a personalized blend of rustic and formal. The walls were adorned with pewter sconces, not the bronze doré customary in Quebec City's choicer residences. Louis de Montigny had brought with him a number of paintings from the family collection. Most were landscapes of the British and Italian schools, but there was also an intimate depiction of Saint Catherine playing a lute by Lorenzo Lotto and a more recent oil of a pastoral subject in the courtly manner by Pater—a gem that must have just been acquired, perhaps given as a gift by a visitor from France, conjectured Jean Luc.

William ushered the guests directly to the upstairs hallway that spanned the length of the house. Jean Luc paused to gaze once more at the naively executed portrait of Emma hanging at the far end by the master bedroom before William showed him and Marie Claire to a handsomely decorated room made all the more inviting by the afternoon sunlight.

"Monsieur, will this be suitable for Madame Lambert?"

Jean Luc turned to Marie Claire. "Do you like it?"

"Oh, yes, it's lovely."

"May I suggest adjacent rooms down the hall for Madame Seguin and Pierre?"

"That's fine, William. Pierre needs to start sleeping by himself more often. Madame Seguin is with him almost constantly. He's going to grow up afraid of being left alone in the dark."

William turned to Madame Seguin and Pierre. "May I show you both to your quarters?" But before he had time to move, Jean Luc interrupted, "And the room next to this one... I'll sleep there."

"But...I thought this time Monsieur would prefer the master bedroom."

"I'm not the master yet. And may never be." Jean Luc's features betrayed only slightly the burden of the impending decision that had been weighing on him over the past months. "Besides, I'll be closer to Pierre if he needs me."

"Very well, Monsieur. I'll give instructions for the room to be prepared."

Marie Claire looked out the window. To the east, a line of firs towered in the distance like so many church spires, tracing an irregular dark green ridge along the horizon. To the north, clusters of maples and birches awaited the arrival of warmer temperatures. For the moment, they were nothing but a series of twisted black and brown lines against an infinite blue-gray sky.

"Such calm and tranquility. As though the world's problems did not exist..."

"I understand now why my uncle was so content here."

He left her to recover from the long ride. She removed her heavy traveling garments and put on a black dress she considered more suitable for supper. Perhaps it would help make her feel less conspicuous in the aristocratic surroundings. The duty of mourning had allowed her the extravagance of new clothing and footwear. When she came downstairs, the halls were empty. There was no one in the drawing room. There was no one anywhere. Barking and voices from the opposite end of the house caught her attention. She followed the sounds that led her to the estate kitchen where everyone had assembled to watch the spectacle.

The room was ample, with a vast open fireplace tall enough to stand in. The trammel, where the pots were suspended over the fire, was built directly into the hearth. Iron pans, casseroles, griddles, caldrons, and several ornate bellows hung along the room's west wall. The elaborately worked brass pothooks bore fleur-de-lis and arabesque motifs. Like icicles magnifying the sun's golden rays on a cold winter's day, they glistened with each moving reflection from the fire burning in the hearth. A small cabinet with glass doors housed an assortment of well-worn cookbooks that Louis de Montigny had either brought with him from France or imported after his arrival in the colony. Among them was the famous *Art de bien traiter*. The chef who had compiled the recipes must have wished to keep his identity a secret, since only his initials, L. S. R., appeared on the frontispiece. Perhaps it was his way of emphasizing the dishes rather than their source. It was uncertain whether the book had been penned by the celebrated cook, Rolland, or the equally popular master chef, Robert. The manor's collection also included Audiger's *La Maison bien réglée*, a work aimed at pleasing lords and gentlemen, city dwellers and country folk alike. Yet without question, the book whose pages bore the most traces of flour and oil was Massialot's *Le Cuisinier royal et bourgeois*. If the vintner's art was not dissimilar to alchemy in the eyes of the elder Baron de Montigny, his brother, the Viscount, viewed gastronomy with equal wonder.

Off to one side, two massive oak cabinets with a diamond shape carved into each of their thick doors flanked a sizeable butter churn. A kneading table equipped with a bin for storing baked loaves stood by the window. Adjacent to the fireplace, high overhead, was the object of the guests' impromptu gathering. They were watching a dog inside an enormous cylindrical cage made of wood. The apparatus was suspended on an axle in the manner of a carriage wheel and turned as the animal attempted to walk. The revolving movement activated the rotisserie in the hearth, thus making manual labor to keep the spit in motion unnecessary. A suckling pig was roasting in preparation for the evening meal. In New France, the dog may have been the poor man's horse, but it was also the rich man's servant, thought Jean Luc as he watched the pungent smoke rise from the slowly rotating pig.

"Let's get our wraps, Marie Claire. I'll show you the grounds if you like. I hope you've brought shoes more suitable for walking."

She was pleased he had noticed her black leather *bottines*.

In the short time Jean Luc had spent on the estate, he had discovered practically every aspect of its functioning. And he shared what he learned with his companion who listened politely, happy to focus on things that did not directly concern her. The seigneury's surface area covered more than fifteen square miles. A portion of it was divided into lots varying from eighty to one hundred acres, and inhabited by settlers who paid Jean Luc's uncle the requisite seigneurial fees, including one for the privilege of grinding their wheat at his mill. The lots were shaped in the form of a trapezoid and all had direct access to a transportation route—a road or waterway. The fields were plowed twice a year, in the fall and again in the spring as soon as the snow had melted, usually in early May. Only half the land was sewn each year for the late August harvest. Wheat and oats were the main crops, but corn and beans were also planted.

William was watching from the kitchen window.

"You see, Jeanne? You see? I knew there was a good reason why Master Louis's nephew wanted the room next to the lady's. I wouldn't be surprised if Monsieur's bed goes unslept in tonight."

"William! What an idea! She's a woman in mourning. Must have lost someone close within the year, poor thing." Resuming her work, Jeanne added, more for her own information than William's, "But if you're right, I won't have as many sheets to wash."

Her husband merely sighed as he went back to the tasks awaiting him in the dining room. It needed to be swept and dusted. Before the table could be set, the porcelain dinner service and crystal glasses had to be buffed to a sparkle with a soft, clean rag. Had Leon polished the silver platters and sterling cutlery?

Jeanne was far from finished preparing the second meat course, *poularde aux olives*, an added work of art to welcome the visitors who had made the long journey to the estate. Because Louis de Montigny appreciated the pleasures of fine cooking, he

saw to it that Jeanne could read well enough to decipher the
instructions contained in his limited collection of cookbooks.
She alone had mastered the procedures that could bring about the
desired transformation. She glanced hurriedly at the large clock
Louis de Montigny had installed in the kitchen in recognition of
the fact that the culinary art needed to be carried out with
precision. The hands were racing. The tick-tock was unusually
loud.

Jeanne had decided to serve the dish her master requested
most frequently. She thought perhaps the man's nephew would
derive equal contentment from it. Louis de Montigny insisted
that capons and poulardes be raised on his estate. After all, why
should a self-respecting connoisseur subject himself to the less
savory meat of ordinary poultry? Soon after the guests arrived,
Jeanne had tied layers of bard to the trussed bird and set it aside,
awaiting the proper moment to place it on a shelf in the hearth
near the roasting pig. Next, she melted pork fat to prepare the
stew in which the poularde would simmer. She added the
spices—salt, pepper, sprigs of dried parsley—to the onions,
capers, and olives, along with the heart, liver, and gizzard.
Working her magic, she caused the elements of the mixture to
skip over the flames before sprinkling in three crushed bay
leaves, some thyme, and a few pinches of flour. Quick. Bouillon.
White wine. Not too much. Pour them gently into the saucepan.

It was getting late and the poularde wasn't in the hearth yet.
She knew that exactly one hour before serving the meat courses,
she would have to remove the bird from the fire and call William
to cut it into ten pieces that she would mix into the stew and let
simmer together for twenty minutes, not a second more. She
worried that some courses would be cooked too soon, that others
would not be ready on time. And the vegetables... They still
hadn't been peeled.

Where was Lucille? She was supposed to be back by now.
Jeanne had told her daughter not to dally at Marie Anne's. She
was just to leave the corn soup with her for her father-in-law.
Old Elzear's appetite would not return. If he could find the urge
to drink some soup, it would give him strength. He might make it
through the winter. Why was the girl still not back? Who was
going to make the mushroom sauce? And would she and William

be able to remove the pork from the hearth and carve it in time? The presentation of each dish at Monsieur de Montigny's table had always been executed with painstaking care. It was a tradition she would not allow to disappear, even now that the master was gone.

Jean Luc and Marie Claire had reached the large barn about three hundred yards from the manor. The four immense sails of the stone windmill where the wheat was ground turned in unison with every breeze. Each creak of the cogs added a mournful note to the wind's song.

"Winter has lingered too long. Spring is impatient to begin," he remarked as they walked through the milky fields. "The first time I saw the place was in autumn. I imagine it has its own particular charm in summer, too."

"Where do the slaves live?"

"Jeanne and William live at the manor with their two children. My uncle had quarters built for the others. Come, I'll show you."

Following a path of packed snow, they forged their way to the dwellings located about a quarter of a mile from the manor. When they arrived, the younger children were playing outside. There were five households in all. Bourville had given Jean Luc the paper on which Louis de Montigny had inscribed the names of the slaves and their relationship to one another:

Jean Baptiste, métis, born 1698, wedded to Marie Anne, Pacotas, born 1700

Gabriel, Pawnee, born 1710, wedded to Hanna, Negress, born 1713

Titus, Negro, wedded to Manon, Negress, in 1727

Toussaint, Negro, wedded to Isabeau, métisse, in 1726

Balthazar, Pawnee, born 1699, wedded in 1717 to Augustine, Pawnee, born 1701

The information was incomplete, especially concerning the black slaves. Most were not sure of their own date of birth or age and had no idea who their parents may have been or what their real names were. Names given to them in a land of warmth and sun... Names lost during the long passage... The records Jean Luc's uncle kept were as accurate as deemed necessary in the event of any further financial transactions.

There were currently three elders—Adelaide and Gregoire,

who were Isabeau's parents, and Elzear, who was Jean Baptiste's father—and twelve children. Jean Luc had learned on previous visits to the property that their dwellings were modeled after colonial farmhouses but, unlike them, had a stone *solage*—a foundation to make them sturdier. Some farmers dispensed with *solages* so they could dismantle their house and take it with them if they decided to move. The slave quarters Jean Luc's uncle built, however, were intended to be permanent. Their dimensions were standard—twenty by twenty-six feet. A small patch of land annexed to each could be used for a vegetable and flower garden in the warmer months. The wooden walls were whitewashed. Balthazar's and Gabriel's houses had thatched roofs. The other three were covered with cedar shingles. The furnishings were adequate, but the only interior subdivision was the large wooden *cabane* where the parents slept. They had to climb up into it, and a door provided them a small amount of warmth and privacy. The children slept on cots with straw mattresses, and kept warm under bear and moose skins, and blankets of cow or dog hide.

As Jean Luc and Marie Claire drew near, heads turned in their direction. Isabeau and Marie Anne peered apprehensively out the front windows of their dwellings. The boys of working age and all the men, except for old Gregoire and Elzear, were at the sawmill or tending to the livestock. A feeling of uneasiness came over Jean Luc as he stood before the enclave. It was an aberration to him, an immense social regression. Inhumane. "From what I can gather, Uncle Louis was kind to his slaves, but..." His words were halting.

"Couldn't you just free them all?"

"The estate doesn't belong to me. And even if it does become mine, freeing them wouldn't be that easy. My uncle's will provides for very little leeway. Besides, many of them have nowhere to go. Conditions could worsen for them if they were on their own."

"But that's a risk they should be allowed to take if they want."

As they spoke, the door to Toussaint's dwelling opened. Old Gregoire slowly edged toward them with a wary smile. Like the others, he was ill at ease in Jean Luc's presence. He did not know what the fate of his children and grandchildren would be. The new master might not be as kind as the old one. Perhaps the children would be sold. He might be separated from Isabeau and Toussaint. Walking past Jean Luc and Marie Claire, he nodded respectfully, and then headed toward Marie Anne's dwelling, pretexting a visit to check on Elzear. The truth was that he'd been sent out by his daughter to size up the woman in black at the side of the man who could well become their new owner.

When Jean Luc and Marie Claire got back to the manor, Pierre and Madame Seguin were in the drawing room. She was playing blind man's bluff with the boy to pass the time. Madame Seguin blindfolded Pierre again and they all took turns twirling him around. As Pierre groped about, trying to find the adults standing in different corners of the room, Marie Claire sensed Jean Luc's anxiety. His face was expressionless. Was he still thinking about the slaves? Or was he disconcerted by her presence? Had he decided she was out of place at his uncle's manor? Not of the proper social rank? She hid her emotions and played the game. Jean Luc's discomfort became more acute when his eyes fell upon the crest carved into the stone fireplace. It was the Montigny heraldic emblem—a shield divided down the middle by a sword with a dragon on the left and a griffin on the right, both set against a background dotted with fleurs-de-lis. A garland of sculpted ivy embellished the crest's border. He'd been to the estate on numerous occasions. How had he never noticed it before? His complexion paled as he read the motto chiseled at the crest's base: *Mon devoir, notre honneur.* He barely heard William announce that the guests could proceed to the dining room.

Supper had ended. Pierre and Madame Seguin had retired, as had Marie Claire. Jean Luc was alone with the words that would give him no rest—*Mon devoir, notre honneur.* He poured himself one more brandy and welcomed the fires of distillation. He put down the empty glass. His body moved slowly toward the staircase. His legs carried him up to the landing, each step more difficult than the one before it. He lifted the heavy iron latch and pushed open the door. Light from the candelabrum he was carrying slowly filled the room where Pierre was sleeping. Jean Luc kissed him on the forehead, wondering what the future held. No life is without suffering, but he hoped Pierre's pain would not be too much for him to endure. He left the room silently, closing the door behind him. Before he took his first step, the floorboards made a loud creak. A shadow that was not his moved over the cedar chest in the hallway.

"Good evening, Monsieur. Is everything to your satisfaction?"

"Yes. Couldn't be better. Thank you, William. Good night."

As hurriedly as his limp would allow, the majordomo made his way to the corridor's end and pretended to adjust Emma's portrait while Jean Luc walked in the opposite direction to his room. He lifted the porcelain pitcher from the nightstand and filled a glass with water. As he did, his gaze swept the stark walls surrounding him. The chamber's sparse furnishings betrayed its sporadic use. The wide bed was cold and empty. Hers was only steps away.

Beau Val, on this Saturday morning the 22nd day of March 1735.

Her countenance is peaceful in the early morning light. I do not wish to wake her from her contentment. It would be unkind to pull her from the arms of Morpheus where she is so serenely nestled. Last night she took me back to a meadow in my mind. I was determined never to return there again.

She untied the cord, opened the white silk shirt, and placed her hand on his chest, on the amulet hanging from his neck. Fire touching fire. He pulled the night garment off her shoulders and down her torso. The manor's remoteness intensified their desire for freedom from convention. Thick down quilts engulfed them. They were again transported to a place where nothing exists but sensation, where memory is dulled to the point of oblivion. They prolonged each moment of their escape, each twist and turn of the passage, tasting the fruits of ecstasy in a way they never had before. Lethe's waters were sweet. But as their passion reached its climax, a Cyclops forced its way into his mind and dragged him back through the landscape of his torment, ever deeper.

Laughter... Hands twirling Pierre round and round. His hair is the color of sunlight. Golden ringlets cluster along the edge of his blindfold like a crown. The laughter changes. Now it is Helene who is wearing the blindfold and twirling faster and faster. Gasping, muffled sounds... Where has she gone? The images are jolted and dizzying. Hands are spinning Madeleine ever more violently. Help her! Can no one help her?

"Jean Luc. Jean Luc. What is it? What's wrong?"

The voice was so distant. Had he lost consciousness at the height of deliverance and collapsed in her arms? All he knew was that at the moment of release, he had been overcome by the terrifying sensation that he was plummeting down a chasm. When she shook him, it was as though she were waking him from a trance.

"It all came back."

"What came back? What do you mean?"

"The blindfold."

Marie Claire knew he had suspended his voyage into the labyrinth of his memory. He had not completed it with her. But it could not remain that way forever.

"Jean Luc, you never finished telling me about Madeleine."

Just as she had brought him into her world of dragons, he had to confront his personal Minotaur. Finally, he began, resuming his account as if it had been grounded in another form of continuance, uninterrupted by mundane notions of reality and how it is measured and recorded. He spoke slowly, each word a difficult victory over silence and subjugation.

"As it had for you and Jacques, time had ceased to exist for us. Or so we thought. Pierre was born. Soon he was almost three and Helene five. It was May. Madeleine and I were sitting in the garden with my father having some port, watching Helene and Pierre play with the dog Father had given us a few months earlier. Mother was in Angers spending time with her sister."

It was still vivid in his mind, although he had done everything possible to eradicate it.

"Jean Luc, I can't believe how quickly they're growing. My own grandchildren...they'll be adults in no time. That makes me terribly old, doesn't it?"

"Helene! Pierre! You're wearing that dog out." Knowing the animal was accustomed to more civilized behavior, Madeleine had decided to intervene. The children were laughing and racing about. "Meteor's tired. Give him a rest. How about playing hide-and-seek or blind man's bluff?" She pulled a white linen handkerchief from her pocket and held it out to Helene.

"Here, *chérie*. Use this for your blindfold."

Jean Luc smiled at his father. "I know the real reason you gave us Meteor is so we'll take care of him for you."

"I have to admit you're right. I need a bloodhound every fall for hunting season, but what am I supposed to do with the rascal the rest of the time?"

"Well, you can have your rascal back for the hunt, but the remainder of the year, he's ours. The children love him. And with all the exercise they give him, he should be the best bloodhound for miles around. Your hunting partners will be envious."

"We'll see about that in a few months." François was anxious to know how the hound would perform in the woods and brush, how quickly he would pick up the scent of boars and roe deer, how accurately he would lead the hunters to the partridges, ducks, and quail they brought down in full flight. But François would have to wait for that. Meanwhile, there were more pressing subjects to broach with his son. "Have you given any thought to what I was saying the other day? Will I ever persuade you to stop practicing medicine? It's getting too hard for me to oversee the vineyards all by myself."

"Oh, François, you know your son can be as stubborn as you sometimes." Madeleine winked at Jean Luc. "And besides, we still have time to ponder it. In spite of what you say, you're not as old as you may think."

"My son, you married a clever woman. She knows how to flatter a man, even an old codger like me."

Loud crying disrupted the conversation. Helene was spinning Pierre unrelentingly. Bolting from her seat, Madeleine went to her son's rescue. "Helene, stop that this instant! Your brother is too little to play the same way you do. You have to be gentle with him. Some day he'll be bigger than you, so you might want to think about treating him nicer now. Maybe he'll return the favor when he's older."

Madeleine took Pierre in her arms, wiped the hot tears from his cheeks, and sat him on Jean Luc's lap. "It's alright now, *mon petit lapin*. Show papa the picture of the king I gave you this morning."

Pierre's crying turned to slow sobs as he pulled a gold coin from his pocket. On one side was the profile of Louis XV. On the other, three fleurs-de-lis in an oval, embellished right and left with laurel branches and capped with a crown. Jean Luc took the coin in his hand and examined it closely, to Pierre's delight. "Very impressive. What a nice picture of His Majesty. Now don't lose it." Turning to Madeleine and his father, he added, "Maybe once the old cardinal's gone, the king will start taking care of the country's business himself. Right now, I don't think he has any idea what's going on."

Madeleine walked Helene over to Pierre. "Now, Helene, say you're sorry. Tell your brother you didn't mean to frighten him."

Helene lowered her eyes and murmured "I'm sorry," almost indistinctly.

"Come on now, give him a kiss," prompted Madeleine.

"Monsieur de Montigny, there's someone here asking for you." No one had noticed Marthe approach. François started to get up from his chair.

"No, Monsieur, they want to see the doctor."

"Well, I guess that means you."

Jean Luc detected a hint of disappointment in the elder baron's tone.

"Who is it, Marthe?"

"Monsieur Gauvin. Says he's sorry to disturb you. He knows it's the midwife's job, but Madame Lebeau is nowhere to be found. His wife's water broke. He doesn't know what to do."

"She wasn't due for another few weeks... Tell him not to worry. I'm coming."

"Well, now I'm glad it wasn't for me," laughed François. "I'd be of no help whatsoever to Madame Gauvin. I guess I'll be off, too. It was about time for me to go anyway. Thank you, Madeleine, for putting up with me all afternoon. I never tire of watching my grandchildren. And I especially never tire of your company, my dear."

Father and son kissed Madeleine goodbye and left.

"Well, children, that leaves just the three of us to do whatever we like. Let's..."

"Pierre's nap, Madame," interjected Marthe, after clearing her throat.

"Oh yes, his nap. Such a pity Jean Luc isn't here," said

Madeleine dreamily. "Oh never mind," she added, noticing the servant's perplexed look. "Yes, please take him. Go see the sandman, Pierre. And when you wake up, you can tell mama what you dreamt. And take Meteor too, Marthe."

"Now it's just the two of us. What shall we do, Helene?"

"I want to go pick flowers by the water."

"What an excellent idea! We can make a bouquet for papa."

Madeleine took Helene's hand and led her through the gardens, past the stone statues of Diana and Pan, out the wrought iron gate, beyond the open fields and meadow, to the pond. They surveyed the array of blossoms—deep red amaranthus, bright blue delphinia, pure white daisies, and so many others whose names Madeleine did not know.

"We'll put them here by the tree, then we'll choose the prettiest ones to take home."

Imitating her mother, Helene lifted her skirt to form a basket in which to carry the colorful plunder over to the old willow. The vagrants hiding in the brush never made a sound. Bertrand and Jacob survived precariously from day to day, any way they could. Their unshaven faces, dirty hands, and filthy clothes were the emblems of a caste condemned to roam. The drifters observed the woman—her slender frame, the fairness of her features, the rhythm of her movements. The blood began to throb in their veins. Bertrand gave the nod to move closer. They were only a few feet from the tree. Each time she came near, they could have reached out and grabbed her, touched the forbidden softness. But they held back.

The sun was about to set when Jean Luc returned home from the Gauvin residence. It was unusually quiet. Helene did not run to greet him as she normally did. Had she and Madeleine concocted some sort of surprise? Or perhaps they were with unexpected company in the green room. He resisted the impulse to call out and instead rang for Marthe.

"Aren't they back yet? I put Pierre down for his nap and must have lost track of the time. I believe they were going for a walk, but I thought surely they had returned by now."

Jean Luc rushed into the garden. The servant followed. Nothing. No signs of life. Only the golden rays of dusk softly illuminating the treetops against a vermilion sky.

"Marthe, run and get Meteor." He had spotted Madeleine's handkerchief on the ground.

When the servant appeared with the hound on a leash, Jean Luc put the handkerchief to the dog's nose and steered him out of the garden. They combed the terrain until finally Meteor began to bark. He had picked up the scent. Within seconds he led Jean Luc to the willow by the water. The dog felt the resistance around his neck loosen as the leash dropped to the ground. He sniffed the bodies and began to whimper and bark wildly as he circled in a frenzy.

Moving in a daze, Jean Luc touched Helene's face. Warmth had not completely left her. When he lifted his daughter, her head fell back like a ball attached to a string. Her neck was broken. Cradling the child in his arms, he placed her by her mother's side, to sleep with her eternally. He looked into Madeleine's sea-blue eyes. For a split second, he thought she was alive. But she could not see him. Her gaze was fixed on distant horizons imperceptible to him. He removed the kerchief from her mouth and gently closed her eyelids with his fingers. As his hand caressed her golden hair, he saw the straight slit, its almost meticulous exactness destined to haunt him every day and every night for the rest of his existence. He would never be able to banish the sight of that thin straight line from his mind. Nor the pool of dark red. Nor the crushed flowers soaked in crimson.

Death and destruction spoke to him, filled the silence, communicated their irreversibility. A bellowing roar came forth from his gut and swelled in his throat. Anger. Outrage. Indignation. At himself...at those who had violated such innocence...at the universe. He fell to the ground, wishing he were not alive, wishing he were with them. Madeleine. Helene. His wife. His daughter.

"When I came to, I was sitting on the ground with her body resting on mine, stroking her hair, for the last time. Marthe sent for my father. He was the one who helped me pull myself away."

They had held back, waited until it was time. Both removed the kerchiefs tied around their necks. Jacob gave his to Bertrand. As the mother and daughter turned once again to collect more flowers, Jacob seized Madeleine from behind, his large hands

immobilizing her body. He held her by the waist with one arm
and pinned her wrists behind her back with the other. Before she
could turn her head to see them, Bertrand tied his kerchief over
her eyes. He used the second to gag her.

But there was the child. Her vain efforts to free her mother
were less bothersome than her hysterical screams. Silence her.
Immediately. Bertrand spun around and clutched Helene just
below the ribcage, his hands squeezing the oxygen from her
lungs like a vice. He lifted her into the air—weightless in the
shadow of his force—and hurled her against the tree. The long
willow branches surrounded the child's limp body forming a
shroud of pale green, streams of tears. Gone was the warmth of
the sun's rays. Gone, her mother's sweet words and gentle smile.

Jacob pushed Madeleine to the ground, pulled up her skirts
and thrust himself on her, placing his pelvis firmly against hers.
The penetration was swift. Over and over he entered her while
she struggled to escape his grasp. When his energy was spent, it
was his partner's turn. Bertrand mounted her like an animal. She
managed to free one hand, push the kerchief up over her
forehead, and look her attacker straight in the eyes. His reflex
was automatic. He pulled the finely sharpened knife from the
pocket of his torn jacket. The soft flesh of her throat offered no
resistance to the long blade. Angel of life. Angel of death.

"I've failed her. Failed them both. They're not at peace. Nor
am I. At night I hear them calling to me. I never avenged their
murders...their terrible murders."

Jean Luc looked down, focusing on nothing. Tears he had
not let fall for so long welled in his eyes. Neither he nor Marie
Claire could speak. No sound or syllable could convey the
emptiness. Words do not have the power to describe such
suffering. They both knew they could not cast off the heaviness
that had enveloped them.

Beau Val, on this Sunday the 23rd day of March 1735.
  *I must accomplish the mission fate has thrust upon me. It
would be ignoble were I not to assume the task.*

Jean Luc put down his pen and quietly headed to the kitchen
without waking Marie Claire.

William and Jeanne were already preparing breakfast. They wanted everything to be just right, and had again donned their best attire for the occasion. Jeanne's plain gray dress was set off by the whiteness of her starched linen bonnet, shawl collar, and fluted apron. William was wearing his white pleated cotton shirt. A long dark green jacket with brass front buttons running from top to bottom was draped over the back of a chair. He didn't want to soil it while getting the meal ready. As Jean Luc walked down the hallway leading to the kitchen, he could hear their voices. When his name was mentioned, he stopped outside the door.

"So I peered around the corner and saw Monsieur's maneuver as he left his room and went to Madame Lambert's. He thought nobody was watching. But I saw him... Jeanne! Just look at what you've done!"

"Oh, William. I'm sorry."

"This is a fine mess. Monsieur Louis's nephew is here and I have to show myself like this."

"It's just chocolate. It won't stain. I really am sorry. Take off your shirt. I'll wash it and put it by the fire. It will be dry in a few minutes."

Jean Luc felt disloyal eavesdropping on their conversation, but thought it would be worse if they heard him leave. He walked in, and regretted it immediately. William was visibly embarrassed to be bare-chested in the presence of Louis de Montigny's nephew.

"I...I was just wondering...if there was any hot chocolate," Jean Luc stammered, red-faced.

"Yes, of course, Monsieur," replied Jeanne with a smile, sensing his awkwardness, and doing her best to act as if nothing were out of the ordinary. "We just made a pot." Knowing he would want some for the lady visitor as well, but not wanting to appear indelicate, she set four cups on a small silver tray. "Here you are, Monsieur."

As Jean Luc went to take the tray from Jeanne, he noticed something on William's shoulder and couldn't keep from staring.

William glanced down. "Oh that. It's from the first time I tried to run away. They branded me."

Jean Luc apologized for his impertinence as he looked closer—a scar in the shape of a fleur-de-lis.

"Did my uncle do that to you?"

"God, no! Monsieur Louis would never have done anything like that. It was when I was down south. I was lucky they didn't cut off my ears."

"What are you saying, William?" Though he knew such things happened, Jean Luc was appalled that the desire for freedom could be punished by physical mutilation.

"It's all written down in the Code. The first time a slave tries to run away, they brand him if they catch him. And usually cut off his ears. If he tries a second time, they cut the hamstring of one of his legs. That's what happened to me."

The majordomo undid the right knee buttons of his breeches and exposed the wide scar on the back of his leg. Now Jean Luc understood why the man had such difficulty walking.

"You see, I tried to run away twice. But with my leg like this, they were sure I wouldn't get very far if ever I tried again. I never did because I knew if I got caught a third time, I'd be hanged."

William needed to say more, needed to tell his story, but it was tale of suffering that so few wanted to hear. "Slaves in my condition are worth much less on the market. I was lucky, if you can call it that. A sea captain bought me at one quarter the worth of an able slave and took me to Quebec City. He tripled his money. Sold me to your uncle for almost five hundred pounds. That's two years of a tradesman's salary. Seems Negro slaves are harder to come by up here, no matter what condition we're in."

William was proud of the high price Louis de Montigny had paid to purchase him. How degrading, thought Jean Luc, that human worth could be measured by market factors. The only personal merit society allowed slaves to feel was the sum they could draw at auction.

"Good thing your uncle bought me. If he hadn't..."

Jeanne handed William his shirt, still damp, but immaculate once more—like his heart, which he had temporarily cleansed of the pain that dominated his past. But the stain would forever return. And much of his story still remained untold—how he and so many like him were betrayed by their own people, taken

captive in Senegal, brought to the *Maison des esclaves* on the
Isle of Goree to be hoarded onto slave ships in exchange for
arms, mirrors, and worthless trinkets. They were crammed into
the lower depths of the vessels, the men in shackles, the women
herded together separately, with at best two miserable feedings a
day.

Sometimes the voyage took more than three months. The
middle passage, it was called. William's took just over forty-five
days. Guns were pointed at him and the others during the entire
journey. There was no room to move. The holds were so
cramped that the captives could not stand to a full upright
position. And when exhaustion overtook them, there was only
space enough for them to lie on their sides. Tubs overflowed
with excrement. The small portholes afforded little ventilation.
During storms or rough seas, they were completely closed,
causing unbearable heat and trapping the odors of blood and
human waste. The air soon became unfit to breathe. Only one out
of six slaves survived the passage. Those on board suspected of
carrying a contagious disease were poisoned with laudanum. If
the disease had been widespread, the whole shipload would have
been exterminated. Hungry for entertainment, the slave traders
occasionally brought their captives up on deck when the weather
permitted and compelled them to dance and sometimes sing.
Those who were reluctant were whipped. Most of the sailors and
officers engaged in sexual intercourse with the women. William
had witnessed and endured all that even before he reached
Guadeloupe. When would he again have the opportunity to
purge his emotions? Would he ever be allowed to recount the
agony from beginning to end?

As William put on his shirt, Jean Luc could do little more
than give him and Jeanne a reassuring nod. The flush of
embarrassment was gone from his cheeks. It had been replaced
by the pallor of shock and disgust.

Quebec City, on this Monday the 24th day of March 1735.
        *The hour is now quite late. We left the estate before
midmorning. I was in no mood to make conversation. Everyone
must have sensed that something was bothering me because they
scarcely said a thing.*

"I've given instructions to the driver," Jean Luc announced as the carriole made its approach to the city. "He'll drop me off first, at the notary's. Then he'll take you home, Marie Claire, and after that bring you and Pierre to the inn, Madame Seguin. I'll join you both there as soon as I can."

It was an unscheduled visit. He didn't know if Bourville would still be in the office, let alone have the time or inclination to receive him. By chance, the notary was there and appeared most gracious as Edouard showed Jean Luc in. He could not wait another day to take action. They discussed the matter for a good half hour. Bourville tried to dissuade him, explaining it was futile so long as the fate of the estate remained in limbo. But he insisted. He had to make the effort, even if it was only symbolic, even if it would serve no purpose.

"Well, it does put a whole new slant on what we've been working on up to this point. I'll reexamine the laws and Louis's will in light of what you've just told me. As soon as I have a definitive answer, that is as soon as I can tell you if it's possible from a legal perspective, I'll let you know."

Jean Luc thanked the notary and hurried back to the inn. Shortly after his arrival in the colony, he discovered the long winding stairway that connected the upper and lower cities. That evening, he headed for it rather than taking the roundabout and treacherous *Côte de la Montagne* as he sometimes did. When he got to the *Auberge*, Sylvie told him Pierre and Madame Seguin had already had supper brought up to their room. It had been a hard trip and both were tired. He decided to have something to eat in the tavern before turning in himself, and sat at the first empty table he saw. *Potage d'oignons au lait*, that would be enough. Sylvie served him before taking pitchers of beer to a loud table nearby. The men had started hours before. As Jean Luc was finishing the croutons lying at the bottom of his tureen, he heard his name.

"Well my, my. Hello, Monsieur de Montigny. I haven't seen you in a while." The fur trader had just entered for his nocturnal libation.

Jean Luc stood to greet him. "Good evening. Would you like to join me?"

"Don't mind if I do."

Sylvie took Desjardins's order, although the gesture was more a confirmation than an inquiry. He rarely strayed from his usual preference—hearty red wine from the tavern's keg. Because of the high volume he needed to procure, the innkeeper had first choice of the barrels arriving from France. After years of experience, and much trial and error, he had learned to sort the good from the bad.

"So, Monsieur de Montigny, have you made up your mind yet? Are you going to stay if the court decides in your favor?" Desjardins was partial to the formality of titles. Despite the fact that he had been one of Louis de Montigny's closest friends, he never addressed the man's nephew by his first name. As he was talking, he pulled out his pipe and filled it. He was a man of great physical and mental energy. In his younger days, he rarely remained idle. Now that he was less directly involved in the commerce of furs, he sought adventure through verbal discourse. Conversations with him were like spending hours in a talking library—and at times entering into dialogue with one's conscience.

"Well, as they say in Normandy, perhaps yes, perhaps no."

"Still weighing the pros and cons, I see."

"I'm thinking of my son. Do I want him to grow up in a country that is only half born? Who knows what the colony will be like when Pierre is a man?"

"Do you think conditions are any better in France?"

"Well, I know things aren't perfect there, but the winds of change are blowing over Paris. Over the entire country. Some of the less frivolous circles are discussing provocative ideas, like those of the Baron de Montesquieu."

"A native son of Bordeaux, is he not?"

"And a vintner as well. My father has been to his chateau in La Brède. What he writes is as good as the white wine he produces. Some say even better. Have you read *The Persian Letters*?"

"I have indeed. A masterful satire, I must concede. How ingenious of him to use a couple of naive Persians to poke fun at the French court and royal authority. It's not surprising it was published anonymously, but everyone knows who wrote it."

"And there's a growing number who think along the same

lines. Separation of powers, respect for every individual's rights, that's what they're suggesting."

"The children of Descartes, Bayle, and Fontenelle I suppose we could call them," added Desjardins, as Sylvie arrived with his wine. Without taking the time to look up and thank her, he continued, "Their books have made their way here, too. I've read what some of them have to say. Seems we colonists are more loyal to the monarchy than you are in France, at least in our own cavalier way."

"Do you really believe that?"

"I most certainly do. While I was at law school, I had to study a case involving a decree issued by the Sovereign Council here. I've forgotten exactly when it happened. Charges were brought against one Paul Dupuy for having made light of the execution of Charles the First of England. Notice, I said England, not France. Regardless of the ongoing feuds between the two countries, Dupuy's words were deemed an offense to the whole institution of royalty. He was stripped down to his shirt, dragged through the streets with a rope tied around his neck, forced to repent in front of the Chateau Saint Louis and beg the king's forgiveness. After that, he was transported to the lower city, retained in the stocks a few hours, and imprisoned again. Oh yes, they branded a fleur-de-lis on his cheek as well."

The fleur-de-lis scar... Jean Luc thought once more about what had been done to William. He remembered a play he'd seen some years earlier, a satire by Marivaux that took place on a distant island where social roles were reversed. Masters temporarily became the subjects of their slaves. It was a bold political commentary masked in the guise of light comedy.

Thinking about the play made Jean Luc nostalgic for his library at Loublanc. It was a special place, cut off from the rest of the world. He visualized the bookcases he'd commissioned from the workshop of Charles Cressent, a cabinetmaker to the Duc d'Orleans when he was regent of France. More than mere repositories for books, the cases were works of art in themselves. Each was adorned with four bronze figures allegorizing the oceans and continents, set against a marquetry of exotic woods. Mesh doors protected the precious volumes from the sunlight. The library was hallowed ground where Jean Luc could vicariously converse with philosophers, poets, and playwrights.

"But change is inevitable." Desjardins's husky voice called him back from his reverie. "You said it yourself. You can't protect your son from it. What's happening in France is the beginning of something that could quickly spread to the point where there's no turning back. Destabilizing any government, good or bad, opens the doors to the unknown. That is, if a viable alternative has not been laid out. Let's just imagine for a moment that the ideas of these thinkers catch on. Unless the monarch acquiesces, there could be serious problems. And if he does, he might lose credibility, and by extension, any real authority. That could lead to a movement to depose him. A drastic measure. If that happened—and suppose it did—it could mark the beginning of utter chaos. Lunatics could seize control and initiate change for short-term goals. That could only result in anarchy."

"Certain achievements of the past will be swept away, I'll grant you, but that's necessary if something better is to be created."

"Something better! What incredible arrogance! What makes you think someone else can do better? Destroy tradition and stability and you become prey to the ephemeral and all its whims."

"Here all along I thought you were the pragmatic one, Monsieur Desjardins. Now I'm getting a glimpse of the philosopher in you."

"Young man, make no mistake, there's a philosopher in everyone."

"From what you're saying, you seem in favor of maintaining the status quo."

"Not at all, but if change is not properly guided, we break the fetters of the past in the name of emancipation only to become victims of our own hubristic folly."

"Perhaps, but isn't it part of the human condition to keep trying, even though we commit the same errors over and over? I want my son to contribute to the new way of thinking."

"Couldn't he do that just as well here?"

"Possibly. Look at me, mapping out his life for him. These are things he'll have to decide for himself."

"Like your own decision to stay or return to France."

"I suppose. But either way, I don't want to be a slave to

memory."

"How so?"

"I've befriended someone...a woman...the widow we drove home after her accident."

"I see you've finally decided to admit it. Believe me, it's no secret. Everyone in town knows."

Jean Luc glided over Desjardins's remark. "I've been trying to help her make the inner journey you spoke about when you gave me the amulet, the one the shamans undertake to free themselves from images of the past that are holding them back. And she's been helping me do the same. I'm not sure how it will turn out, but I need to know if I'm in love with her. In love with a woman—or a ghost. Right now, I'm not sure. And I don't know if she's in love with me or a shadow from her past."

"Well now, you'll have to reach that conclusion on your own. I'll gladly talk politics all night. My friends will tell you that. But affairs of the heart, that's another kettle of fish."

Quebec City, on this Monday the 14th day of April 1735.

I appeared before the Sovereign Council today, just as Marie Claire did in February. The council heard testimonies from both parties, called witnesses, and asked question after question. Jeanne and William were intimidated by the proceedings, but they responded admirably. Boisvert's theatrics bordered on melodrama yet succeeded in arousing the pity of the magistrates. He is a crafty villain. Surely he would attempt to lure Satan himself into any trap if he thought he could profit from it.

The plaintiff waived his right hand in the air as he concluded his emotional plea to the court. The hand seemed to speak another language, convey a message unrelated to the words being pronounced. William could not take his eyes off the dark jacket's wide cuff as it moved up and down, in circles, never stopping. Finally, the hand ceased to move. The plaintiff went back to his seat. The council members conferred. Nods and gestures accompanied their inaudible words.

The atmosphere was tense as the chief magistrate addressed the chamber. "It is the opinion of this court that Monsieur Philippe Boisvert has put forth convincing arguments. The financial difficulties Monsieur Robert Langlois, here present, experienced with the plaintiff are irrelevant to these proceedings. Furthermore, the letters introduced as evidence appear fully authentic. Moreover, with regard to Monsieur Albert Bourville's allegations, I do not think we can begrudge the deceased a change of preference as far as his stationery is concerned. Lastly, the whereabouts of the plaintiff on the night of September the twenty-first of last year is a moot issue. Two material witnesses have signed affidavits confirming he was in their company on the evening in question."

As the magistrate spoke, William watched Boisvert struggle to contain a smile of satisfaction and mask his contentment by raising his left hand to his face to conceal the corner of his lips. William gazed once more at the man's dark coat, the wide cuff of the sleeve. Why had he not seen it sooner? He had to act. He had to tell what he knew. But would anyone believe him, a slave? No matter, he had to do it. He jumped up and walked to the front row of seats as quickly as he could.

Annoyed by the interruption, the magistrate fell silent and stared at the estate's majordomo, who was gesticulating wildly and talking breathlessly to the Baron de Montigny. He appeared to be placing something in the baron's hand.

With growing anger, the magistrate bellowed, rapping his gavel repeatedly. "Order! Order, please! Would everyone be seated? The council will not tolerate any further interruptions."

But the baron paid no attention and bolted in the direction of the plaintiff. He held the small round object he had received from William next to Boisvert's cuff. It was a perfect match. "If it please the council," he declared, "the servants found this article in the kitchen on the morning of the twenty-second of September." Gasps of astonishment filled the chamber. It was at that moment that Boisvert realized he was missing the fifth button on the left sleeve of the only jacket he owned.

Bourville was right after all. He was convinced that both of the letters Louis had allegedly written to Boisvert were forged and that it was Boisvert himself who had done it, probably copying my uncle's handwriting from a letter going back many years—one written to Emma's brother, perhaps. But Bourville was unable to explain how the unsent letter found its way into my uncle's edition of LaRochefoucauld's Maximes. The break-in William told me about on my initial visit to the estate seemed to be the only possible explanation, but after Boisvert succeeded in documenting his alibi, there was no way of substantiating the accusation. All that could be proved was that he had contracted enormous liabilities as the result of a series of failed transactions and had already set plans in motion to sell my uncle's property in order to liquidate his debts. He was going to start a new enterprise with his own cheap labor force—the slaves from the estate. Why William still had the button in his pocket is a wonder. He claims that several days after my first visit to the property, Louis came to him in a dream and told him to cherish it as if it were a precious stone.

So many things in this world are beyond our comprehension...

Quebec City, on this Monday the 21st day of April 1735.

Boisvert has been sentenced for fraud and willful obstruction of justice. Upon further interrogation, and corroboration from William, it came to light that he never set foot in the manor's kitchen during his one and only visit with Louis. That information, coupled with the fact that his button was discovered near the forced kitchen door, only bolstered Bourville's contention that Boisvert had returned to the estate after my uncle's death. The scoundrel's two accomplices have been sentenced for signing false affidavits.

The whole affair has shown me that justice can at times be had. Never should we recoil from pursuing it.

"I have the papers ready for you to sign. Both documents." The notary had reverted to his matter-of-fact mannerisms. With the exception of extraordinary occurrences such as those related to the estate controversy—an issue of great personal interest—he was not the type to display emotions or waste time on pointless chatter. "In rereading the will, I was able to see it from a different perspective, that is, from the standpoint of what we discussed last month. It might at first seem we're bypassing your uncle's wishes in doing this but, in reality, it still achieves what he wanted. I don't feel I'm betraying Louis in any way. We're simply honoring the spirit rather than the letter of the law. Given the wording of his testament, it's perfectly legal."

"Excellent. How did you come to that conclusion?"

"It boils down to the fact that when your uncle drew up his will, he never listed the slaves as part of his estate. By law here, slaves are property that can be bought and sold. Your uncle was in legal possession of them, but from a philosophical point of view, the idea displeased him. That's why he refused to include them in the estate inventory. None of their names appear in any of the ledgers or on any of the legal rosters. Besides the titles of ownership, the only document he left pertaining to them was the unofficial list I gave you."

"So that's why there was no mention of them in the will."

"What this means for you is that, because the slaves were not included in the itemization of goods, they can be treated separately...off the record, if you prefer. But you have no legal power to do anything until you actually become the owner of the estate. The will specifies that in order for that to happen, you are to reside on the property and continue activities there as though nothing had changed."

"I know. I still haven't decided whether I want to abandon everything in France or..."

"This document will facilitate the procedure no matter what you choose to do. Let's consider the contingencies outlined in the will. You've already spent some time in Beau Val. Technically, that could qualify as having lived there. From what I understand, the slaves are carrying on as before, in memory of your uncle, waiting to see what their fate will be. So that condition of the will has likewise been fulfilled, which means you are qualified to sign this document giving you the full legal right either to move in or sell the property, knowing that the proceeds will not go to you, but rather to the Basilica."

"And the slaves?"

"You'll become the sole owner of both the estate and the slaves. I'll leave you alone to look over the papers yourself."

Bourville closed the door behind him. Jean Luc pored over each clause, every stipulation to make sure it was what he had requested. He wanted to be absolutely certain he wasn't backing himself into a corner or accomplishing something other than what he intended. After a time, a discreet cough from the antechamber signaled the notary's imminent return. The door swung open.

"So then, Monsieur de Montigny, is everything in order?" Bourville asked the question with the assurance of a man confident he had done his work well.

"It's a masterpiece of legal finesse. If the other document I asked you to prepare is as meticulous as this one, things will run quite smoothly should I decide to return to France."

"That one is fairly straightforward. You'll see. I have it ready as well. But first, sign here to indicate that you accept the estate and have become its rightful owner. I'll then affix my seal to it."

Jean Luc took the quill from Bourville's hand, dipped it into the now familiar inkwell, and signed.

Quebec City, on this Saturday the 10th day of May 1735.

Her mourning has come to an end—at least as far as the requirements of society are concerned. She is free to appear in public unchaperoned in the company of a man and clothe herself in colorful attire if she wishes. Twelve months in black for widows. Six for widowers.

The violet trim of her shawl lent freshness to her appearance.

She knows now that my bereavement last autumn was not due to the death of my uncle. Yet removing the darkness without does not dispel the night within.

We went to the port late this afternoon. The sun glistened against the masts of the ships docked there. The crew of an incoming vessel was pulling down its sails. The massive whiteness fell in gentle folds like silk off a bolt. Someone said the boat was coming in from Saint Malo, which was an unusual event so early in the season.

A flotilla of rowboats set out from the docks in the direction of the vessel amidst excited hollering. Bags of mail were lowered to the extended arms of a throng eager for news from across the sea, longing to read an "all is well" or some declaration of affection written in a familiar script. Merchants lined up at the water's edge to snatch up the best goods. What remained would be sent on to Montreal and beyond. The wealthier women of Quebec City were among the primary beneficiaries of the chaotic negotiations. They were reputed to be the most fashionable in the colony despite the fact that styles were more than a year behind those of Paris.

Marie Claire's gaze was fixed on the ship.

"I wonder if I'd like France."

"Perhaps one day you'll see."

We took rue Sault au Matelot from the port. It is an exceedingly narrow passage. The setting sun cast a golden light on the buildings. And on her. She seems a different woman now.

They turned left onto *rue Saint Antoine*, then right onto the wooden footpath of *rue Saint Pierre*. Not far from the corner was a small cabaret. They entered its universe of noise and smoke, edging their way through the tight network of tables. The sour smell of hard cider hung in the air.

"The town is rarely this active."

"It's the end of winter. That's always cause for celebration. When the sap of the maple trees starts to flow, it means spring has arrived. Sugar and syrup...the beginning of a new season. It's weeks overdue."

A chubby hand shoved a tin plate piled high with small, crispy mounds in front of them.

"They're Christ's ears," said Marie Claire, seeing the need to explain.

"You mean...?" He pointed to his ear.

"It's really just fried pork rind."

"Only in a country overrun with Jesuits could someone come up with a name like that."

Neither of them could turn the conversation to the imminent decision that had to be made. Both had instinctively resolved to enjoy the night to the fullest for what it was, regardless of what might happen later. He picked up a curled rind with his fingers, knowing better by now than to use a fork. As he nodded in approval, a voice cut through the din. "Fricassee or wild boar. That's all that's left."

Darkness had fallen by the time they finished supper and proceeded to the *Place Royale*.

I put my arm around her shoulders. I can do so now without concern for her reputation.

The yellow-orange of small bonfires illuminated the square. Both Marie Claire and Jean Luc had crossed through the *Place Royale* on a hundred occasions since that October day when the

Goéland docked in the harbor. It was impossible not to. The *Place Royale* was the very root of the colony, the locus of France's origins in the New World. Once Samuel de Champlain's private garden, it had now become a market square, a theater of difficult beginnings marked by both permanence and change. Fire destroyed the original wooden buildings. The present ones of stone were inherently European in style yet uniquely colonial in function. Soon after being placed there, the bust of Louis XIV had been removed so that horses and commoners could move about more freely, as if the old Sun King had been deposed by his subjects.

He felt her shoulders tighten beneath her shawl. She was remembering—the branding, the execution, the effigy. The flames dancing around them there in the square that night brought it back to her—and to him—with intensity. But they did not wish to take the specter of remorse by the hand. His was not the company they were seeking. The merriment and music pulled them gently from his grip.

They stopped in front of *Notre Dame des Victoires* where they had attended Christmas services. "To commemorate two battles we won against the British," she said in answer to his question about the church's name. "One in 1690 and another about twenty years later. If they ever gain control of the port, it will be the end of New France. Oh, there's Monsieur Gilbert's stall," she said, almost in the same breath. "Let's get some candy." The threat of the enemy was another specter that refused to leave. Neither did she care to ponder its somber features or look into its merciless eyes that evening.

The seller's children had filled the trough with snow they'd collected from the colder shaded areas of the woods. Jean Luc fished through his assortment of stamped cards and handed one to Monsieur Gilbert, who inspected it with an experienced eye before putting it in his pocket and performing his ritual. Picking up a spouted can containing maple syrup, he poured some of the dense liquid over the icy white granules. In a matter of seconds, it hardened. Once he was satisfied with the texture, he invited Jean Luc and Marie Claire to peel the ribbony strands of amber off the frozen crystals. The ceremony was a blending of the seasons that transformed the sweet syrup and chilling snows to usher in the warmth of spring.

"Gaze upon your destiny. Predictions. Fortunes. Revelations. Your questions answered."

The old Sioux woman beckoning was from the western regions. She had come into possession of her tarot cards long ago from a French sailor in exchange for some beaded armbands. How she had learned to read them was as mysterious as her art.

"You have questions for the cards. Ask them." She extended the worn, oily deck directly in the path of Marie Claire, who took the cards from the woman's hand without hesitating. Jean Luc was struck by the quiet spontaneity of her reaction, as if obedience were her only option.

"Hold them tightly. Think about what you want to ask. Shuffle them well." The fortuneteller retrieved the deck. "Violence. Much suffering in your past. You. And the man, too. Maybe the cards will not tell you what you want."

"It doesn't matter."

The Sioux woman pulled the first fifteen cards off the top of the stack and placed them face down in five rows of three going from right to left. "This is the present. Your present," she said as she turned over the first card—the Lovers. Marie Claire blushed. The fortuneteller did not react.

"The next row is about the question you are asking. Things that will happen." She turned a card—the King of Cups. "Responsibility. And obstacles. These will be revealed in the third row." The set's dominant card was the King of Wands. "Devotion, duty, honesty." The fourth set pointed to things that would come to pass unbidden. Again the old woman turned a card—the Three of Swords, reversed. "Sorrow, separation, absence."

The seer's hand stopped before moving to the last set. "These show what you can hope for. The answer to your question." Among the cards she turned were Death and the Hanged Man. "Do not fear them," she responded to Marie Claire's wince. "Their meaning is sometimes not what it seems. I see an end to things present. Birth, change."

Marie Claire never told Jean Luc the question in her mind when she held the tarot cards. And he did not ask.

A boom lit up the night sky. The smell of gunpowder filled the air. Reds, blues, greens, golds, and whites glittered overhead.

Hundreds of shooting stars illuminated the passing clouds. Fireworks were being set off down by the port. A canon blast accompanied each burst of light.

They walked to the *Auberge du Roy* as the last sparks dissolved into the cosmos. The spectacle ended as abruptly as it had begun—a passing diversion that disintegrated like a transient dream.

The inn's windows were pitch black. "They must have closed early to go to the festivities, but I've got a key. We'll have to be quiet. If I'm caught bringing a woman into my room, they'll kick me out. They made that perfectly clear the first day." He imitated the innkeeper's gruff voice. "Monsieur, be assured, this is not that kind of establishment."

As the innkeeper had promised, there were candles by the entry for occasions such as this. Jean Luc lit one from the small oil lamp on the low bench. Its flame could not be seen from outside. It was a secret shared only with the lodgers. The light of the candle allowed the two sojourners to find their way up the stairs and to the end of the corridor. He closed the door behind him, lit the candelabrum on the table, then sat on the chair, and drew her onto his lap. Who did she see as she looked into his eyes? He unlaced the ruffled bodice of her dress. She tugged on one side of his cravat, pulled it from his neck, and let it fall to the floor. He caressed her smooth flesh as he slowly removed her *robe volante*, its delicately flowing folds reminding him of another, ever more evanescent presence.

Quebec City, on this Sunday the 11th day of May 1735.
*   I have once more made the pilgrimage to Cythera. But with whom?*

~~~

The isle of love, elegance, peace and harmony. Pierre thought of his father's quest for the absolute, his unremitting efforts to make Cythera a reality. The ideal had become increasingly elusive as the years went by. Each small victory over some form of tyranny was countered by a larger defeat in the face of iniquity. Pierre remembered his father's unsuccessful battle with local

authorities during the last months of his life over the slave depot
the city wanted to create by the port—jails where slaves
accompanying their masters to France were to be detained. It was
a means of curbing the growing number of chattel in the mother
country without outlawing the practice of bondage.

Jean Luc de Montigny would not accept compromise, could
not settle for personal happiness at the expense of the freedom and
dignity of others. Yet many around him did. It was fashionable for
members of Bordeaux's nobility and wealthy residents to be seen in
public with their young black servants, who were looked upon as
exotic curiosities. Having a servant of color painted into family
portraits was the ultimate emblem of sophistication and refinement,
a sign of prosperity and influence, a way of emphasizing social rank
through antithesis.

A dark speck appeared on Pierre's hand. It was a fly. The
mosquitoes had retreated into the shadows and the insects of
daylight had begun to replace them. Pierre looked more closely
at the tiny creature caught in its own fight for survival, while the
immense human drama of suffering was beginning to unfold
once again. There were footsteps and voices, commotion in the
corridor just outside the cell. The changing of the guard. Dawn
was coming. Soon the massive door would open. Soon they
would read the names aloud from the roster, the list everyone
feared, the list that had no end. Those summoned would be
herded outside into the sunlight, into a world where darkness
was life, and light the harbinger of death. The filth and stench,
the dread and pain were less terrifying than what awaited.

As Pierre anticipated the first glimmers of his last dawn, he
could not stop thinking of the Marquis de Condorcet—the man
who fought so unselfishly for the principles those now in power
had spurned. The marquis's belief in moral and intellectual
progress seemed ludicrous against the spectacle of horror and
bloodshed. Condorcet was fortunate enough to avoid the
guillotine but not death. Pierre wished he, too, had at his disposal
a vial of poison that could spare him the cold blade and allow
him to follow Condorcet's example even into the next world.

~~~

Aboard the Quatre Vents, off the shores of New France, on this Friday the 30th day of May 1735.

The winds fill the sails pushing us steadily over the rough waves, ever further from the coast. Yet I still see her eyes, reddened with sorrow as we embraced for the last time. My guilt cannot be ignored, cannot be shared. I am responsible for my fate and must continue the voyage. I am no longer certain where home is, though I remain hopeful I will one day find it. I return to France not out of vengeance but out of love. A single wrong left unpunished is intolerable. I must requite their senseless deaths. I owe it to Madeleine and Helene, my own flesh and blood, those dearest to me. And Pierre. I must bequeath to him as perfect a world as possible. I owe it to Marie Claire, too. For how can our love truly exist unless I wash my hands in innocence? Inaction is complicity, a form of guilt. I must render my new love pure and noble. If you were here with me, Desjardins, I could give you the answer to the question you asked me so many months ago. I now know with certainty I am of the philosophical breed. But surely you knew that to be the case long before I.

Our past is a part of us we can neither escape nor deny. Of that I am sure. And our destiny is the sum of our actions.

Jean Luc and Marie Claire paid no attention to the passengers scurrying to board the *Quatre Vents*, or to the porters hoisting trunks and parcels from the dock onto the ship.

"I'll return once I've accomplished what I must. I promise."

She forced a smile, but her green eyes were an ocean of sadness.

"Suzanne will always have a brother in France," was all Jean Luc could say.

"And he, a sister in Canada."

In their struggle to free themselves, to forget what could not be changed, they had accomplished something they had not counted on. They had embraced once more those taken from them, prolonged their love for one more season.

"Last boarding call. All passengers please board now." The shipmate walked up and down the dock, ringing a bell as he blared the announcement.

"Last boarding call. All passengers please board now. The

ship will depart momentarily. All ashore who are going ashore."

He pulled himself from her arms...or was pulled by a force greater than his own. After kissing Anne and Suzanne, he took Pierre by the hand and began walking toward the *Quatre Vents*, resisting each step that carried him further from her. Then she saw him turn and run back to her. He reached into his jacket pocket and gave her a packet.

"Don't look at it until the ship has left."

The card money he had not spent and could never use in France, she thought as she watched him rush to join Madame Seguin. Midway up the gangplank, they stopped to gaze one last time on New France, on everything it had given to them and taken from them.

Tristan in exile, nevermore to behold his fair Iseult. But banishment and separation cannot extinguish the love that unites us...

~~~

Pierre put down the journal—the last traces of the journey. It was filled with events that transpired when he was too young to understand and emotions he never knew his father experienced. The moment had come. Pierre pulled the leather cord up over his head, slipped off the amulet, and tucked it inside the pocket of his breeches, afraid it would be taken from him. Nothing could remain that might obstruct the blade's descent. Pierre had treasured the small bone carving ever since his father's death, ever since he discovered its existence and the significance it held. The figure of the warrior had always hung inside his father's shirt, on his chest, close to his heart, not for the eyes of friends or strangers. Pierre removed it the day his father died and placed it around his own neck to prolong the memory, prevent it from fading into nothingness. Now he would carry the amulet with him into the darkness to meet his father. And the spirit of the warrior.

Bordeaux, 1794 (continued).
I must write quickly now, Suzanne. There is little time left. I

realize why my father made the choice he did—a choice that most would find incomprehensible. He renounced all personal contentment until his small role in creating a better society had been fulfilled, the way Antigone had. Was Antigone's defiance in vain? Were my father's efforts futile? If he had succeeded in his mission, if others had followed his commitment to justice, I would not be in this prison awaiting death.

Your mother more than anyone knew of all the years he spent searching for the men who murdered my mother and sister. Their capture and punishment became his obsession. So many times he came close to succeeding and felt certain his work would come to an end, making it possible for him to return to New France, to your mother. He desired it with all his soul. In spite of everything, he did achieve justice for some. His search brought him in contact with countless numbers of people wrongly accused of crimes. He came to their assistance whenever he could. But the culprits he was seeking were never apprehended and my father regretted that bitterly to his dying day. Time has surely exacted the justice he could not. My poor father. He never found Ithaca. Only glimpsed Cythera from afar.

Among his papers, I discovered a letter your mother wrote to him more than twenty years after we left New France. It is testimony that their love transcended time and space. I am enclosing it with my own. I hope to slip them both to a friend on my way to the scaffold. If God is with him, he will see to their safe transport out of France. Should you read these words, it means he escaped the butchery and reached England safely.

The guards are approaching. My night has ended.
Adieu,
Pierre

The folded pages arrived, addressed to *Miss Suzanne Lambert, Beau Val, Quebec.* The supplication on the reverse side had ensured that they reached their destination: *May God protect the bearer of these letters from perils both at sea and on land and guide him to a safe haven.*

Beau Val, this 30th of May, 1758.
    My Dearest Jean Luc,

Today marks the twenty-third anniversary of your departure from New France. I can still see the plank being lifted. At that moment, I knew we would be forever separated. Never would I gaze into your sweet eyes again. You left harboring secrets you thought you had shared with me, but there was still so much you kept to yourself. And how many of my secrets did I truly share with you?

I watched with sadness as the ship pulled away, slowly extending the divide between us. It was only when I could no longer see your face that I looked down at what you had handed me. Monsieur Bourville's red wax seal made the document look so official, I was almost afraid to open it. I had no idea what to expect. Then I realized what it was. Anne had Suzanne in her arms. I held the paper for her to see. When she finally understood, she didn't know how to react. She couldn't believe you had given me your uncle's entire estate. "And he never told you anything?" I remember her asking in astonishment. Dear Anne. I miss her deeply. It's still difficult for me to imagine she's been gone this long. But I take solace in knowing her final years were bright ones. She loved it here.

I'm grateful that Suzanne has taken charge of things. Sometimes I wish she had married. Who knows what might have happened if you and Pierre had stayed on? But I've accepted the fact that she is too devoted to the land to share her heart with a man. Like her aunt, Suzanne will never wed. She is subjected to the same banter I was when I first took over the property. People aren't used to seeing a woman run a manor of this size.

Those early years were challenging. The deed you transferred to my name had its conditions, of course, the way your uncle's had for you. But yours were easy conditions and I was content to comply. Employing any slaves who wanted to stay on as free workers was more a blessing to me than a condition. I was good to them, just as your uncle had been. I've lost track of those who went off to begin their own lives. Those who stayed have all passed on now. I think fondly of Jeanne and William. Each year, Suzanne sees to it that the graves are tended from spring through the first snow.

How ironic it is that you gave the slaves their freedom, and you freed me of my poverty and lightened the weight of my memories, yet you could not do the same for yourself. Your letters have been a comfort to me. So often they held the promise that you would at last accomplish the task that was yours. So often they gave me hope that you would return. But time has been victorious.

The British are an ever-growing threat. They outnumber us, by fourteen times some say. Should they succeed in taking over, which seems more likely with each passing day, all communication with France will surely be cut off. I want to tell you, perhaps for the last time, that despite the distance and years, we are still together in heart and spirit. If you receive no more letters from me, it is not because I have forgotten you. It is because New France is no more.

All my love to you, my dearest,
Marie Claire

EPILOGUE

In 1755, the British began separating French families in Acadia and deporting them. Seven thousand people were forced to leave in the first year alone. Most of them wound up in Louisiana. Deportations continued until 1762, uprooting thousands more.

In 1763, France signed over the majority of its New World territories to England. New France ceased to exist. Slavery lingered on under British rule into the beginning of the nineteenth century.

In 1777, the French monarchy passed a law in an attempt to ban entry of slaves into France. The law was virtually impossible to enforce and met with little success.

In 1792, the Reign of Terror swept through France. An estimated 17,000 people were tried and executed. Another 25,000 were executed without a trial, merely on the basis of their lineage.

In 1794, the revolutionary government abolished slavery throughout France and its remaining territories.

In 1802, Napoleon re-instituted slavery in the territories. It was not definitively abolished until 1848.

In 2001, the French Parliament adopted an act declaring slavery a crime against humanity. The motion was put forth by the deputy from Guyana to honor the millions of men and women enslaved throughout the colonial territories over the centuries.